TERROR PEAK

EDWARD J. MCFADDEN III

Let the world know:
#IGotMyCLPBook!

Crystal Lake Publishing
www.CrystalLakePub.com

Join the Crystal Lake community today
on our newsletter and Patreon!

ISBN: 978-1-957133-02-7

Cover art:
Ben Baldwin—http://www.benbaldwin.co.uk

Layout:
Lori Michelle—www.theauthorsalley.com

Proofread by:
Paula Limbaugh
Sue Jackson

WELCOME

TO ANOTHER

CRYSTAL LAKE PUBLISHING

CREATION

"It has not been in the pursuit of pleasure that I have periled life and reputation and reason. It has been the desperate attempt to escape from torturing memories, from a sense of insupportable loneliness and a dread of some strange impending doom."

—Edgar Allan Poe

1

January 12th, 1951, Sawatch Mountain Range, Colorado—Elevation 9,871 feet

THE WILLYS JEEP Wagon fought through slush and snow, windshield wipers thwapping as they swept away large white flakes, dirt speckled snowdrifts towering over the road. Jesse hunched over the wheel, gripping it with both hands as he peered at the steep slope, the Jeep's headlights bouncing around, finding nothing but swirling white specks against blackness. The truck's engine whined, its thick tires spitting dirt and gravel as it struggled up the incline.

Ahead, a single light flickered in the gloom, but it appeared to be getting further away, not closer.

The wind gusted and screamed, whistling through the wagon's weatherstripping, murmuring and singing. Swirling cyclones of snow danced across the road, and shadows writhed just beyond the reach of the headlights. A bump rocked the truck, and it fishtailed, pushing through two feet of fresh snow, sliding and twisting as Jesse worked the wheel and kept the Willys on the road.

To the north, Abominable Peak rose like a monolith. The Sawatch mountains are high, vast, and gentle in contour. Abominable Peak was rugged and chiseled, its sharp summit a frozen hook. The peak had a tall, overbearing, ominous look, like it wasn't part of the Sawatch Range at all, but rather its master. At 16,971 feet,

Abominable Peak was the tallest mountain in the US Rockies, and Roland meant to be the first person to ride it.

Jesse glanced over and said, “This thing might make it after all.”

Roland said nothing. Nobody in their right state of mind traveled to Fort Fortune during winter, because there was no good reason to be there, at least there hadn’t been before Roland had his crazy idea. Without a reward, why take the risk? Spend the money for fuel and supplies? On the occasions when the camp did need to be reached when the Rockies were blanketed in feet of snow, a slow-crawling snowcat was used.

The road had no snow ruts or channels, which told Roland nobody had been up this way for a long time. A civilian vehicle had never made the trip in winter, and Jesse and Raymond had debated at length the best way to get to Fort Fortune.

The 1946 Willys Jeep Wagon was one of the first four-wheel-drive vehicles available for purchase by the general public, and Jesse had argued it wasn’t up to the task. He’d wanted to buy a military surplus vehicle, but Roland didn’t have the money and he’d insisted his Willys could make the trip. So far it had, though not without issues. Two flats and a broken ball joint had delayed them two full days, but there was no schedule in the mountains except night and day, black and white, right and wrong.

A cloud floated across the moon, and shadows writhed, thick darkness pressing on the road.

Jesse slowed and downshifted, the truck bucking and creaking, the equipment in the back of the vehicle shifting and clanging. “Check on that stuff, will you,” Jesse said, eyes locked on the road.

Roland leaned into the backseat and scanned the cases that contained Jesse’s camera gear. In the far back, their backpacks were stacked next to ski poles and boots. Two shotguns in leather bags were laid atop the ski poles. Their main function was to trigger avalanches, but they were also for defense. "Everything looks fine," Roland said. "Can't those cases be dropped from a hundred feet or something like that?"

Jesse pursed his lips, eyes darting from the road to Roland like that was the dumbest question he'd ever heard. "Well, sure, but if the lenses aren't packed perfect, or the padding shifts . . . " He gave Roland one last withering look before locking his gaze back on the road.

Roland knew the look well. It was his assistant's way of telling him it should be Jesse that was famous. He should be the world downhill champion, not Roland.

"I don't want to hear, 'What? You didn't get that?' when you launch off a cliff or bomb a patch of powder," Jesse said.

Roland sighed but said nothing.

The road narrowed, and the Jeep cut through two feet of snow like a plow, tire chains crunching, engine straining. A building materialized out of the thickening snowstorm, its single yellow light flickering in the darkness.

Jesse brought the truck to a stop, brakes squealing, wiper blades smacking back and forth.

The structure was made of wood, and it was half buried, drifts of snow covering the lower portion of its two boarded up windows. There were no signs, no identification of any kind, but Fort Fortune was known to everyone who ventured to Abominable Peak. In 1943, hikers discovered an exposed vein of gold in a cave, and during the other three seasons of the year, the base camp housed miners and support staff. The gold diggers were gone by Thanksgiving, at which time the place was mothballed until the following season. A caretaker was supposed to check on the place regularly but judging by the condition of the road he hadn't been around lately.

Roland and Jesse stared through the windshield, the snow sparkling under the glare of the Jeep's headlights. The wind howled, snow pelting the wagon like sand, fog-like breaths clouding the interior of the truck.

"Natural gas?" Jesse asked.

Roland nodded. He wasn't certain how the building's light was fed, but it was clearly a flame.

"Let's take a look," Roland said. The snow was too deep to open the door more than a few inches before getting stuck. He pulled the door closed and cranked down the window, snow blowing in his face, cold biting at his exposed skin. The temperature gauge attached to the truck's side view mirror registered eight degrees Fahrenheit.

Jesse made no move to get out of the truck, and as Roland wiggled through the open window he said, "You coming?"

"I'll follow you. No sense having both windows open. That is unless you want the car filled with snow?" Jesse said.

"Why do you always have to be such a wisenheimer?"

"Just trying to be one step ahead of you," Jesse said. "I thought that was what you wanted?"

Roland said, "What I want is for you to hand me my snowshoes." He sat in the open window with his legs in the snow, a stack of skis and equipment on the Jeep's roof racks behind him. The wind gusted, a deafening roar that whistled and sang like an out of tune orchestra.

Jesse handed the snowshoes to Roland, who dropped them in the snow. They were made of ash, with rawhide webbing and leather straps. He carefully slipped into each shoe, buckling the straps tight over the toes of his boots as he sat perched on the edge of the Jeep's open window.

The storm kicked up, and Roland found himself in a whiteout as he crossed the thirty feet between the wagon and the building. The Jeep's headlights pushed away the blackness, but he couldn't see Jesse or the truck. There was nothing except the cold black nothingness of the blizzard and the angry wind.

Roland hugged himself and pulled his coat tight around him, stomping the ground with his snowshoes, checking gloves and zippers to make sure he was sealed up. The

Jeep's cab had grown warm, the 134 cubic inch Go-Devil F-head four-cylinder engine throwing plenty of heat. The engine wasn't much of a powerhouse, but it was the main reason he'd selected the Willys. The motor was virtually indestructible, having proved itself in the harshest conditions imaginable during WWII.

Snow and ice pelted his face, and Roland raised his arm to shield his eyes as he pressed forward. His damp T-shirt and the perspiration running down his back grew cold, a chill spreading through him that threatened to seep into his bones.

A mournful cry followed by a bark-growl echoed over the howling gale. Roland stopped walking, listening hard, trying to edit out the wind, the push and brush of the snow, the growl of the truck's engine, and his galloping heart. The biting storm cajoled and whispered, searching for exposed skin. Roland felt his nose running, snot freezing in his mustache.

He spun around and a dark shape came at him through the sheets of snow. Roland reached for the strap holding his shotgun, only to remember it was back in the Jeep.

The crunch of footsteps and harsh breathing.

Jesse emerged from the white-speckled blackness, flashlight in hand, eyes frantic. "Did you hear that?"

"What?" Roland wasn't sure what he'd heard if anything. He'd been on enough mountains to know that wind is a siren's song, and when you're alone, cold, and miserable, the wind had a way of telling a person what they wanted to hear.

Jesse's eyebrows lifted beneath his goggles, and Roland felt stupid for not wearing his.

The duo's snowshoes crunched as they worked their way to the building's door, which was half buried in snow. "Mr. McMatheson said there were shovels under the overhang. Do you see them?" Roland asked.

Jesse disappeared into the whiteness, flashlight beam

bobbing. He returned moments later with two rusted shovels with ash handles, and the pair used them to clean the snow away from the door.

"Damn," Roland said. He traced claw marks in the scarred wood with his gloved index finger.

"Bear?" Jesse said.

Roland nodded, but he wasn't so sure. The gashes were high up, and if a bear had made the marks, it was a big one that had been standing on its hind legs.

"You have the key?" Jesse asked.

Roland huddled close to the door and shielded himself from the wind and snow as he pulled off his right glove. The key was in his jacket pocket, and as he unzipped the heavy poplin coat and wind and snow worked their way under his protective layer, tiny shards of pain knifing through him.

He pulled free the key and zipped up. The lock was iced over. Roland breathed on the lock, then pressed his thumb to the metal, and after a few minutes of the brass leeching all the heat from his hand, he was able to work the key into the lock and force the door open.

A blackness deeper than the darkest night filled the room.

Jesse stepped inside, his flashlight beam arcing through the space.

The place reminded Roland of a military barrack. Rows of bunk beds with an aisle down the center, tables covered in empty washbasins on either side of the door, and lines of empty hooks for jackets and gear. A one-inch cast iron pipe ran along the upper edge of the wall and fed the perpetual flame of the exterior light. Roland didn't see a valve to shut it off. The air smelled musty, like a room that's been sealed for a long time, with tinges of dirt and natural gas.

Wind whistled through every crack and gap, and Roland thought he heard the miner's voices, their laughter, their fears. He felt eyes on him, ghosts in the blackness.

"Everyone lives here?" Jesse asked.

"The miners, supervisors, cook," Roland said. "The entire crew of twenty-four."

Roland followed Jesse up the center aisle, his flashlight finding tiny piles of powder where the wind had wedged snow through cracks and holes. Icicles hung from rafters in several spots, and Roland eyed the corresponding water stains on the plank floor. The place was frigid cold, but without the constant attack of the wind, it felt like they were strolling in the Bahamas.

"That's it?" Jesse said, pointing at the smallest potbelly stove Roland had ever seen. Thick icicles stuck out like spikes around the spot where the vent pipe penetrated the roof, and the wood holder next to the unit was empty.

"Doesn't matter, mate. We can't use the water. Pump is off and winterized. Same goes for the stove and all the other systems. Even the generator. But we've got a roof over our heads, walls to keep out—" He looked around. "—most of the wind and snow."

Jesse sighed. "Let's get to it then."

Blackness dulled Fort Fortune, snow already covering the Jeep's headlights. Jesse lugged the gear inside, while Roland dealt with the truck.

They would make the rest of the ascent on foot, and the Jeep needed to be prepared for several days of nonuse. He checked all the windows, tipped up the windshield wiper blades so the rubber didn't stick to the glass, and popped the hood. A shriek, like a dying cat screaming, pierced the whiteout, metal on metal screeching as Roland lifted the hood. He pulled off his gloves and stuffed them in a pocket, and his hands began to numb immediately. He disconnected the battery, a light covering of snow blanketing the engine as he worked.

Roland stared down at the battery, pondering if he should bring it inside the barrack. Would it be warmer there? He concluded it would, so he removed the holding bracket, put his gloves back on, and jerked the battery from the engine compartment.

Snow crunched and something snapped, a piece of wood or a branch, but there were no trees around Fort Fortune. He paused, turning in circle, his arms protesting the weight of the battery. He saw nothing in the white speckled night, the beckoning call of the wind urging him on.

Roland stepped out of his snowshoes, leaned them tight against the barrack, and opened the door. It shrieked, but there was no accompanying growl of metal. He went inside and put the battery on one of the wooden tables, then closed and locked the door behind him.

A tent had been erected in the center aisle, the glow of a cooking stove within painting Jesse's shadow on the green canvas.

"All good?" Jesse inquired.

Roland peered through the mesh of the tent's entrance. "Yup." He stomped his feet and brushed snow off his jacket and pants.

Jesse chuckled. "Weeks of planning and a treacherous three-day trek up Abominable, all for a six-minute ride."

"To make history."

"For you, maybe," Jesse said.

Roland sighed. "Hopefully, the ride will be a tad longer than that, and you'll get footage and pictures that will make you a few clams and might make you famous. You want the cover of Ski Magazine, right? Or was all that bragging in the bar in Denver BS?"

Jesse said nothing. He stared through the mesh at Roland, his face expressionless.

Roland knew the look well. The two men had once been close friends, and he still knew his partner, perhaps better than he knew himself. He said, "What you got there? Stew?"

Jesse nodded.

Roland shook himself like a wet dog, unzipped the tent flap, and slipped inside. He sealed everything up tight and stripped off his jacket, boots, snow pants, gloves, hat. It was like removing a second skin or a wetsuit.

The two men ate in silence, drinking melted snow and whiskey. When they were done, they crawled into sleeping bags, doused the lights, and settled in for what would be their last night of solid sleep for three nights.

The old wood building creaked and moaned, boards popping, the door rattling in its frame. Sniffing . . . or snow pushing over snow like sand. Scratching, grunts, Jesse's labored breathing. His partner had no trouble falling asleep.

It would be a long night for Roland, his brain running through an imaginary minefield as he pondered the claw marks, the strange sounds, the call from the wild. Experience told him the animals that called the mountain range home were nestled deep in their warm lairs, nibbling food they'd gathered when the leaves began to fall in October. Yet his imagination argued and persuaded that there was something outside in the storm. Someone, or something, calling for him. Searching for him. The storm crooned and whispered, finding every crack and hollow, the tinkle and pop of snow pelting the wood like trillions of cockroaches scuttling over ice.

***

The next day dawned clear and bright, sunlight refracting off pristine snow, kaleidoscopes of color sparkling across a crystalline ocean of white. The wind hummed, ice cracked, and snow shifted in a dull roar, like a distant wave rolling on the white ocean as it crashed on a mountainous shore. Abominable Peak rose in the north, its summit a twisted white knife.

Roland pulled on his eye protection. Snow blindness was common on high snowcapped mountains where the air is thinner and provides less protection from UV rays, so he had to remember to always wear his goggles. He was bundled up, snowshoes and backpack on, skis and poles strapped to his pack. He was already sweating under the double layer of long underwear and the full hood that covered his head and most of his face.

Leaving the barrack was like stepping from a space capsule onto the surface of the moon.

Jesse knelt, examined the ground next to their small equipment sled.

Spears of dazzling light knifed through the whiteness like electricity, the crunch of Roland's snowshoes echoing in the silence. In the light of day, he saw other buried buildings, but nothing larger than the barrack. There was equipment under all the snow. Barns and stables. A compound buried like Atlantis beneath a sea of frozen waves.

"Find something?" Roland said as he peered over his partner's shoulder.

A red dot marred the immaculate white, but that wasn't what made his breath catch in his throat like a fishbone.

Huge four-toed footprints in the soft snow formed double tracks like those of a bipedal creature, three-inch slices at the tip of each digit delineating claws. The tracks trailed away into the milky whiteness.

2

January 27, 2018, Abominable Peak, Colorado—Elevation 16,971 feet

THE JET-BLACK HELICOPTER streaked across the clear blue sky, sharp sunlight reflecting off the new-fallen snow, dimples of color sparkling like diamonds. The rattlesnake tinkle, rhythmic bass, and psychedelic rift of Aerosmith echoed through the cabin, drums pounding as the band shrieked about sweet emotions.

Chance rolled his shoulders and cracked his neck as he zipped his shell and pulled up his gloves.

Steven Tyler crooned, rolling guitar thunder rushing through Chance like an electric shock. It was a time warp to the past, he and his crew psyching themselves out for a run the way they had when they'd been on the circuit together, competing, but as tight as a group could be. All that had changed when Chance fell from grace.

The *womp-womp* of the copter's rotor blades pounding the thin mountain air was like an additional drum track, the steady beat out of rhythm with Joe Perry's screeching guitar. The helicopter was an AStar designed for high altitude missions and was powered by an Arriel 2B engine equipped with a digital engine control unit with a mechanical backup system that made flying in strong winds at high altitudes less insane. The AStar 2B was the first helicopter to land on the summit of Mount Everest, and the whirlybird's pilot, Trevor Lindy, was one of the most experienced drop guys in the business.

The AStar was configured in a five-passenger setup, plus the pilot and co-pilot. Tina sat in the co-pilot's seat because she liked talking to Trevor over the headset, helmet in her lap, her red knit cap with blue pom-pom on top inched back on her head. The hat was a gift from her deceased father, and she wore it whenever she wasn't riding under competition rules. Big Bob, who everyone in the crew affectionately referred to as Biggie, sat next to him on the forward bench seat, lost in the music, eyes closed, head bobbing up and down with the beat. Colin, Jibber, and Bomber sat behind him, and he heard Bomber thrumming his fingers on the copter's glass window, Jibber's horrible singing, and the occasional rhythmic chirp-snore of Colin.

Chance smiled. He felt like a member of a special ops unit on his way to a drop-off, everyone dialing in their inner strength, calling the demon that made them want to fly to the top of the world and ride a hill that had no business being ridden.

Those looking in from the outside thought his crew had abandoned him, and there were times it felt like they had. As he thought of his friends, a warmth blossomed in his chest that wouldn't have been possible a few short months ago. These people hadn't abandoned him like his sponsors had or the many others he'd called friends. Sure, he hadn't seen any of them in the months leading up to their trip to Abominable Peak, but he didn't blame them. They were still on tour, chasing a dream that had deserted him for little white pills.

When he'd stopped blaming the injury for his downfall, his life had come back into focus. Like a run, he once again saw life's drops, its fine lines, freshies, curves, and pitfalls. He could anticipate it all before it happened, dropping into each bump and curve life threw his way, avoiding every bony spot. That was when things started to change for him, the future no longer clouded in a drug-induced haze.

Sweet Emotion pounded through the cabin like an anthem.

He gazed west at the army of dark clouds marching across the horizon. The incoming storm was expected to dump a foot of snow on the Rockies starting late afternoon. Wind pushed against the copter. Trevor kept the nose of the craft dipped as he climbed, turbine whining, rotors battering the air as he gripped the yoke with both hands.

Chance said, "Storm looks bad."

"We'll be drinking martinis at Lucky's before the first snowflake hits the ground." Biggie elbowed Chance and put his arms around him. "This must be really special for you, huh? I'm happy for you, man," he bellowed.

Chance glanced at Tina, who was wearing cans, mic before her moving lips. He looked over his shoulder at his three amigos, and they pretended they hadn't heard the question. He turned back to Biggie, but words failed him.

Whether it was the look on his face, his lack of response, or the general uncomfortable vibe that leaked through the cabin like sewage, his friend added, "What with your grandfather passing on up here and all."

Chance felt his face go taut and his eyes grow wide.

"Sorry, man, I just . . . " Biggie looked away.

Charles 'Chance' Hance's grandfather had died on the peak back when skis were made mostly of wood, and it was a three-day hike to the summit for each ride. Chance said nothing as he stared at the snowboards strapped to the copter's landing skids. Bomber's orange Burton with black stripes, Tina's aqua number with Hawaiian flowers, and Colin had brought his competition board, which was covered in logos—Salomons, RIDE, Burton and Nitro. The other three boards, including his custom Burton Reaper, were out of view on the opposite landing skid.

The chopper banked hard to port as Trevor circled the mountain, giving the boarders a good view of the conditions on the peak, which was formed from a huge overhanging cornice like a curved fang that bulged out over the eastern slope. The summit's sharp angle reminded Chance of Mount

Crumpit, where the Grinch hung his hat. The northern face was a series of cliffs, crags, and tumbled boulders dusted like glazed donuts. The southern face was treacherous but rideable, the eastern and western faces nothing more than shoots where the rock splintered into vertical crevasses, slender seracs like teeth in a boney jaw.

Spindrifts rolled down the mountainside like a frozen river, eddies, chutes, and falls coming together like puzzle pieces, a route forming in Chance's head. Sheer drop-offs marked by brown rock faces cast long, thick shadows over virgin powder. From above, Chance saw all the cracks in the snowpack and ice, all the blocks and runners that had shifted, the many overhangs of built-up snow and ice hiding bony areas and rough sections of chowder caused by falling ice.

Aerosmith died away and Trevor's voice crackled over the inboard comm speaker. "Looks good, wind shear at a minimum. Chance, you gonna blow out the candle?"

There was no place to set down the bird, so the team would have to rappel to the peak, but first potential avalanches needed to be dealt with.

Chance gave a thumbs up. With the sun glaring down through the thin air the snowpack weakened as it became wetter and heavier, and the weaker layers are forced to carry more weight. Blowing out the candle referred to trigger shots or explosives used to free snowpack on the verge of moving or falling.

Biggie passed Chance the case containing the explosive charges. Each charge, which boarders called M-180s, had detonators with digital timers and equaled roughly a stick of dynamite. He slipped on his belay harness and snapped the carabiner at the end of his safety strap onto a steel ring mounted next to the cabin's sliding door.

"Buckle up," Trevor said. "I'll tell you when, Chance."

The helicopter wheeled, spiraling in close, the thunderous roar of the rotor blades and the rumble of the turbine slicing the air. Rivulets of snow and ice cascaded down the face of the mountain, and several large cracks formed in the snowpack, dark lines spidering over the field of white.

Chance checked his safety line, put on his goggles, pulled his helmet chinstrap tight, and opened the case containing the charges. Then, he slid open the AStar's side door, and wind gusted through the cabin.

Tina whooped, the roar of the rotors like a hurricane.

Trevor eased back on the yoke and the chopper hovered four hundred feet above the peak. Trevor's voice squawked over the comm. "Now!"

Chance pulled one of the charges free, two white three-inch rectangles held together via black electrical tape with a small circuit board attached to it. The activation switch was covered with a safety shield, and Chance thumbed it up, flicked the toggle, and dropped the charge out the open door.

Trevor cycled up the copter's engine, rotors hammering as he pulled on the yoke, and rolled the helicopter east.

The companions all strained to see out the port windows. Three seconds slipped away . . . four . . .

The thump of an explosion echoed over the mountain, bouncing off the cliffs. Crowds of snowballs rolled down the wave of white, a geyser of snow shooting fifty feet into the air. Dull thuds and deep cracking rose above the wind and thumping rotors, but none of the snowpack gave way. Chance repeated this process two more times with no success, but his fourth attempt was the charm. A third of the snowpack clinging to the sharp peak shifted and broke free, sliding down the mountain at two hundred miles per hour, a tsunami that could flatten skyscrapers and drown cities.

The roar of the racing snow was like river rapids, the occasional snap and crack of a tree breaking, or the pop of boulders tumbling free like gunshots.

Trevor backed off as the peak was obscured in a cloud of white, the whirlybird's updraft spiraling like a cyclone, the copter trembling and vibrating.

As the snow-mist cleared, Chance saw that the run had changed like magic. Clean lines had been replaced with jagged cliffs, powdery bowls filled with sharp spires of ice, and windswept drifts had become impenetrable walls. With the snowpack still undulating and shifting, Chance picked up fresh lines, his mind connecting dots and creating a new path down the sheer face.

Clouds of snow erupted over the peak as Trevor dropped in, the helicopter's engine whining as he brought the yoke to center and hovered eighty feet above the snowpack.

Chance sat by the open door, so he would drop first. The winch mounted above the door had a length of red nylon dry rope spooled on it, and he checked the knot holding the carabiner at the end of the line, then snapped in. He thumbed the carabiner's lock into place and gave a thumbs up.

Trevor's voice cracked as it came over the speaker, "Wave if it's okay."

Chance inched to the edge of the seat, wind gusting into the cabin. He checked his snowboard boots, adjusted his goggles and helmet, zipped his shell all the way up, pulled his gloves tight, and stepped out into the void, placing his feet on the foot pad atop the chopper's landing skid. Dazzling sunlight reflected off the blanket of snow below, and he closed his eyes as he stepped off the skid. The wind spun him like an infant's mobile as he clung to the rope, the harness biting into his chest, snow wash and angry cold gnawing his cheeks.

The winch droned and he looked up and saw Biggie, line running through his hand, Chance hanging from a red rope above a field of pure white reflected in his helmet's face shield.

Chance's feet hit snow and he sank knee-deep. He

stomped, creating a small patch of snowpack, then he waved up to Biggie who began peeling the snowboards out of their racks and feeding them down the red line. When all the boards were down, Biggie funneled down six yellow Ortovox Free Rider emergency backpacks before the crew began dropping from the sky like spiders on silk strands.

The helicopter's rotors tore up the peak, spindrifts cascading like water, a hurricane of snow and tiny ice pellets piercing his face like mouse claws. He cursed himself for not wearing his full hood.

When everyone was down, Trevor saluted through the side window, dipped the whirlybird's nose, and flew off.

The six boarders pulled on their safety packs in silence, the wind like a gentle breeze without the help of the copter's rotor wash. Chance gazed out on the Sawatch Mountains and thought of how his grandfather had stood on this same peak, saw this amazing view.

The Sawatch Range runs along a northwest-southeast axis, extending roughly eighty miles, forming part of the Continental Divide. Its eastern side drains into the headwaters of the Arkansas River. As Chance gazed southeast, Mount Elbert's round top towered above lesser peaks, but not by much. The range contains fifteen peaks over fourteen thousand feet, and to the north, Mount Massive soared almost as high, but Abominable Peak towered above them all, piercing the clouds.

Chance sat in the snow and snapped into his bindings. His axe was a Burton, black, with a cloaked Grim Reaper holding a ski pole scythe with bony hands adorning the front surface, death's robes and skinless arms feathering back around the bindings to the tail. The board's rails shone in the sunlight, no rust, gashes, or dents. The ride was new, but he'd tested it once, checking the binding settings, and learning the flex and speed of the board. Knowing your plank's capabilities was crucial when riding a rail of ice or hitting a tabletop of stone.

The winch-like clicking of bindings being tightened echoed over the peak. The riders adjusted gear, cracked necks, tightened emergency backpack straps, stretched, and straightened goggles and helmets.

Jibber said, "So, did I hear that right? Your legendary grandad died up here?"

Chance nodded as he stared down the southern vertical slope, finding a line, creating a mental map.

"That's why you wanted to ride here so badly?" Bomber said.

"So, it wasn't just about not seeing people from the circuit?" Tina added.

"Riding a hill you've never ridden?" Colin piled on.

"Do I really need to explain myself to you stooges?" Chance said, but he was smiling. He puffed out a cloud of condensed air. "It's not something I go around telling folks, and it's not like I saw you guys. We never . . . talked about coming here. You turds just said you'd come."

Tina said, "Why wouldn't we?"

"I don't know . . . " he said.

Tina hopped to the edge of the precipice, the snowpack giving way, her board slipping down the face. "I'm sorry I never came around. I've got no excuse, man. None."

"You were on tour," Chance said.

"Yeah, so? See you at the collection spot." Tina hopped again, straightened her board, and crouched low as she disappeared over the edge and down the southern slope. The others watched as she cut a line, fresh powder spraying like water.

The distant *womp-womp* of the helicopter faded into the wind.

Colin was up next. His thick gnarly beard was already covered with tiny icicles, his goggles iced around their edges. He put his huge paw on Chance's shoulder and squeezed it before dropping off the shelf and jumping into Tina's track.

Bomber said, "Tina's right. We should've skipped a stop and come to see you. Shit, we didn't even come to the hospital after the injury. I'm sorry about that, dude. Sorrier than I've ever been in my life."

"I told you guys not to come," Chance said. "I didn't want to inconvenience anyone." The truth was, he hadn't wanted anyone to see him that broken.

"Yeah, we shouldn't have listened. Can't wait to catch up over drinks tonight," Bomber said, and hopped onto the slope. He didn't follow Tina and Colin's track, but instead lived up to his namesake and divebombed straight down the seventy-five-degree slope, hopping and air gliding, and passing Tina and Colin as they carved wide loops in the virgin powder.

Jibber clapped him on the back. "I'm just happy you're back, dude. Can't wait to kick your ass next season." He pushed off and was gone.

Chance hadn't made up his mind about competing again. He still loved riding, but the drive to compete just hadn't returned.

Biggie inched close to Chance. "Sorry about before," he said. "I thought everyone knew."

Chance smiled as he adjusted his goggles, rolled his shoulders, and checked his bindings one last time. "No worries," he said.

Biggie inch-wormed forward and slipped over the precipice. He didn't look back.

It was out, and now his crew knew that not only was he chasing his demons, but also a ghost.

3

EXTREME SPORTS ARE an addiction. There's no other term that fits, that embraces the lunacy and recklessness which leads a person to bomb down the side of a mountain, rocks and trees buried under feet of frozen water waiting to gobble a rider up and spit them out before said junkie had a chance to take a breath. When the gnarliest of groomed trails ceases to get your blood pumping, you've become a full-fledged adrenaline addict. All riders seek their own ultimate rush, pushing their limits. It was akin to drugs or surfing a wave. There's nothing else in the world at that moment, and it was the only time Chance let go of his past.

Sunlight danced on snow as he gazed down the sheer incline, ridges and dunes casting long dark shadows over the field of white, ominous black patches filling bowls and furrows. Flutes and cracks lined the snowpack, wide and deep.

His nerves jangled, the tips of his fingers stinging. It had been a long journey to Abominable Peak, both mentally and physically. He thought of his grandfather, what it must have been like to reach the summit after a three-day climb. Would he be as thrilled to take the plunge if it had taken three days of hiking to get up here, not a ten-minute heli jump from base camp? He'd climbed from the shit, risen above, and here he was, ready to take the leap again and head on back down so he could start all over again. It was exhilarating and frustrating.

The sun glare made it difficult to see, though Chance's polarized goggles helped. His crew was cutting swagging lines down the face, except Bomber, who'd disappeared within his own wake cloud. Chance jerked his hips and wiggled forward, the snow crunching as his Burton started to slide.

Boris Karloff's voice rattled in his head, the pop and snap of the crunching snow bringing the image of the Grinch sliding down the face of Mount Crumpit to mind. Something about a growing heart.

He bent his knees, got low, and inched over the lip, dropping into the groove created by his crew, throwing a wall of snow as he cut hard right, slowing, his edge slipping as the board dug into powder. Wind tore at his face as he picked up speed, hitting a pristine line and carving into a white dune, then slinging downhill, working his legs back and forth as he snaked through loose snow.

Uneasiness and dread knifed through him, spine aching and tingling, sweat rolling down his back. He was moving too fast, the board sliding out from under him. He was losing control and had to slow, but he was afraid to carve hard for fear of catching an edge or hitting a stone. Muscles tensed, a loud ringing filling his head like he'd been hit in the head with a bat.

Chance fell back, the tip of the Burton coming up, the board flexing. He eased his right foot forward and slipped his left back, bringing the board vertical to his body, his legs shuddering under the strain. His momentum arced him onto a bulletproof section of snow, and he dug in the board's inside edge, the sound of metal tearing over ice like a scraper clearing a car's frozen windshield.

Tina, Colin, and Biggie launched off a low cliff, splashing into the snowdrift at its base, disappearing as if underwater only to burst free, covered in white, a rooster tail of ice and snow trailing behind them. A field of rocks and chowder trailed away to the east, so Chance dug in with his toes, gliding through a thick field of powder as he arced toward his friends.

The sun glare blinded him for an instant, and panic punched him in the gut. He'd talked to a race car driver at a party once—Giuseppe something—and he'd told Chance about what it was like being on the track during an accident, racing into clouds of smoke at a hundred and fifty miles an hour, not knowing if you were going to make it out.

Pain knifed through Chance's stomach, fear and doubt stabbing him, telling him he was a fool to think he could just ride like he had before, no training, no prep. What had he been thinking? Yet, as muscle memory took control, he stopped thinking, let his body do what it had done many times before.

He arced left, anticipating the sliding snowpack, hopping off a rock and landing on a cloud of snow before launching off a low cliff.

Dazzling sunlight, sharp lines of a bright rainbow, whiteness filling the world.

The freefall ended and he thumped into sugar, knees shrieking as his board flattened and he bounced forward, picking up speed as he emerged from a wave of cascading snow.

Tina whooped but didn't stop. Colin pulled up short to make sure Chance was alright, then turned downhill and was gobbled up by the deep snow.

The incline lessened, but rocks, moguls, and the tops of evergreen trees poking through the snowpack created an obstacle course. Chance stayed well away from all such impediments because there was no way to know what dangers lurked beneath the snowpack. Catching the tip of a snowboard on a branch or stone when moving at a hundred miles per hour could be catastrophic.

He cut between the tops of two evergreens, his balance coming back, angst and fear draining away. He cut hard right, carving into a mound of snow, and launching into the air. He grabbed his board out of habit, though there was nobody there to see it. Dazzling sunlight as he landed, fell on his ass, but he used his momentum to bounce back to his feet. The Burton Reaper flexed its tip catching snowpack. He leaned back, sliding the board back and forth as he sculpted a line down the last section of the upper peak.

The crew had veered to the east and were playing in a shallow snow-filled bowl that looked like a natural skate park.

Tina cut a wide ribbon through a field of chowder, and jumped onto a flat rock, riding its edge before pulling hard left and continuing through the bowl. Colin rode the rail of a fallen tree, its exposed trunk free of branches. Biggie and Jibber vaulted back and forth between two massive snowdrifts, like a natural halfpipe, the boarders zigzagging and hopping through the open snow tunnel.

A hollow roar echoed over the mountain, like a T-rex voicing its displeasure at the intrusion into its peaceful habitat. He searched the slope before him, looked back, fighting the sun glare.

Chance and his crew had dropped a thousand feet, the grooves of their passage dark lines of shadow in the immaculate white. He breathed heavily, nerves walking the highwire, sweat dripping down his back.

He dropped into a flute, rivulets of ice and loose snow cascading through it. He got low and let the moving snow push him along as the frozen river engulfed him. He was knee-deep in powder, and he carved east, struggling as he sprayed snow, board flexing and popping under the strain.

A dull cracking sound echoed over the mountain like a giant ice block had broken in half. It was the sound nobody wanted to hear when they were walking across a frozen lake . . . or when racing down a seventy-degree slope on a waxed piece of wood coated in fiberglass that had no brakes.

Chance tried to take inventory of his team, but the only one he could find in the blinding whiteness was Bomber. He was way down the face, a long trail of snow behind him. A worm of worry writhed in his stomach and started its crawl up his throat to his brain, then he remembered he was the one who hadn't ridden in months. They should be watching him, making sure *he* was okay.

He leaned back, lifting the nose of the board as he cut right, avoiding a bony area where treetops stuck from the snowpack like bumpers in a pinball machine. Tree limbs reached out, and he figured the patch of forest provided solid terrain riding in early winter, but with the snowpack burying the forest and only the tops of the tallest trees visible, riding through the glade was too dangerous. He cut away from the trees, heading over a boulder and down the slope.

A field of pure white opened before him, the slope leading to a drop that had been marked on the survey he'd reviewed. The cliff was thirty feet high and too tall to glide off.

He worked west, legs swaying back and forth as he carved an endless S in the powder. Sunlight sparkled, and a tiny rainbow arced over his line. He smiled, sucking in a deep breath of chilled, clean mountain air.

He was back.

The ground gave way beneath him. One moment, Chance was drifting along the snowpack, easing into a groove, then he was falling, his board finding no resistance as he plummeted in a maelstrom of snow and ice. He reached out in the chaos, not knowing what he hoped to find. He twisted and thrashed, trying to bring his board flat and stay above the river of snow. His board hit something, and the shock jarred Chance's knees and back, pain running through him.

Everything went dark for a heartbeat as the wave of snow broke. He leaned back as far as he could, snow covering him like water. He fumbled for the red plastic release grip to activate his backpack, but he couldn't find it in the whiteness. A load of snow dumped on him, and his board was thrust upward, the Reaper at the end of the Burton eyeing him for a heartbeat before disappearing in tumbling snow. He wiggled and writhed, the board flexing, but staying together. Finally, his hand found the safety release, and he yanked it down.

A rush of air, like a parachute opening, and Chance was tugged up, straps biting into his armpits and chest as the backpack airbag inflated and pulled him to the top of the avalanche like a surfer being sucked from the depths. His board caught an edge on a massive ice ball, and he was pushed forward as he broke free into sunlight, riding the face of the avalanche, the inflated airbag twittering in the wind.

Chance pushed his back foot down, hard, keeping the tip of the Burton up, trying to stay atop the flow. Tree branches, snow rocks, and chunks of ice tumbled in the spindrifts, a wall of snow traveling at over a hundred miles an hour. Visibility was near zero, but it didn't matter. He had no control and was doing everything he could to avoid being rolled in the undertow like a pebble when the snow wave broke.

A dark evergreen appeared before him and the Burton crashed into the thick trunk, the tip of the board snapping off, the Grim Reaper disappearing in the swirling snow.

A loud *pop* echoed over the chaos and Chance felt himself falling as he lost the lift of the airbag. Yellow nylon jumbled with the white—his punctured airbag—and he leaned back as far as he could, driving the broken board into the torrent of ice that threatened to sweep him under.

An updraft of snow pushed him forward and up, the board cresting on the frozen wave, the Burton's shattered tip kicking up slushy spray. Blue sky filled his view as he plummeted down an eighty-degree slope, a sheer drop-off advancing like an unavoidable task, an inevitable failure.

Chance heard screaming . . . Tina, but he couldn't understand what she was saying.

He twisted and flipped in the deluge, trying to dig in the jagged front of the Burton, but there was too much snow, and it was moving too fast.

Chance was swept over the cliff.

He let his body go slack as he was jostled and tossed, his stomach sinking with the feeling of falling. Whiteness with a backdrop of blue spun and shimmered, his goggles still somehow on his face. The rough leaves of an evergreen scratched along his side, and he reached out and grasped it like a child snatching a toy dangling before their greedy eyes.

Chance held on for a second before being torn away, pain stabbing his shoulder. The second of resistance did more harm than good. Brown rocks were added to the churning blue and white speckled canvas of his vision, and he put out his hands to stop from hitting an outcrop of stone. He cartwheeled, the splintered edge of the Burton catching a boulder, and what was left of the board was cleaved in half, the plastic bindings breaking free as an eddy of snow slammed Chance into the cliff face.

The blow jarred him to the core, sharp edges tearing into his jacket and snow pants, pulling at his torn airbag, pain blooming in his head like an arterial hemorrhage, his vision going blurry, muscles taut with adrenaline and panic. A roaring waterfall of snow poured over the cliff, evergreen branches and boulders of ice tumbling in the deluge.

He covered his head with his arms as he was buried, warm blood leaking down his face. He pushed with his legs, still wearing the broken bindings, shards of snowboard clinging to his feet like flattened teeth. He plowed, thrusting his legs out, pressing the snow away and pushing himself tighter beneath the overhang, nestling into a crag in the cliff face.

Darkness filled the small space as Chance thrust out his legs, pushing back the snowpack, which creaked and crunched under its own weight, always compressing, ever pressing. The snow reached his waist, he took a deep breath, preparing for Abominable Peak to dunk him.

The rumble of falling snow died away, Chance's harsh breathing out of rhythm with his thumping heart. He twisted, loosening his torso and lifting his arms. His hands met a rock ceiling two feet above his head. He was trapped under the avalanche's wake-wash and had maybe half an hour of air.

He needed to start digging, but that was fraught with danger. With the snow still settling he could cause a cave-in or open a new funnel, and Chance heard cracking and rending as tons of icepack shifted and slid. He wiggled and dug, clearing enough room to pull off his emergency backpack. The popped airbag was twisted and wrapped around the pack, but Chance wedged his hand into a side pouch and drew out a headlamp. He snapped it on and sucked in a sharp breath.

A ceiling of brown rock ran on a downward angle from the cliff face, disappearing into a sparkling white wall. The space was the size of two coffins side-by-side, and the sheet of white before him was splattered with his blood.

Chance's legs were going numb, and his hands trembled as he pulled off a glove and caressed the knot on his head, blood soaking into his black polyester glove liner. The wound throbbed, but he didn't remember hitting his head. He pulled free his folded utility knife, and the blade glinted as Chance flicked it open. He inched his headlamp over the front of his helmet, cut the airbag free, and closed and stowed the utility knife. He always carried the mountaineering Swiss Army knife when in the backcountry, and its five-inch stainless steel blade with notched spine regularly came in handy as did the collection of other tools the utility knife provided: needle-nose plyers, screwdrivers, can opener, and the always useful small saw and corkscrew. The knife had been his grandfather's, and his dad had passed it on to him on his twelfth birthday.

He slipped his pack back on and started swimming, thrashing, and wiggling his legs, compressing snow, making space as he worked his way to the top of the spilt powder, sinking in the frigid whiteness. With the shards of his snowboard still attached to the bindings, which were still strapped onto his boots, he was able to get some leverage and work his way along the underside of the ledge, snow leaking into every gap in his jacket and pushing down his neckline. His body temperature was dropping, his ski gear not up to the task of prolonged exposure to extreme cold.

The faint roar of a beast in pain fought through the snowpack, and he froze. It wasn't the scream of a searching friend or the pounding of helicopter rotors. It was something else. The worm of worry that had retreated squirmed into his stomach and setup camp.

He continued digging, warming as he worked, his mind spinning through an endless series of possibilities. His team returning to the collection point—even if only one made it—would trigger a full search. Rangers, helicopters, snowcats. They were probably already looking for him. When he didn't arrive at the collection point, Trevor would spin-up and look for him.

Chance did some mental calculations and determined it had been less than fifteen minutes since he'd started his run. The odds of finding or catching up with his crew were perilously low, even if he could fashion crampons from his broken Burton and his bindings or create snowshoes using evergreen branches. Hope grew in him as he realized none of that was necessary. All he needed to do was wait it out. Dig out of the snowpack, spread out the popped yellow airbag, and wait to be seen. The storm wasn't due until the end of the day, so there was plenty of time to get off the mountain. He'd been lucky.

Slipping snow and cracking ice echoed through his hole, and he stopped digging, listening to the moaning and heckling of the snow shifting, sliding, and compressing. He moved forward gingerly, sweeping loose powder behind him, and he inched along the underside of the ledge. When he reached its end, he could turn upward and follow the cliff face to the surface.

Another bestial roar and snow flowed into his face, filling the small space. The crack and snap of ice breaking, and then he was falling again, engulfed in sugary powder that wrapped him in its icy embrace.

4

CHANCE WHIRLED IN the whiteout, stomach protesting, fear taking hold, mind spinning.

This was it. He was done.

He reached out desperately into the maelstrom, searching for anything to grab hold of, but there was nothing. He plummeted for three heartbeats before landing in a pile of powder that exploded upon his entry. He sank into the snow, still dropping, ice pellets peppering his face. Bursts of light sparkled before his eyes as he thumped to a stop, the dazzling starbursts like shooting stars. Air rushed from his lungs and pain cut through him as he gasped for breath, the frigid air stinging his lungs.

A snow waterfall poured onto Chance, and he covered his face with his arm as he tumbled off the snow pile, landing on frozen stone. He rolled onto his side and vomited, bits of powdered egg and ketchup-tinged sausage splattering the pure white. He lay there several minutes in stunned shock, the light bursts fading, his eyesight slowly coming back online. What had happened? Time slowed, his mind tried putting the events in order, but there were too many missing pieces.

His headlamp had slipped off his helmet and hung around his neck by its strap. It cast a cone of wavering light through a narrow crevasse. He flexed his arms, legs, and back. Crashing cymbals rang in his head, cold seeped into him along with the realization that he was screwed.

He got on his hands and knees and crawled away from the torrent of snow pouring through the hole above. He pulled his headlamp back onto his helmet, and loosened the helmet's strap, rubbing the area where it had dug into his neck.

Thirty feet above a blue ceiling of ice covered the narrow crevasse, pale light arching through the hole he'd made, but there was no blue sky visible, no darkening clouds. The hole he'd fallen through was beneath the cliff face's overhang and might not be visible from the air. He searched for the popped airbag but didn't see it. The thing was most likely buried under tons of snowpack.

He got to one knee, panting, his muscles screaming as the adrenaline drained away, his vision going in and out of focus, the cold burrowing into his face like a swarm of mosquitoes. The torrent of snow lessened to a trickle, miniature spindrifts rolling down the pile that had saved his life. Beyond the mound, the wet, dark brown stone of the mountainside disappeared into the snowpack above. Icicles the size of broadswords hung from outcrops and ledges, but even if he had the proper climbing gear, he wasn't experienced enough to attempt an ascent. Getting out the way he'd entered wasn't an option, so he turned all his attention to the opposite end of the crevasse, which vanished into grayness, the light leaking through the ice above casting undulating shadows in the haze.

Chance inched forward, the crack in the mountainside no more than ten feet wide. The floor was slick with a coating of frost, and he almost fell twice before sitting on a snow boulder to consider things. The idea of creating crampons returned. With some manipulation, he might be able to fashion the shards of his broken board in such a way that his bindings could serve as crampons.

He snapped out of his bindings. Cloudy stretchmarks lined the black plastic, the upper buckles on both had torn away, and the base of one was cracked from the stress of the snowboard breaking in half. He pulled his knife and popped out the pliers. Working with his gloves on was hard, but he was already getting chilled due to his lack of motion, and he didn't dare take his gloves off for fear of not being able to get them back on because of the sweat and moisture on his palms.

The ice ceiling cracked but didn't cave-in, the thump of helicopter rotors pounding through the crevasse. He dropped his work and vaulted to his feet, watching a faint shadow arc across the roof of blue ice. The *womp-womp* faded and he fell back onto his ass.

He'd never felt as alone as he did in that moment. Not after the injury. Not after he lost everything. Not even when he'd hit rock bottom and woke in the basement of the ski lodge in Breckenridge with no idea how he'd gotten there. Icy fingers massaged his neck, those worms in his stomach swirling and agitating.

Chance went back to his task, and after an hour of fumbling with pieces of the Burton, he managed to screw three shards of broken board to the toes of each binding.

He strapped in, got up, and dug in his toes—wood covered in fiberglass shrieking in the stillness. The shards flexed but didn't break. He had no idea how long his makeshift crampons would last, but they'd be better than nothing if he needed to ascend a steep slope or stop himself from sliding.

Wind whistled through the tunnel, the tinkle of powdery snow leaking through holes and cracks in the mountain, spears of ice hanging from every notch and crag. He sensed something awful hidden in the pouring streams of snow and within the sharp icicles, felt the mountain tremble and sigh beneath his boots, heard the wind whistling, cajoling.

He hadn't gone far before he reached a spidery intersection where the crevasse splintered off in four directions. Two tunnels with rock ceilings no more than a foot-wide angled up and down, a third nothing more than a narrow chute filled with a slope of ice-covered scree that fell into blackness. The fourth route lay straight ahead, a continuation of the current crack, the blue ice ceiling continuing like a fluorescent light fixture. Chance stepped forward, intent on going the obvious way when a growl slithered up from one of the tunnels.

A paralyzing fear rooted Chance to the frozen ground, eyes flicking back and forth between the dark maws of the larger tunnels. The wind mumbled and chortled, singing through cracks and shrieking around sharp edges. His headlamp arced through the half-light, shadows fleeing into darkness.

A clicking sound—the gurgle of an angry animal—floated on the rank breeze that pushed from the tunnel plunging downward.

He lurched into motion, following the main tunnel, pseudo-crampons scraping the iced floor, his harsh breathing bouncing off the walls, the blue glow above a poor replacement for sky. But even as he mentally complained, the ceiling became opaque. Specks of dirt and debris mixed with the ice, and as he hurried along more dark particles mixed with the ice ceiling, the blue faded to a dull brown. The cave grew narrow and dark, sheets of frost ending in thick icicles that melted into the slick ice-covered ground.

The cave floor pitched steeply downward, the crack in the mountain running deeper. The ice roof was gone and had been replaced with a mix of watery ice, stone, and dirt. Chance dug in the makeshift crampons, water dripping onto his cracked helmet from a row of slender icicles as he leaned back, peering downslope, his headlamp beam dying in blackness.

A loud pop, like a giant metal rivet tearing away from a steel support, ripped through the cave like a gunshot. The ground trembled, thin cracks forming in the verglas that coated every surface.

Another explosive pop echoed through the cave as ice

and stone broke away and Chance slipped into a chute like a child riding down a playground slide. He landed on his ass, headlamp bouncing in the darkness, ice shards pelting his face, starbursts of color filling his vision as the LED light bounced off crystalized snow. His backpack snagged on a rock, a shoulder strap tore, and he was again plummeting downward.

Chance rolled onto his stomach and tried to dig in with shards of broken board on his feet, but the stone was slick with water and ice, and the wood shrieked and cracked, but didn't take hold. He bounced off the wall, his helmet smashing into stone along with his headlamp, and Chance heard the cracking of plastic and rending of metal as the light went out and the enormity of his situation struck him like a hammer to the temple.

He'd made peace with his death as he fell through the ice pack into the tunnel, only to survive unscathed, and as the incline of the chute lessened, hope spread through him like a warm fire after of lifetime in the cold. The burn of whiskey, the scent of charred meat. Things that made him think of better times, better feelings. Chance dug in with renewed effort, and one of the shards of wood broke away, but that didn't hurt the effort.

The chute looped upward, and Chance slowed, stopped, then slid back into the hollow bowl at the bottom of the chute. He lay on his back in darkness as he shifted, checking to make sure all his connections worked. Wiggle toes. Check. Fingers. Check. He rolled his shoulders as he stared up, cold biting his face, his shell pulled up to his shoulders, frigid fingers massaging his back.

But his chill wasn't from the cold.

Two red pinpricks of light appeared in the blackness above. They moved, levitated. He stared, the tapping of dripping water growing louder, his vision tuning out the darkness. The red spots grew in brightness as if advancing. Random thoughts of rescue danced through his subconscious like birthday wishes he'd known weren't going to come true the instant he blew out the candles.

With a sickening dread akin to his acceptance of plummeting to his death, terror seized him, and he couldn't move. He knew he wasn't hurt, yet now his body was on strike, refusing to follow direct orders. Insubordination of the most vicious kind. As he stared, his body itched, millions of invisible ice ants crawling inside his long underwear, biting and stinging.

The red lights blinked out and returned. Fear played Chance's nerves like a harp, the realization that there was something in the tunnel with him pushing through his protective cocoon of denial. A growl rumbled down the cave, followed by a thunderous roar that triggered small spindrifts, ice and powdery snow falling from the walls and ceiling like some god shook the Abominable Peak snow globe.

He gave in to the primal urge to flee and screamed in his head, ordering his body to move. Pain filtered through him, and he wiggled his fingers and toes. Chance got to his feet, his right ankle and knee protesting as he slid down the pile of snow to the rock floor.

The two blazing red specks had grown to the size of golf balls, and they swayed as they advanced.

Chance ran blindly on, his harsh breathing thumping in his ears, heart hammering and heading for a redline. He slid on ice, arms out as the shards of the Burton dug in, trying to jerk him to a stop.

Cracks appeared in the cave walls, thin crevasses that would one day widen and split the surface of the peak. His mind spun with the idea that an animal of some kind had built itself a den within the confines of the natural cave, but he didn't think bears made their homes up this high. He didn't know for certain how far down the mountain he was, but he'd descended at least two thousand feet before the ground fell away beneath him, so he figured he was at around fifteen thousand feet.

So far, he'd only experienced a slight shortness of breath, but the longer he stayed at this altitude without food, water, proper sleep, his body would begin to break down and the cold and elevation would eventually kill him. He looked over a shoulder but didn't see red points of light in the blackness.

He went on like this for an hour, gliding and skidding as he jogged, before the crevasse became more cave-like and opened into a wide chamber that extended into blackness in every direction. His eyes had adjusted, but it was impossible to tell the size of the space. The wind whispered and sighed . . . or was it growling? Things crunched beneath his feet, like chicken bones, and he felt a rancid breeze on his face, the icy fingers scratching his spine again.

Chance pushed on through the darkness, the air tickling his nose like when a cat was near, a faint light glowing in the distance. He focused on that light. Made it the most important destination he'd ever tried to reach. It was the cave mouth. Had to be.

The beast—his mind had convinced him it was some type of—was behind him. Fear drained from him, and his muscles slacked as adrenaline fled, his body trying to pump blood through his freezing body.

A memory from one of his grandfather's letters flitted through his head. A memory one didn't know they had until there was a use for it, a purpose.

In his sprawling hand, his grandfather had written to his son on a sheet of brown paper, the script flowing diagonally downward as he addressed his son's complaints of a bully at school. "The bigger the bully, the bigger the baby. That holds true for animals as well. They're usually more scared of you than you are of them. Leave them be, and they'll leave you alone. If not, go for the eyes."

Chance had never known whether he meant the bear's eyes or the bully's, and as he stared back into the blackness of the cave, he wasn't sure he wanted to know.

The tunnel ended in a barrier of ice, pale light leaking through an opaque wall, long white and gray hairs clinging to it like a dirty bathtub. He felt the ice with his gloved hands and worked his way along the barrier until he was able to dig his fingers into the snowpack around the ice wall's edge. Above, pale light reflected off huge missile-like icicles that clung to the massive block of ice, water dripping to the floor, forming frozen stalagmites pointy enough to penetrate the strongest of animal hides.

A howl bellowed through the cave, blackness pressing in around Chance like a fever, heat burning his cheeks, head pounding in rhythm with his heart.

He frantically dug through the snowpack at the edge of the ice wall, arms stinging, the tips of his fingers going numb. Joy and relief flooded through him when gray light streamed through a hole in the snow. He dug with renewed effort, the snowpack giving way before him.

Chance tumbled out into a gray daylight, his head slamming into a rock, the cracked helmet cleaving in two and finally giving up the ghost and falling away along with the broken headlamp and goggles.

He saw the black and white picture on the mantle of his childhood home in his mind's eye. It was a yellowed snapshot of his grandfather and another man standing on the summit of Abominable Peak. For the first time, he wondered how the photo had been taken.

The whiteness faded to black.

***

Flashes of light, black and white images burnt into the back of his brain, still frames of his life curling at the edges, the snowfall thickening into an impenetrable dark curtain speckled with diamonds that sparkled in the steady cone of light thrown by a streetlight. Black silhouettes writhed within the storm, shadows argued with the wind, and the scent of bloody meat floated in the air.

The snow thinned, the gray forms of buildings taking

shape along a street. He felt the cold on his face, a fresh throbbing in his head, yet he knew what he was seeing couldn't be real.

"Why not?" soothed his father's voice.

Chance's nerves jumped, tiny needles poking his skin, unease making his back muscles spasm, his mind careening down an endless hole that got deeper every moment he went without his meds.

He chuckled to himself. To call the pain killers medication would be implying he required them for a recovery, but he was fully healed, and covering up the bleeding wound that was his pathetic excuse for a life had become his primary focus. Even the shadiest of doctors had cut him off. But paying fifty dollars a pill on the street was no big deal. Money was bullshit, anyway.

The snow stopped and a dark entrance to a familiar alleyway stood before him. Yellow lights arced down, and garbage pails, empty boxes, crates, and several dumpsters lined the sides of the alley. A dark form stood just outside the nearest cone of light, leaning against a wall.

Chance looked over his shoulder and saw only a wall of black dotted with falling snow. The alley was quiet, and he heard faint breathing, or perhaps it was just a push of the wind. He inched down the narrow lane, the windows of the surrounding buildings like open eyes.

When he was ten feet from the shadowy figure, he stopped, a rank stench wafting on the air. He covered his nose with the back of his hand, coughed lightly, and said, "Hello? It's Chance." He squeezed the dollar bills balled up in his pocket.

The dark form stepped into the light, lifting its head so Chance could see a face.

"Dad?" he squeaked, his stretched nerves twanging with tension and fear.

His father's eyes flashed red, then fell to gray as he appraised his son. His old man wore the suit he'd been buried in, except the white shirt was covered in brown dirt and his tie had been loosened. Coal-black bags hung beneath his eyes, and open sores dotted his face. The wounds squirmed and writhed as if maggots slithered therein, and when his dad smiled a tooth fell from his bloody gums.

"What is this?" Chance stammered. "Why are you here?"

"Why are you here?" his father yelled.

A shutter of uncomfortable angst surged through him, skin crawling, pain splitting his head. "My medicine."

His father laughed and a spider tumbled from his mouth.

Chance jumped back.

"Easy, boy, easy," his father said. "Listen, I don't have much time, and neither do you."

"What do you—?"

The specter of his dad hissed and surged forward, momentarily turning to snow, then reforming a foot away.

Chance jumped again.

His father laughed. "Don't worry about the how, because I don't know how I'm in a form you can see and talk with. I have sat beside you for some time, always watching, and I have grown greatly disappointed with your decisions."

Snow gusted down the alley as if trying to break the spell and remind Chance he had more important places to be, but heat like the hottest desert wind pushed down the narrow alleyway from the opposite direction, driving away the cold.

"I am here to save you," his father said. "You may still change your fate, there is hope that you may turn your life back to the path it was meant to travel. All is not lost if you will just listen."

Snow swirled in the alley, the floodlights dimming as darkness crept down the lane like an approaching storm.

"Listen to those who knew you best, who took the time

to care, for they may guide you through," his father said. His voice was getting faint, and frost appeared on his eyebrows and his skin grew whiter than flour.

"I don't understand," Chance said. "Maybe if you gave me a pill, just one to clear my head, I might—"

The apparition screamed a thin piercing wail that cut into Chance like a blade. "For your own sake, remember the past, recall all that I have said, and what they will say."

Chance looked at the ground, which was now white with snow. When he looked up, he found his father's face inches from his own. Strange noises floated on the air, arguing voices, calls for help, and a constant murmuring chant filled with grief and regret. Sorrow washed over him, the dirge burrowing into his head like maggots feasting on his brain.

His father lost his form, coming apart, and his snowy remains swirled up into the bleak, dark night.

The growl-bark of an angry beast echoed down the alleyway, and blackness engulfed him.

5

CHANCE'S EYES SNAPPED open, tiny snowflakes falling on his checks, his entire body covered in a sheen of snow and wet ice. The wind howled as it ripped across the peak and Chance was momentarily paralyzed with fear, a deep sense of loneliness that crept through him like a disease. He rubbed the ice off his watch and saw it was 3:18 PM. He'd been out for hours and only had two hours of daylight left, if you could call the dull dirty glow that leaked through the snow and dark clouds light.

His head throbbed, and he reached up to find his broken helmet and shattered headlamp gone. Chance hated wearing the helmet, but it had saved his life, no question about that. He glanced around, half expecting to see a giant shadow falling over the mountainside, but there was nothing but swirling snow and grayness. Upslope, the ice-covered boulder he'd hit looked down on him, a section of bare stone visible, probably where he'd smacked his head.

Nothing moved within the maw of the cave. No red eyes peered from the darkness. Had he actually seen that? He was colder than he'd ever been in his life, and he had to assume his perceptions were being altered by fear and weariness. He knew this, understood it, but was unable to stop the feeling of desperation from taking hold. He felt the urge to sit in the snow, give in to the cold as it beckoned to be let inside.

With the arrival of the front edge of the storm, rescue

operations would be severely limited, and as the snowfall increased and night came on, the search would be abandoned until sunup, which meant he'd have to spend a night on the mountain.

He rose unsteadily to his feet, putting out a hand to support himself on the slope. He was knee-deep in sugar, spindrifts running into a wide crevasse, the parent of the one he'd fallen into. The crack widened as it got deeper, leaving a stack of stones, and at its base was the cave mouth.

Somehow, he'd ended up on the jagged eastern slope where a descent wasn't possible. The rescue team wouldn't even be looking on this side of the peak. Exhaustion threatened to take him down, and he had no food, no water, no shelter, and night was coming on. He had the clothes on his back, the makeshift crampons, and whatever was left in the emergency backpack.

Chance was loathed to go back into the cave, though that seemed to be the safest course of action. Hunker down, wait for the storm to peter out and hope for rescue. Once Trevor got the whirlybird back up, it would only be a matter of time before he was spotted. There were dead trees in the cave. Wood that would be dry enough to start a fire. He could boil snow, and hot liquid would make all the difference.

Except the rational side of his mind, the one supervised by the voice of his mother, reminded him of what he'd seen and heard in the cave. Something lived within. Something he didn't want to meet.

But that's crazy, said the portion of his brain that thought it was a good idea to take a helicopter ride to a peak fifteen thousand feet up and slide down a seventy-degree slope on a piece of waxed wood and fiberglass.

Rationality or fear . . . fear.

Chance moved away from the cave mouth, working his way diagonally down the vertical slope, searching for a spot to make a snow hole. He scanned the ridgeline that ran several hundred yards above him, a brown scar of stone running through the snowpack. He was searching for a cornice or a large drift where the snow consistency would be heavier and compressed. He smiled amidst his grief as he remembered his survival instructor saying, "When digging a snow hole shelter, you want to find the kind of snow used for building a snowman."

A gust of wind swept up the mountainside, running through Chance like a bad chill. His stomach grumbled, his legs trembling under the strain. To the east, an endless sea of white fell away to blue sky, giant pillars of stone in the foreground. He angled upward toward the exposed ridge, leaning forward, and digging in his makeshift crampons, the wood shards screaming under the strain.

He drained his mind of the arguing thoughts, every department in his body trying to get their say, plead their case. He ignored the pain, the worry, but fear niggled into him like a damp draft. His gaze kept shifting to the cave mouth which was getting harder to see as he moved steadily up the incline.

A waterfall of snow poured over the ridge, ending in a mound of snow that was continually growing and shrinking, like the top of an hourglass. Sun glare bounced off the snow in a kaleidoscope of color that hurt his eyes, and without his polarized goggles, Chance saw none of the contours in the snow, no stone shadows, or wounds of rock. He lowered his gaze to the snowpack and headed for the snow falls.

The sugary snow tinkled and snapped as it fell, the wind brushing it east, creating snow mist that floated over the peak like a dense cloud. Spindrifts danced across the slope, the snowflakes getting large and less wet.

He picked a spot just south of the snow pile created by the runoff. A good-sized cornice had formed at the top of the pile, eddies of snow and wind shaping the snow like clay. The area was perfect, and there was enough snow for him to dig upslope.

Chance dropped onto his butt and sank two feet into loose powder. The clicking of his bindings being opened rang over the wind, and when he had both free, he commenced using his makeshift crampons as hand shovels. He worked slowly but methodically, hollowing out a sleeping area. He threw snow behind him like a dog digging for a bone, not worrying yet about the hole's shape.

Digging felt good. Heat built inside his cocoon of polyester and polypropylene, and sweat ran down his back, though his hands were freezing as they worked. When he was down five feet, the snowpack became thicker and denser, so he started digging upward, slowly creating his bivouac, which would be shaped like an upright bell. This shape was ideal because the bell shape is structurally strong and would prevent the roof from sagging due to the heat created by his body.

Heat. That was the purpose of this excavation. When the bell was big enough, he created a sleeping platform that sat ten feet higher in elevation than the snow hole's entrance. This design created a heat trap that allowed the cold air to cycle out and the warm to stay in. Chance smiled again as his instructor's voice rasped over his brain like sandpaper. "It's like how beavers build their lodges," he'd said.

This was Chance's first snow hole, but as snow poured from above and the spindrifts swirled, the entrance to the shelter began to close. He estimated within an hour the hole would be covered, and he'd be entombed.

While he still had light, he pulled free his pack and took inventory.

First thing out was his stainless-steel water bottle. He stuffed it with snow the best he could, sealed it, and put it in the inside pocket of his jacket. He had no way to boil the water, but he was relatively certain there'd be no significant harmful organisms in the frozen water. Still, one never knew. He was more concerned with lowering his body temperature by drinking cold water, but the shelter was already warming up, the walls of the snow hole becoming slick and shiny.

He pulled off his leather Burton gloves, leaving on the polyester linings. He felt like a historian handling ancient documents as he emptied the side pockets of the emergency backpack, the main compartment having held the deployed—and now missing—airbag.

Chance pounded a shelf next to his sleep platform and laid his treasures out on it. A red safety whistle, a basic first-aid kit which held tape, bandages, alcohol pads, three packets of aspirin, hydration tablets, and the thinnest blanket he'd ever seen folded in a neat square and sealed in plastic. Though the thing was made of mylar, it wouldn't warm his ass in the Caribbean.

The opposite pocket contained patch tape, a kind of thin duct-tape, and a fifty-foot length of thin rope with a small grappling hook on its end. Its purpose was to anchor the airbag.

He glanced down at his snowboard bindings with the broken wood shard toes, then at the ice shelf and everything he had. It wasn't much, but he thought it was enough. Even if the storm lasted more than twenty-four hours, which it wouldn't, he could go without food for that long.

The snow hole's entrance was almost sealed with sliding snow, a beam of gray light spilling through the closing opening. He placed the thin blanket of mylar on his sleep platform, creating a barrier between him and his mattress of compressed snow. He saw his haggard reflection in the mylar; cheeks windburned, his eyes tired. He nestled into himself and drew out his water bottle. It tinkled with thawed snow, though the metal container was freezing. Chance would've preferred hot water, and a chill ran through him as he drank deep, nothing more important in that moment than satisfying his thirst.

When he was done, he packed more snow into the

bottle, sealed it, and slipped it back into his jacket before zipping up, pulling draw strings, and adjusting his position atop the ice cube he called a bed. He pulled down his skull cap and buried himself in the collar of his shell, so no skin was exposed.

Heat blossomed in him like a small fire had been ignited at his core, warmth radiating outward to his extremities, his mind drifting as the gray beam of light streaming into the snow hole dulled and went out. Impenetrable darkness filled the bivouac as wind scoured the snowpack above, the constant sound of shifting snow like sand pouring through a crack.

His thoughts shifted to Fort Fortune. Right about now, he'd be opening the Lucky Strike, getting ready for his shift. Now that he no longer had sponsorship money rolling in, he had to earn his heli fees, travel expenses, and food. So, when he was offered the option to mix his magic cocktails at Lucky's, he grabbed it with both hands and didn't let go. Shelly would open for him, and he and his crew would most likely be the main topic of discussion.

Though Trevor had bugged out, the cloud of snow from the cave-in would've been visible for miles around and seen by the weather monitor in camp. Stormie spent his days monitoring Abominable Peak—that's how he paid his heli fees—and since there were several other parties that had been scheduled to ride, the entire camp would know of the avalanche.

Outside, a scraping sound mixed with the wind. Chance thought he heard sniffing and grunting, but with the storm raging it was difficult to determine if his imagination was conjuring images based on the day's events, or if his friend was clawing around the entrance to the snow hole, looking for a warm morsel.

He pulled his knife, flicked it open, and stabbed the blade into the snow. What he'd do against a huge black bear he didn't know, but as his eyelids drooped, he drew comfort from knowing the knife was there. As he drifted into a fitful sleep, he saw his father's destroyed face in his mind's eye and remembered his words.

***

Whirlwinds of snow raced across the beach like phantoms, the white specters running, spiraling, and murmuring. Waves crashed on a sandy shore, the undertow of snowy spindrifts tumbling back into a crystal blue sea. The cry of seagulls and laughing children was hushed by the pop and crack of ice as the ocean froze and unfroze as Chance breathed. The cyclones of snow formed shapes, people sitting in lounge chairs, swimming in the froth, or standing in the sea's undertow as dogs caught frisbees.

His mother sat in her beach chair entrenched in her blue half-dome cabana, gazing out at the ocean. Despite being protected from the harsh sunlight, she still wore her large, floppy straw hat and large dark sunglasses. Her blue one-piece bathing suit fit her well, and the floral sarong wrapped around her waist made her legs appear young and attractive. She looked good, a frozen drink beside her on a cedar table.

Frigid cold bit at the back of his neck, the echo of a roar fading as he walked across the beach and plopped into the empty beach chair next to his mother.

She turned to face him, like a skull lulling to the side atop a skeleton, and nudged her shades to the tip of her nose. Pinwheels spun in her eyes, gray hair falling around an unblemished face that looked like paper pasted to bone. Corded muscles ran down her suntanned arms, her nails painted a shade of pink with a starfish on each pinky. The golden sea creatures writhed and crawled. His mother's mouth slithered, "Well, look who it is. So, you've crawled off the mountain, have you?"

Chance felt the brush of snow on the nape of his neck.

"Why have you come? I heard . . . " His mother looked away, the creak of her neck bones popping like shells being dragged over stones in the undertow.

"Good to see you too, Mom."

Her hand shot out and grabbed her frosty drink, tiny spindrifts of snow cascading down the side of the curved glass. For an instant, a tiny figure boarded down the side of the glass, only to disappear in an ice slide as Chance's mother tipped her glass back, sucking in frothy white pina colada.

She sighed, and in the moment her face softened, and the carelines of her years returned. "I'm sorry. Are you okay?" she asked.

He nodded. He was so far from okay he'd lost his way.

"It's just . . . I've told you so many times you could be doing so much more with your life."

Chance tossed his head back and stared at the blue canvas roof of the cabana. This was an old argument.

Despite the heat washing over the sand, a chill ran through him, snow blowing across the beach, forming tiny drifts at his feet. He heard his father's voice. "Listen to what they say."

"Bouncing around the world with those ski bums, no ho—"

"Hey!" Chance interrupted. "Don't talk about my friends that way."

She recovered like a salesman that had been rebuffed by a customer. "Oh, sorry, don't be so sensitive. You've got no home, no goals, always partying and smoking the marijuana, having a grand old time. What happens when the music stops, Chance? Hmmm? Are you going to come here and rake the beach? That's all you'll be qualified for."

His mother's frustration and disappointment in him burned his stomach and made bile creep up his throat. He understood it all came from a place of love, even if he disagreed with her. He'd been sent to the best schools, been exposed to amazing things, given every opportunity, and he'd chosen to barrel down the side of mountain on a polished piece of wood.

"Not that I blame you. Genes are genes and insanity runs deep on your father's side of the family."

Another common refrain, it was all his father and grandfather's fault.

"One of these days you're going to get hurt, and . . . "

Her voice faded as Chance gazed out to sea, a thick white line appearing on the horizon and growing like a nightmare.

"Are you listening to me?" his mother said. She shook her head, sunhat flopping around. She inched her sunglasses back over her eyes and lifted her empty glass. "I'm sorry. Do you want a drink?"

A young man with slick black hair, wearing a very tight bathing suit and little else, arrived to take his mother's empty glass. "Another?" he said.

She smiled at him, fangs hanging atop rose-colored lips as her head lolled to the side, vacant eyes finding Chance.

He shook his head no.

"One more, *please*," his mother said.

Snowflakes floated into the cabana and the air grew cold, the puddle of perspiration on the cedar table from his mother's drink tinkling and cracking as it froze.

The thick wall of white on the eastern horizon was coming on fast.

The ground trembled, and a loud sucking sound rose in a tumult and was replaced with a thunderous roar. A mighty wind tore across the beach, sugary snow tinkling against the cabana, and his mother's hat blew off.

A massive wave of ice and slush crashed onto the shore, an avalanche of snow breaking over the beach as whiteness filled every empty space. The rumble of boulders, screams of pain, and the harsh whistling wind spun like a cyclone as Chance was sucked off his chair and drawn into the maelstrom.

The last rancorous words of his mother pierced his head like an icicle. "Stop riding!"

6

January 28, 2018, Abominable Peak, Colorado—Elevation Unknown

CHANCE AWOKE WITH a start, jerking to a sitting position, his head hitting the ceiling, forehead sinking into slick snow. He slid his jacket cuff up, and pale green light from his watch illuminated his snow coffin. The walls sparkled like tiny green diamonds coated the snow, and his gear was exactly where he'd left it on the ice shelf. The interior of the snow hole was warm, a tropical fifty-eight degrees according to his watch. He pulled his gloves off and rubbed his eyes, something gnawing at his subconscious like a grain of sand in his eye, or a toothpick splinter caught between his teeth.

He propped himself up on an elbow, the mylar blanket slithering and crackling beneath him, the wind howling and shrieking. It was 4:49 AM and the storm was still raging outside. Hunger pains twisted his stomach, and his head throbbed, his legs cramped and rigid. At least, he had water. He pulled his bottle and drank deep, angst tearing at him as he shed the dull mental blanket of sleep, reality slowly taking hold.

Strange sounds mixed with the wind and driving snow. Something foreign, yet natural. His addled mind went to work, putting pieces together, making ridiculous assumptions, churning out ideas and dangers that couldn't possibly be.

He wanted to get high in that moment more than he'd wanted anything in months. He longed to lose himself in the haze, to gleefully dance around rational thoughts, and plunge into the pool of denial. The urge was so strong he touched his breast pocket, the single pain pill in its sealed plastic vial close to his heart. Once he'd made up his mind to get clean, he'd never seriously considered breaking it open. It was a memento, a taunt, a constant pressure to remind him where he'd been, and how so small a thing could bring him right back there.

Sniffing, claws scraping over ice and raking through snow, the harsh panting of a large beast digging. In the green light, tiny spindrifts cascaded from the snow-packed entrance. A sharp beep, like an electronic alarm, rose in Chance's head, heart fighting to get out of his chest.

He slid his coat sleeve over the watch and darkness wrapped him in its cold embrace.

The sounds of grumbling and wheezing persisted, sugary snow tinkling on ice like sand blowing across concrete.

A thin shard of gray light penetrated the snow hole.

Growling, wheezes, coughs of exertion, and harsh breathing filled the shelter as the gray beam of light expanded, a growing horror blooming in Chance's chest. Whatever was coming for him was probably hungry, and with the mountaintop covered in snow and ice, he probably smelled like a charred T-bone, the sweaty body odor spreading over the mountain like mesquite scented smoke.

He pulled his knife from the snowpack. The five-inch blade looked small in the faint light, but it was better than nothing. He flipped the blade in his hand, sharp edge out, ready to punch and strike.

Chance's mother chimed in his head, the beach and cabana coming into focus for a heartbeat, her voice shrill, yet clear. "Run!"

His split-second flight or fight evaluation ruled out

escape, but when a large hairy finger ending in a three-inch claw broke through the snow Chance reconsidered. He stuffed his belongings into the backpack, pulled it on, snapped the knife closed, and dropped it in a pocket. He buttoned himself up and used the makeshift crampons to dig out the ceiling above his sleep platform.

Snow poured onto Chance as he dug, and he pushed the excavated snow downslope toward the shelter's entrance. The gray light dimmed. He doubled his efforts, tossing snow, his fingertips stinging with cold, lungs burning from the exertion, the elevation and lack of food taking its toll.

A guttural roar cut through the wailing wind, the clicking and gasps of the creature so close Chance thought he felt the beast's warm exhalations on his face, smelled its rank breath. The sounds of digging ceased, and only the wind's serenade drifted over the frosty night.

Chance reached loose powder and the roof of the snow hole sifted down like flour, burying him to his navel. Above, dark cotton candy clouds marched through the blackness, stars blinking through the gaps, sheets of white twisting and swirling like dirty phantoms. The wind widened the gap above, cascading snow filling the shelter. The icy hands of doubt and fear massaged his shoulders, sending a shiver down his back and pain jolting to the tips of his fingers and toes.

Bright red eyes appeared above, blinking down at him.

The staring contest loosened Chance's bowels, the rank stench of rotten meat and blood filling his nostrils. Long strands of mop-like hair fell about the shadowy head, the creature's apelike breathing chanting over the wind.

He slipped out his knife and opened it.

The creature sniffed, snorted, and growled as it dug, a white-haired claw raking the snow two feet from Chance's face.

He lashed out the knife and felt the blade press through flesh. It came to an abrupt stop.

Wails of pain rocked the night, and the dark shadow reared back, then surged forward as a warm, moist cloud hit Chance's face.

A hand grasped his backpack and yanked him up, a primal scream of fury cutting through the fierce wind and driving snow.

Chance was tossed through a snowdrift. He landed face first, sank into sugar, and lifted his chin, wind and snow stinging his unprotected eyes. Gray and black snow speckled the emptiness that stretched out before him, like he was floating in an infinity pool, a sheer drop of a thousand feet falling away below him.

He lay still, half-buried, his eyes locked on the void of endless black and white dappled nothingness. The snow beneath him crunched and popped, the wind hooted and yelled, and beneath it all a steady harsh breathing and clicking that sounded like teeth mashing together.

The urge to flee crept through him as he inched backward, moving away from the drop-off, the lizard side of his brain spinning irrational tales of escape. He felt the creature's presence, that instinctual sensation that tells a person something's stalking the darkness and waiting to pounce.

Chance tried to press free of the snowpack, but the snow below him was too soft, and he sank deeper.

That probably saved his life.

As he floundered in powdery sugar, red eyes appeared in the whiteness, and a claw slashed his flailing arm, missing his head by inches as he sank deeper into snow. Warm blood dripped down his arm into his glove as Chance screamed, but his hand still gripped the knife. He swung it wildly, slicing snowflakes and slaughtering air.

He crawled through the snow, the eyes fading to white. He hit a stone and used the rock for support as he got to his feet, the sheet of snowpack covered in verglas, the memory of the drop-off planted in his frontal lobe.

A hollow roar echoed off the mountain, the cry so loud Chance flinched as he jerked into motion. The storm picked up, the wind gusting, white sheets blanketing the peak.

He slipped, boots sliding on ice, the wind pushing him around like a leaf. He put his arms out like an old man, willing the air to support him. The howl of the wind seemed to die away as cold worked its way through the rip in his jacket, the gashes on his arm shrieking and throbbing.

Panic squeezed his chest, heat rising in him despite the cold, the sweat of unease and worry dripping down his back. He turned, peering into the storm, searching, but the contours and landmarks of the mountain had disappeared and his view in every direction was an indistinguishable whiteness. The horizon was gone, the ledge of the southern slope, and he realized with a deepening dread that he had no idea which direction he was facing. The landscape was featureless, snow clouds lifting from the snowpack and blending into the thickening snowfall.

Dizziness and fear paralyzed him. The beast could be five feet away, and he wouldn't see it. Cliffs, crevasses, chowder, bony slopes—they all waited in the whiteness to gobble him up. If he fell and broke his leg . . . His face stung with pain, his eyes stinging as they were pelted with snow and ice. He didn't know which way to go. A step in any direction could mean death.

Chance had never been big on waiting. He knew people—his father—who lived their entire lives timing things, waiting for the right moment, the right opportunity. People who rode down ungroomed fifteen-thousand-foot mountains tended to be an impatient lot, and Chance was no different, even after everything he'd been through.

His palms itched as he stood on slick verglas, the storm raging around him, blinded by a whiteout, with no goggles, a torn shell, and no food, and . . . He looked over his shoulder, but no red eyes peered through the whiteness.

A hollow, fleshy clicking snapped above the gale. The gurgle of something big. It got louder, steadier, closer.

He gripped the knife so tightly his knuckles hurt, and he peered around frantically, knowing even if there was something to see he wouldn't see it. He covered his eyes with his arm and wept, sorrow and helplessness washing over him.

Chance had known he'd hit rock bottom when he'd woken in a pool of his own vomit in the basement of a ski lodge in Breckenridge with no earthly idea how he'd gotten there. His little friends, the white pills, had talked him into doing some drinking, snorting a little powder. The smell of his urine-stained pants, the dried puke in his beard, and the memory of how he'd gotten that way had rocked him like never before. He and Amy had a fight, and those were the last words he'd said to her.

Something moved within the white, a dark amorphous nothing.

He focused, his mind a slick icy surface where nothing would stick, stomach fighting for attention, knees and ankles aching, the wound on his arm throbbing. The bleeding had stopped, and the dried blood pulled and jerked on his skin as he moved. He tried to keep the arm still, let the scab take hold as he filtered out the shrieking wind, the scrap of snow over ice, and the drumbeat of his body, listening.

The slow crunch of footsteps sinking into snow.

A dark shape appeared in the whiteout, a hulking, massive absence of whiteness. The ghostlike figure came forward, two dull pinpricks of red taking shape and piercing the gloom.

The shadow howled and lunged, moving like black steam, surging through the snow so fast Chance jerked back in surprise and lashed out with the knife. He missed and slipped, the ice beneath his feet tinkling as he fell.

The creature's swipe also missed, but Chance felt the brush of air as the claw almost caught his face, even with the wind scouring him.

He crawled over the ice-covered snowpack, directionless, fully expecting to drop off into nothingness. But he didn't fall, and a boulder materialized before him, the verglas giving way to powder as he climbed up the slope. He gasped for air, face burning. Chance was barely able to keep his eyes open, the icy snow biting him like angry fire ants.

A dark appeared in the whiteness, but he didn't see the red eyes. Deep melancholy soaked him, and he felt no urge to run, his flight reflex done, kaput. He didn't even raise the five-inch blade as the monster came on.

The blinding snow swirled and danced, the dark form breaking into snowflakes, tiny sprites whirling in the blackness. Chance felt the sun rising on the eastern horizon, a dull glow behind the tumultuous clouds. The wind talked and argued, thousands of voices fighting for his attention, but one voice rose above the others.

The floating dark specks of shadow rushed together and reformed into a shape much smaller. It came forward, undisturbed by the gale and whiteout. The form floated above the snowpack, angelic, a faint light growing stronger as the shape came together like a puzzle.

Chance got to his knees, hurt arm folded by his side like a broken wing, his other outstretched, reaching for the dark shape as it took its new form.

The dark specks and snow were sucked together, and Amy stepped through the curtain of white, her long blonde hair neat and dry. She wore a sundress, unaffected by the wind and driving snow as if she stood within the protective cone of a sunbeam sent by God.

"Amy?" Chance's vision blurred as he reached for the vision, the early stages of snow blindness poking his eyes with needles of pain.

His ex stopped when she was five feet away, snow swirling around the apparition, adding definition to her face, color to her dress. She smiled, revealing two long, curved fangs. Her piercing blue eyes were lasers, and they'd always seen right through him. She tilted her head to the side as if looking at something in the distance. A past remembrance of another time and another place.

"Why . . . ?" His voice was nothing, a whisper on the wind, a pathetic expression of everything that had gone wrong in his life. Anger welled in him, a growing pressure and heat. Snow worked its way into the collar of his shell, into his wound, numbing the throbbing pain. She'd left him. Just like the rest. When he had needed her most, she'd abandoned him.

"*No!*" the apparition screamed, reading his mind.

Chance flinched, the shriek like an icepick jammed in his ear.

"You," she said, flames shooting from her mouth, puffs of smoke mixing with the driving snow. "You abandoned me. Abandoned your own self-worth. Reason. All to get high. Remember?" Her eyes blazed with a flame that cut through the storm.

"Did you love me?" he asked and was ashamed of the pathetic sound of his voice. Why did he even care?

Because he did.

She nodded.

"Then why . . . ?" He wanted to ask why she hadn't helped him, forced him to see what was right in front of him. The injury had knocked him off his pedestal, but it had been the pain meds that brought him to his knees, though he understood better than most there was nobody to blame but himself. He'd accepted that, yet new anger and resentment burned like the heat of a thousand disappointments. He said, "So, when the going got tough, you got going."

Her fiery eyes appraised him, but she said nothing. She didn't need to say anything. Chance was making excuses, pushing blame, doing exactly what addicts do. She waited, the wind and snow curling around her, eyes smoldering.

"You know I've been clean for six months?"

She nodded.

"So, why didn't you come back?"

Her face sunk in on itself like many years had come upon her all at once, black bags shining beneath her eyes, dark lines of sagging skin marring her liver-spotted face. "Do you really think that's possible? After everything?"

Words are deeds, his mom used to say, and Chance didn't know what he'd said in the throes of his drug-induced anger, but he was certain it wasn't good, and he surely recalled what he'd done. "Just words," he said, a spear of pain stabbing his stomach.

She hissed, her eyes blazing, her tongue flicking out like a snake's. "Just words? Still, you *lie.*" Her voice screeched, a million fingernails on glass.

Memories crowded out his current situation, the whistling wind fading, the biting snow easing. The walls of a room formed—blue wallpaper with slashes of white. He watched himself yell and scream, Amy backed into a corner, tears leaking down her face, eyes wide as quarters.

On he'd raged, how he'd get everyone who'd left him for dead. Crush every sponsor, all the teams that shunned him. They would all pay.

She would pay.

Chance stared through the snow at the specter, tears streaking down his face. "I didn't . . . That wasn't me. You know that."

She smiled, lips peeling back, but instead of clean, orderly white Chiclets, her two curved fangs bookended a mouth of bloody shark-like teeth.

7

THE FALLING SNOW undulated and swayed, the wind twisting and shaping it, the snowpack shifting beneath his feet. The blue wallpaper with slashes of white boxed him in, a forgotten hotel room during the steepest portion of his tailspin. Amy huddled in the corner, arms folded over her chest, wide eyes filled with tears. Chance raged on; she never loved him, was just using him for his money, fame, the trips around the world. What had she ever done? She was a hanger-on, a leech, a snowboard groupie. As he watched his former self, the knot in his stomach crept up his throat and settled there like a tumor. He'd said those things. Him, and there was no drug excuse, no excuse at all that was adequate.

Some things can't be unsaid, and sometimes what can't be unsaid can't be forgotten.

Chance stood before the woman he claimed to love, breathing like he'd just run a marathon, chemicals surging through him, his bloodshot eyes burning, but not from swirling snow.

The imaginary walls started to fade, and Chance wept because he knew what was coming next, and shame washed over him like a tidal wave.

Amy's voice was sharper than any knife. "You're gone. Get away from me. I never want to see you again."

Chance watched his own face sift through a menu of emotions—confusion, sorrow, then anger. His cheeks blossomed red, and he clenched his fists as he stepped toward her.

Amy put up her hands as if to ward off a blow, and Chance's former self reeled, pulling back. She tried to squeeze past him, blue wallpaper with white slashes sliding by like a passing cloud.

"You disgust me," she said.

Chance closed his eyes, snow hitting face, but the vision came anyway, playing on the inside of his eyelids.

Red hot anger ignited in his chest, and it spread through him like he was made of straw. So much hatred and fury that it boiled over. He reached out and grabbed Amy's arm and jerked her to a stop. "Who the fuck are you talking to like that? You think you get to decide? It's over when . . . "

Chance opened his eyes, and the vision was gone. All that remained was Amy staring at him in her sundress, the white fangs hanging over her lips now tinged with blood, the whiteout clamoring around her.

"I didn't mean it," he said. He'd never put his hands on a woman in his life, save that one time. It was a blemish on his consciousness he would never be able to erase, like a wound that never healed.

"It can heal," Amy said, reading his mind again.

"Thank you," he said. "For sparing me." He hadn't hit her, but the bruise he'd left on her forearm put him over the edge and sent him into freefall.

Amy's face smoothed, her wrinkles fleeing as fast as they'd appeared, blonde hair spilling around her face, the flowers of her dress bursting with color. "You must never forget where you were. I know you understand that, but you need to feel it, live it every second of every day from here on out. Can you do that for me, Chance?"

He nodded.

"You are at the start of a new path, but it's winding and narrow and steep. There are many pitfalls." She started to come apart, snow spinning around her.

“I . . . I still love you,” he said. It felt good telling her, but the heat ball growing in his stomach told him he’d gone too far.

“It’s too late for us, but not for you,” she said. “You can still make it.”

A gust of wind roared over the slope, scattering Amy, snowflakes spinning like a whirling phantom.

Then, she was gone.

***

Chance stared into the white, the wind ripping at his torn shell, darkness washing away as the sun inched over the rim of the world and fought through the cloud cover, its dull glow spreading in the east. The throb of his arm had slowed, the bitter cold chilling the wound like a gentle flame. With the fading night, the whiteout got deeper as the light that managed to leak through the cloud cover was diffused, clouds of thick mist rising from the snowpack like smoke.

There were no sounds of footsteps, no crunch of snow or throaty gurgling.

Now he had a frame of reference in the east and knew which way was south. Chance straightened, back screaming, neck stabbing him with a shock of reality. His arm hung by his side. When he lifted it and flexed his fingers everything worked, but the price of the effort was excruciating pain. He didn’t think the arm was broken, but the creature had torn through skin, muscle, and tendon, only stopping when the curved talons hit bone. He wasn’t very concerned about the onset of infection because he knew it was difficult for a virus of any kind to thrive in extreme cold. He also knew intense cold suppressed the immune system, so the possibility of infection actually increased.

The emergency backpack still clung to his back, the knife in his pocket, and a few mouthfuls of water sloshed in the metal bottle. The wind bellowed, spitting and whistling and yelling. As he angled down the slope, he searched for a cornice or hollow bowl, a boulder or overhang, any spot to get out of the driving snow so he could dress his wound, but it was next to impossible.

He pushed through the two feet of dense sugar, the snow compacting beneath his feet. He lost his footing several times as he stepped on unseen stones, treetops, and debris. To his right, a dark edge appeared out of the whiteout, brown stone trailing to the east toward the stacks of snow and ice that made up the eastern slope of Abominable Peak. Chance struggled toward the stone cliff face, the snow getting deeper. Gusts of wind tore over the ledge, forming a cornice that extended many feet beyond the cliff's edge.

Beneath the overhang, the swirling snow lessened, the wind skipping over the cliff and funneling down the southern slope. Chance gaped up at the underside of the cornice, its sharp icy tip curving down like a fang. Mice danced on his spine, clawing at his lower back, memories of almost being buried alive clouding his mind.

"You don't have a choice," the diligent voice of his mother protested inside his head. Her voice was so clear, so close, Chance glanced around expecting to find her specter appraising him, but all he saw was swirling clouds of white.

He grunted. As usual, his mother was right. He gingerly pulled off his pack and pulled out the first-aid kit with his good arm. The left arm of his jacket was shredded, as was his Chili's long underwear. Four red gashes cut across his forearm, the two center cuts longer than those on the edges. Dried blood covered the slashes, and in spots, the fabric of his long underwear was fused to the wound, part of the scab.

Chance slipped off his right glove, but left on the liner, and opened the small medical pouch. He tore open a packet with an alcohol pad in it. Before he pressed it to the wound, he paused, the mumble of his mother rising in his head and pushing away the arguing winds. If he cleaned the wound, it would start bleeding, which was good, but he might lose the natural bandage formed by his long underwear, and that was bad. The other side of the sword was infection. He tensed as a gust of wind pushed a flurry of snow beneath the cornice. The odds of him making it down the mountain were shrinking with each tick of the clock, but the probability would fall to zero if the wound festered.

He used all the alcohol pads, and when he was done a steady stream of blood flowed from all four tears, draining any harmful bacteria determined enough to survive in the blistering cold. He let the wound bleed as he downed both packets of Tylenol with the rest of his water and repacked the bottle with snow. Chance cleaned and iced the gashes, used two large bandages and all the gauze to dress the wound, then used patch tape to seal the rips in his shell.

With all that done, he leaned back, closed his eyes, and listened to the wind fight and holler, the tinkle of sugary snow falling over ice like sand blowing across a beach. He thought he heard a faint howl but couldn't be sure. It was enough to stoke the fire of urgency, though, and he tucked the stainless-steel water bottle into the shell's pocket, zipped up, pulled on his glove, and repacked the backpack.

The aspirin started to take hold, and though it hurt putting on the pack, the pain was less sharp. He felt the folded knife in his jacket pocket, considered taking it out and carrying it open, but decided against it. With his luck, he'd lose it in the snow, and what good was the five-inch blade against the beast, anyway? Chance smiled through his pain, the memories of his knife hitting bone, and the shriek of the creature still fresh in his mind.

An insane thought cajoled its way past the guards patrolling his brain for lack of reality. He could make a spear with the knife. A weapon with reach so he could take the beast down. His father laughed, his deformed specter filling Chance's mind. His eyes hurt, his face stung, and when he pushed to his feet his knees protested, his stomach a roiling sea of acid that splashed up his throat, the burn worse than the highest proof alcohol.

The thought of alcohol made Chance wish he had a martini. He saw the clear glass, the green olive, smelled the vermouth. Shelly was most likely behind the bar, slinging drinks, as all of Fort Fortune talked and speculated about Chance's demise. Most in camp would think he was dead on the mountain, like his grandfather, and that narrative would run through camp like Tijuana tacos.

He stepped out from under the cornice, the wind grabbing and thrusting him downslope. The snow had lessened, and Chance could see twenty feet downhill, the slick sheet of white undisturbed. Tiny spindrifts cascaded into whiteness, clouds of icy mist lifting from the snowpack. Chance was tempted to slide down the incline, but he had no idea where and how it ended. He searched his mind, trying to remember the typographical map of Abominable Peak he'd studied, but without a frame of reference—other than he was somewhere on the southern slope—he had no way to pinpoint his position.

Ahead, the tops of evergreens poked through the snowpack and a surge of hope lit a fire in his chest, but as he watched the green cones shifted, changed color, shimmered, and disappeared. He stopped trudging through the snow, his legs buried and freezing. He blinked, and in his mind, he heard his skin crack and split. He'd hadn't felt any sensation on his cheeks in some time, and he assumed they were gray with frostbite. His world spun in a snow globe, the dark haze of day spreading over the peak. He was dizzy. How had he gotten here? What was he doing?

He walked on and stumbled over the top of a tree, its slender tip encrusted with ice and tiny green needle-like leaves. He focused on the treetop, not believing it was really there. He reached down, heard the scrape of his glove on frozen needles. It was real, and as he shifted his gaze, he realized he was standing atop a buried glade, the green tips of evergreens sticking from the snowpack like miniature Christmas trees.

Chance pulled free his knife and tried to open it to the saw option, but he couldn't with his gloves on. He screamed in frustration, a long, guttural wail that fell dead in the driving snow.

The wind answered his call, murmuring and coaxing in a language he didn't understand.

He looked at his hand. It would only take a second. Without further contemplation, he pulled off his right glove, along with its liner, and the biting cold attacked immediately. Pain cramped his fingers as he wedged his thumbnail into the groove on the side of the saw blade. He struggled with the utility knife for several seconds, the frigid air penetrating his skin, snow covering him.

The small four-inch saw flicked out of its red plastic cocoon. His hands were sweaty, and as Chance struggled to put his glove back on, his nightmare was realized. The glove lining was damp with sweat, the fingerholes inside out and twisted. Mind spinning, he fought to remain calm as he carefully worked his fingers into the glove liner. After five minutes of patient work, his lower back exploding with pain, wounded arm wailing, he managed to get the liner and glove back on.

Chance knelt in the snow, relief hitting him like a cold drink of water after you've crossed the desert. He went to work, clearing the snow away from the top of the tree, then sawed at the flexible pine with his tiny saw. With his shell patched and everything zipped and tightened, he sweated from the exertion. His joints ached, his stomach a roiling knot, his heart pounding in rhythm with his arm wound.

When the two-foot section of treetop broke free, he paused and took a few sips of water, letting his body rest before moving on to tree number two. After thirty minutes of sawing, cutting, and tying, Chance managed to attach the dense tops of the evergreens to the bottoms of his boots using the airbag anchor rope. He stomped and shifted, and the natural snowshoes worked well.

Down the mountain he went with a new urgency, the sense that something followed, staying just outside his whiteout vision bubble. One foot down, support, move the next foot down, support, repeat. He went on like that for two hours, slowly and carefully descending the storm-swept southern slope. He remembered the lines of his run, tried to calculate how far he'd come down the mountain. But with the horizon still nothing but frozen clouds in every direction, he was unable to estimate.

The incline fell away, the grade getting steeper, a layer of ice coating the snowpack. He used the heel of his boot to break the ice, each step taking three times as long. He stomped and climbed, stomped and climbed.

Crack! Pop!

Chance froze, waiting for the ground to give out beneath him again. It didn't.

The wind sang, a voice working its way above the fighting murmurs and whispers.

He continued, one step after another, sticking the heel of his boot into the ice—stomp, climb, repeat. The frozen mist of the whiteout dissipated as he descended, replaced with driving snow, but he could see farther downslope, and like a run, he began calculating angles, finding ways around boulders, cornices, cliffs, and patches of chowder.

His heel hit solid ice, slipped, and Chance fell on his ass, sliding down the hillside, out of control, no way to stop. He raced through the whiteness like a kid on a sleigh. Snow beat his face, wind and cold tearing at him.

Chance flipped on his belly and pulled the knife. He tossed and twisted as he fought to get the blade open but couldn't with his gloves on. He held the closed knife in a fist and plunged it into the ice. Scraping, cracking, and scratching, as the closed knife bit into the ice, throwing shards in his face. Chance wasn't stopping. He weighed too much, and without the open blade, the knife wasn't penetrating deep enough into the verglas.

He came to a crashing halt, striking a boulder, the knife flying from his hand and landing in the snow. He watched its red handle sink as wind whipped and shrieked, snow attacking with renewed hatred. He dug himself out and shook off the snow and ice, leaning against the boulder that had stopped his slide. To the south, a shallow valley was filled with snow. He gazed east but jerked his head back around.

A spark of light flickered below, the orange flames cutting through the white. He did several fast mental calculations. Height, distance, sheets of snow, and clouds of frozen mist. That was no candle down there.

Chance pushed off the stone and his grandfather stood beside him, staring down at the flickering fire.

He reeled, his mind functioning on reserves, the rational side of his brain losing the battle of insanity and rationality. That couldn't be a fire down there, and the apparition before him wasn't his grandfather. He was a tease, a construct of his tired, food deprived, frostbitten brain.

Yet . . . it was his grandfather . . . or he looked somewhat like him.

He'd never met his grandfather because he died before Chance was born, but he'd seen all the pictures, read his journals, and in many ways, Chance felt closer to his grandfather than his own father. Worms wriggled in his stomach; his throat filled with razor blades.

His grandad's face was twisted with age well beyond any normal lifespan. Skin hung from his skull like double cheeks, the few strands of white hair he had left clinging to bone thinly coated with skin. His eye sockets were blacker than night, but the eyes within were bright with mischief.

"What do you make of that?" the old man said, pointing his bony finger at the valley below.

8

LIFE IS MADNESS. For some, that disconnection from reality is dark and foreboding, others monotonous and predictable, while still others live in a constant state of otherworldliness that allowed them to let go, to stop trying to figure things out, understand what it all meant.

Life is also reason, for there can't be madness without reason. Chance had always tried to see the light, err on the side of rationality, but he was having trouble seeing anything but darkness as he looked upon the apparition of his grandfather.

Unlike when he'd met his other loved ones, his grandfather's protective shield that kept out the raging storm encased him as well, the snow swirling around their forcefield, never touching them. Heat built in Chance, and he pulled off his gloves and unzipped his shell to the breast. The aspirin had helped, but tiny needles still pierced his face, knees, and lower back, his stomach gurgling with acid, heart thumping in rhythm with the scratches on his arm. His vision was clearing as the snow melted off him, his grandfather X-raying him.

The wind argued and yelled, shrieks and howls, snow sliding over snow, the scent of rot and decay filling the protective bubble.

What did it mean to be mad? The fact he was asking himself that question was proof enough, to him, his sanity was slipping away and may already be on a beach in the

Bahamas. His parents, Amy, now Grandad? His past thrown in his face, all his wrongs. He was a snowball rolling downhill and collecting bodies. This was why he was going to die on the mountain . . . He deserved it.

Yet . . . most of these awful things he'd done to himself, though the disappointment, sorrow, worry, and fear he'd brought on those who'd loved him made Chance feel lower than the most useless piece of stinking garbage. Shame rolled off him in waves. Was he mad? Or was this his new reality? Was he dead?

His grandfather laughed, and when he looked away, one of his ears fell off.

Chance jumped back, staring at the ear as it lay atop the snow.

His grandfather laughed harder. "I bet you were squeamish as an infant as well." He stared down into the snow-filled valley at the flickering light. "You're not dead, though I could see how you might think that. Plus . . . " He turned and looked at his grandson. "Plus, you do look well on your way. How's that face feeling?"

"It doesn't."

"Well, that's okay. Nothing better with the ladies than war wounds."

Chance said nothing.

"So, we meet at last. I've been watching you, my boy. Very proud. You would've been world champion if . . . " His grandfather's eyes twirled with smoke. "That was some spill you took at Veleta," the old man said. "The way you tumbled, then that last part . . . Shoot, your leg snapped like a breadstick. I heard it over the TV."

Chance gazed down at the light in the valley below and didn't speak.

"So . . . I know you know all about me. That's one of the reasons you're here, right?"

Acid bubbled up Chance's throat and he swallowed, pushing down the growing unease. Chasing his grandfather's ghost—figuratively—had been one of the reasons he'd come to Abominable Peak.

"Must've been hard always living in my shadow," his grandfather said.

"Sometimes."

"I'm proud of you for getting back on the horse. Riding again, I mean. There are many people—me included—who would have never again strapped on skis after what you went through."

Chance nodded, the worms in his stomach twisting and churning. He knew what was coming next.

"But this thing with Amy . . . your parents. What happened? I mean, I know you're not that weak."

Anger stirred in Chance at the word "weak". He knew drug addiction had nothing to do with strength. Quitting, maybe, but getting addicted was as easy as telling your doctor you can't deal with the pain. That's what he'd said as he sat in the dark, alone in his hospital room, day after day. No visits from his friends, his crew. They texted, called, sent pictures, but they had continued with their lives, left him behind, and the pain had been too great.

Reading his mind, his grandfather said, "I understand, but . . . Do you know what I used to tell your da when he complained things weren't fair?"

Chance said nothing.

"The world doesn't care. It will pass you by."

"Well aware."

His grandfather sighed, smoke puffing from his mouth. "Look at that down there. What do you see?"

"I don't know what I'm seeing anymore."

"Fair enough. What if I told you it was your crew? That they wouldn't leave without you? That they established a base camp to search for you?"

Chance's nerves fluttered. Could that be true? He stared down the slope, judging distance, depth, the time it would take to reach the light. He said, "Is that what it is?"

"There are many things I know, and many things I don't," the old man said.

"And . . . ?"

"Oh, yes . . . " The old man gurgle-laughed, like he had thick liquid in his throat. A thin stream of blood leaked between his lips, ran down his chin, drips splattering his jacket.

"You've got—" Chance reached out like his granddad had mustard on his lips.

The old man's image shifted and swayed, Grandad becoming young for a blink of an eye before returning to his state of decay. "The legend is true. I saw the monster with my own eyes," the apparition said.

"Is that how you died?"

Grandfather's eyes smoldered with fire, then went dark. "You're not focusing on the right things. To get off this hill you have to turn your addiction inward."

"You just said it. I'm clean, and—"

"Not that!" Grandad yelled. "Your little pills can't help you now. Focus, knowledge, fortitude. You know what you need to do."

The light in the hollow below grew brighter with each breath, the flames in tune with Chance's breathing.

"Do not look back. Only ahead."

"Will I see you again?" He sensed his time with his grandfather was almost at its end.

"Forge your own path. Let me go."

"But there's . . . "

His grandfather patted the air with his hands. "Listen." His voice slithered from his lips, his hair turning to thick strands of snow and ice. "I ask one thing of you."

"What? Anything." Chance's heart galloped, the tips of his fingers and toes stinging.

"It may come to pass that in your struggle to survive you discover . . . certain things about me that will make you question my past, wonder if I was the man you thought I was. Know I only did what had to be done, and if it comes to pass that you feel I acted unjustly, please forgive me."

Howling wind, the thoughts of every life he never had, every life he'd ever wanted.

"Oh, and don't forget my knife."

Chance tore his gaze from the valley and said, "Forgive you? For what?"

His grandfather was gone, a swirling tornado of snow was all that remained.

Wind tore across the slope, his cone of protection gone, snow working its way into his jacket, his hands freezing. He zipped up, pulled on his gloves, and started downslope.

The echoes of his grandfather's words bounced around inside his head. If the visit was intended to clarify, it had failed.

The light below flickered and swayed in the wind, the flames becoming brighter as he worked diagonally downslope. The feeling of being watched returned, icy fingers of fear kneading his flesh, crawling over his skin like so many tiny spiders.

The snowfall churned and spun, the wind pushing and bullying. For an instant, Chance got a good view of the southern face. He was still way up on the mountain, the flat gray sky extending like a plush carpet. All he had to do was step out onto that carpet, wriggle his toes, and suck in the comfort.

His grandfather's voice rattled in his head. "You're almost there, son." Chance noted it was his grandfather, not his father urging him on. Chance's dad had always favored his older brother, the accountant. He was stable, predictable, and could be counted on to act and jump with every whim of his father. He was the good kid. The one who listened and applied himself, while Chance hung out with snow dogs and spent his time partying and risking his life. His mother had mostly spared him during her celestial visit, but she had often told Chance he was wasting his life. What would he do when he turned thirty and he couldn't compete with the young kids?

Chance had worried about that, but not much. He'd planned on being world champ, and that would've brought fame, money, and all the issues of his past would've slipped away. Instead, he'd gotten a fractured leg, and—

A hollow growl-bark floated on the breeze. Chance stopped climbing, tuning his hearing. He looked back up the mountain but saw nothing but the driving snow, tops of evergreens, and slashes of brown stone poking through snowpack.

Crunching footsteps, grunting, hissing.

Chance bounded down the incline, no longer zigzagging for safety. He slipped, arms out in the riding position as he skidded down the hill.

Looking back, he saw no red eyes hovering above the snow, no blood. He doubled his efforts, jumping and sliding, half out of control, pain jolting through him, rattling his bones like a tuning fork.

Flames licked the grayness below, a fire giving off an enormous cloud of warm light. Dark shapes moved around the bonfire, shadows dancing and writhing against the white. He called out, but his voice fell dead in the frigid air and raging wind.

His mother yelled, "Hurry, son. Hurry."

Harsh breathing and footsteps crunching in the snow rose above the wind, and a dark shadow loomed before him.

A creature unlike any he'd ever seen materialized from the churning snow. It was humanoid in shape; two arms, two legs, a head. The first thought that broke through Chance's disbelief and fear was the beast looked like an albino Chewbacca. Red eyes blazed through the gloom, thick strands of natty white hair wrapping the beast in a shaggy suit, black leather-like skin covering its face. The beast's left hand was stained dark with blood where he'd slashed it.

Chance fought through the knee-high snow, using his right foot as a brake, his left bending and thrusting, driving him forward. His wound shrieked, and he felt a fresh trickle of blood running into his glove.

A cry echoed off the surrounding hills, reverberating as it faded. Was it human? Had it called his name?

When Chance looked back, he couldn't see the creature. He chuckled, finally putting the beast together with the name of the peak. That was just too perfect of an epitaph.

He didn't slow. The fire became a growing orb in the whiteness below. If he could just get there everything would be okay.

Fear robbed him of his confidence and reminded him the fire might be nothing more than a mirage, a fantasy, wishful thinking brought on by his delusions. Ghosts weren't real, and when you were dead, you were dead. There'd been no visits from his past, no reckoning, yet he felt like there had been, like something had slipped, some wheel inside his brain getting stripped, its teeth broken and its ability to connect with the other cogs that made up his reality also gone.

His brain told him he smelled smoke, but he only half believed. The cold had become a constant pain, like his backache, or a grain of sand caught in his eye.

Popping, cracks, the gentle murmur of the mountain as it pressed its bulk upon Earth. White lights, like the headlights of a car, bounced around in the whiteness. The wind no longer fought but instead urged him on in his madness.

The fire below grew fuzzy, black smoke rolling up the hillside, the flames wavering. He heard the fire hiss and scream as the light faded, sputtered, and went out.

Chance screamed, letting loose all the fury, the desperation, the idea that somehow he was going to survive. It had all been bullshit, a fake, a painting his mind created to fool him into thinking everything was going to be okay.

Consciousness slipped as his fading mind attempted to ease his transition into the next world by replaying his pitiful life.

He dropped to his knees, his wounded arm wailing. He had nothing left, no energy, no control. Voices rattled and urged him on, but he didn't care anymore. There was nothing left to do but die.

Chance dumped face forward into the snow, his nose bending in pain. His frostbitten cheeks were numb, but his ears and neck stung as if the cold was orange steel. He laid there a long time, the wind whistling and screaming, the twisting snow finding every crack in his Polyester armor. Where was his father now? His mother? Amy? Sorrow fought his self-pity, the adrenaline addict in him cajoling and pressuring the drug addict, telling him one little pill would make everything alright. They could ride. No worries. Chance lifted his head and peered down the slope, but there was no fire, no rescuers, no monster, and no hope.

9

January 28, 2018, Abominable Peak Collection Site—Elevation 12,119 feet

AS CHANCE FOUGHT his way up from sleep, the murmur of voices, the tinkle of snow pelting neoprene, and the rush of the wind rose in volume like a tuning orchestra. He was warm, almost cozy, and he sank deeper into the smooth sleeping bag that wrapped him like a burrito. His stomach churned, his mouth dry, lips cracked and frostbitten. The gashes on his arm throbbed with dull pain, and he was afraid to open his eyes for fear of what he might find. Dots of color danced behind his closed eyelids, like wheeling stars in sundrenched blackness.

Blurred events, half memories, tossed and turned, and he hugged himself, burrowing deeper into the sleeping bag. He was dead and it was time for him to rest.

He thought of happier times, cutting it up with his crew, the spray of snow, the feelings of exhilaration and accomplishment that came from plummeting down a seventy-degree incline at a hundred miles per hour. It was the only time in his life when his thoughts fled like so many birds heading south on the autumn breeze. Finding his line was all that mattered.

"Hey," said a male voice. "I think he's coming out of it."

"Biggie?" Chance mumbled, hope growing in him like a blooming flower.

Whoops and hollers, slapping hands, congratulations, and a "thank God."

Chance forced open his sleep encrusted eyes. Green neoprene rippled in the breeze above. He was in his tent. That couldn't be.

"Hey, mate?" Tina's face appeared. She was smiling.

The entire tent came into focus, the world coming together, edges curving and straightening, the scent of stew making his stomach scream with anticipation. Biggie and Jibber knelt on his left, Tina and Colin, his right. The tent wiggled and swayed, the gusting wind pushing it around.

Tina leaned in with a water bottle. "Have some of this." She put the bottle to his lips, but Chance snaked his hand out of the sleeping bag, and she handed it to him. He tipped it back, and water dripped into his beard as he greedily drained the bottle.

Tina watched with wide eyes, the pom-pom on her hat tilted right. Biggie coughed, and Jibber stared at the black canvas floor. All four of his friends smoked as if on fire, their cold garments giving up their moisture in the warm tent.

"Where's Bomber?" Chance asked.

"When we got to the collection point and you weren't here, Trevor and Bomber searched from the air. Trevor had to head back because of the storm, and Bomber went with him to be our man on the ground at Fort Fortune."

Chance felt the fresh bandage on his arm as he cracked his neck. Biggie handed him more water and he drank. "Where am I?" he asked when the second water bottle was empty.

"We're at the collection spot," Tina said.

Chance's face hurt when he lifted his eyebrows. "How? When? The fire . . . "

Colin laughed, his dark curls spilling over half his face, the scar on his left cheek, which he had gotten from a skate blade, was white against his windburned face. "Jibber held the fort here while we established a base camp higher on the mountain. We knew if you were hurt there was no way you'd be able to get down the mountain yourself."

"So, we used the sled we carried you down on to haul wood up," Biggie said.

Chance shook his head. "Still, that was a pretty big fire, and there's no—"

"You're worrying about the wrong things, mate," Colin said. "Does it look like the top of the mountain was bombed because of all the holes where we cut off the tops of evergreen trees? Yeah, it does."

"That glade is gonna look strange come spring," Jibber said.

"Flat top," Colin said. He patted Chance on the shoulder. "We'll hike up there this summer and see it for ourselves."

"Hungry?" Tina asked.

Chance nodded, and she went about filling five stainless-steel mugs with stew. The crew ate in silence, the wind scouring the tent, the tinkle of snow-on-snow maddening.

"Feel better?" Biggie asked as he gave Chance a large second helping.

Chance smiled. How did he feel? Like he'd cheated death, gotten a fresh start, a new life card with no punched holes in it. The worms in his stomach reminded him it wasn't that simple. His moxie was gone . . . Or at least on hiatus, and he felt no urge to ride, no burning desire to go back to the top of the mountain. Yet, he did want to go back up the mountain, but not to ride.

He said, "I'm doing awesome all things considered." He looked each of his friends in the eye. "Thanks for not leaving me. I . . . if you hadn't stayed and come looking for me . . . Well, thanks, and any guilt or misgivings you have about the past, things you think you should've done, you can wipe your slates clean. We're even-steven."

Laughter, smiles, and giggles. It was like old times.

"How long have I been out?" Chance asked.

"We plucked you from the snow at around 10 AM, and it's 3:19 PM now, so . . . " Jibber counted his fingers.

"At least five hours," Colin said, his blue eyes bright with happiness.

Chance sighed. "So, we're here until morning?"

Biggie nodded. "We considered trying to get you down to Fort Fortune, but we didn't think you'd be able to travel, and your wound isn't bad. Trevor can't fly until the storm passes, so we figured waiting it out was the best move. There was talk of sending snowmobiles, but with the storm it just wasn't worth the risk."

"We told them you were a tough old bird," Colin said.

"Has this thing almost blown itself out?" Chance said, lifting his hand and motioning toward the entrance of the tent.

Tina nodded. "Should be a crystal clear sunrise."

"We gonna ride after we drop Chance off?" Jibber asked.

Nobody spoke except the incessant wind and sandy snow.

"You going to tell us what the hell happened up there?" Colin said.

"Leave it alone," Tina said. "Let the man get some rest."

"No," Chance said. "It's okay. I've done enough resting." He spun his story, not exaggerating or leaving anything out, except the visits from his former loved ones. The cave-in, the ice-covered crevasse, the strange sounds . . . the eyes peering down at him. The beast.

"Wait," Biggie said. "Like a bear?"

"No, not like a bear at all." Chance went on, and when he got to the attack, his attention went to his wound. He paused, rubbing his bandaged arm like a child.

"Those claw marks sure look like a bear got you," Biggie said.

Tina shot him a glance so hot it would've caused an avalanche on the peak. "I gave you some antibiotics and pain killers. How does it feel?"

"Not too bad," Chance said. "I think I'm ready to go."

"Easy, big boy," Tina said. "You have a fever, and the claw marks are red and puffy at the edges."

Chance nodded. Just how lucky he'd been was coming into focus. He was like one of those people in the movies that are constantly being shot at, but never hit.

"So, the elephant . . . bear in the room is—if you don't think this thing was a bear, what the hell did you see?" Tina asked.

Silence again. Wind. Driving snow. Harsh breathing steaming up the tent.

"I don't know," Chance said. "But you've all heard the legend. Know why this place is called Abominable Peak."

"You're saying you saw a Yeti?" Colin said.

"Bigfoot?" Jibber said and chuckled as he surveyed the faces of the crew. Everyone was doing their best not to smile except Biggie, whose smirk was so wide Chance wanted to smack it off his face. "Look, sorry, but that's a tough bone to swallow."

"The other night in Lucky's, Trevor mentioned there were a lot more bears and cats on the move due to recent blasting to open a new mine. Could be why bears . . . animals are out and about when they shouldn't be," Tina said.

Chance nodded, content to let the issue die. He needed to think.

"Get some rest," Jibber said. "We'll have more chow later."

"And I've brought some refreshment," Colin said.

Chance smiled. "Thank you all again. Really."

"No worries, mate. You'd have done the same," Colin said.

Would he have?

The bright green neoprene turned a shade of deep green as the sun went down, and the gray milky day faded to darkness speckled with white. The wind let up, the sheets of snow thinning as the storm passed on to the Great Plains. When the storm reached New York, it would be rain.

They ate dinner in Tina's tent, which was the largest. More stew, along with apples and cheese. Colin's surprise was a quarter full bottle of Kraken rum, and the companions passed it around as they ate. They talked about their rides and the struggles of the last twenty-four hours. Chance felt like he'd survived some grand adventure, and his friends were ready to head right back out into the jungle, get back on the horse. He knew that's what he was supposed to do—shoot, it's what he'd been doing every day the last year—but in this case, the horse had changed into a donkey, and his priorities had been shuffled, reorganized by the lectures he'd gotten from his parents, Amy, and Grandad.

When they were done eating and drinking, everyone merry, spirits on the rise, Tina said, "You up for a walk?"

Chance nodded. "Sure. Where to?"

"There's something I want to show you."

They bundled up and she handed Chance a flashlight. The others shuffled off to their tents, lights bouncing around inside colored half Easter eggs. Biggie had music playing, and the sound was oddly comforting on the roof of the world. It made him think normal thoughts, the idea of madness receding like a bad dream. But the beast. He couldn't get it out of his mind and there was no way it was bear, not even a mutant. The way the thing had looked at him. There was reason behind those eyes. Purpose. He pushed the thought away and trailed after Tina as she followed a beaten trail up the slope and through a field of large boulders half-buried in snowpack.

The top of the mountain was still shrouded in billowing clouds of white, and below the dark milky horizon stretched into nothingness in every direction. The path meandered up the hillside, a large cliff face standing before them, brilliantly slick black in the darkness, ice spilling down its face like a waterfall frozen in time. The wall shone under the flashlight's beam, tiny specs of quartz and mica sparkling like diamond flakes.

Chance's curiosity peaked as he watched Tina's pom-pom sway in the wind, which had fallen to a gentle breath. The snow fell vertically now, big wet flakes that stuck to everything they landed on, and the scent of wet stone and earth filled his nostrils. A faint tremor strummed his nerves just below his skin, like his brain was campaigning for the raising of goosebumps but had been outvoted. He looked over his shoulder every few moments, though he felt nothing watching, heard no footsteps other than his own and Tina's crunching up the stomped path.

Tina cut behind a huge boulder. A large overhang of stone jutted from the cliffside like the mountain was sticking out its tongue, and beneath the snowdrifts fell away to dry stone. It wasn't a cave, more of a notch in the mountain that, by the coincidence of how the rock cleaved, had a level floor and a perpendicular northern wall.

"Wow . . . " Chance ran his gloved hand over the smooth, cold stone. "Safe to camp in here? It's out of the weather."

Tina nodded. "We didn't know the place was here, or rather, we did, but not exactly where."

"Now I'm totally confused."

"Look at this." Tina marked a spot on the slick stone wall with her flashlight's beam.

Large letters that looked like they'd been drawn on with a crayon by a child were chiseled deep into the rock. The letters spelled 'Harvey and Hance were here.'

She said, "Didn't you tell me there was a picture of this in one of your grandfather's journals?"

He had. "Grandad and his partner argued over this. Crazy. It wasn't like anyone was ever going to find it."

Tina raised her eyebrows and harrumphed.

Chance stepped forward, flashlight cutting through the inky darkness. He traced the letters of his name with his index finger. "Amazing that he stood on this very spot."

"So it would appear."

"How did you find this?" Chance said.

"Just a bit of luck, really. Jibber was checking out the area. Heard the wind piping through here like a sousaphone and he checked it out."

"You get pictures?"

"Yup. Coordinates also so you can come back at a . . . more convenient time."

Chance nodded, his face stinging with pain despite a coat of salve.

"There was this time in Dis—"

A wet strangled scream echoed over the mountain, the wail of someone in great pain.

Tina and Chance stared at each other for a heartbeat before hurrying back the way they'd come. The glow from the dome tents below cast shards of pale light across the frozen ocean, snow blowing around like ashes. The duo arrived back at camp to find Biggie and Colin standing by Jibber's tent.

"We got a problem," Biggie said.

Jibber's yellow neoprene dome tent was slashed open, streamers flapping in the breeze as they clung to fiberglass poles. Bloody smears marred the canvas, and drips of blood and huge clawed four-toed footprints trailed away into the darkness and fading snow.

Chance jerked his flashlight around, feeling red eyes on him, but there was nothing in the darkness except endless specks of white.

Tina followed the footprints, her flashlight beam striving through the night.

"You really think that's a good idea?" Chance said, but he was already trailing after her.

Jibber's twisted and bloodied body was dumped in the snow forty feet from his tent. His right arm had been severed, and one side of his face was torn away, bloody muscle clinging to his skull, skin flopping like a puppy's ear. His left leg was twisted back on itself, the right gone from the knee down, and his clothes were clawed to tatters, his chest flayed open, entrails slopping out onto the snowpack. Jibber's bowels had given way as he died, and the stench of human waste blew over the mountain, the wind singing a mournful melody.

10

January 14th, 1951, Abominable Peak—Elevation 12,119 feet

THE RING OF Jesse's ice axe as it struck the metal tent stake echoed off the mountainside, bouncing around inside the confined space. A huge boulder blocked the entrance to the crag in the cliff face, and above there was a dark overhang of stone. The duo had dug out a hollow, using the snow to make walls to keep out the whistling wind. The notch in the mountain had a level floor, and their tent was set up on verglas covered stone. The northern wall beneath the overhang was slick with water ice, but Jesse had broken away a good section and he'd just finished chiseling the E in their marker and was done.

He let the ice axe and makeshift chisel fall to his sides, arms cramping.

Roland said, "Happy now?"

"Yeah," Jesse said, but he wasn't. Roland was really getting on his nerves. They'd been alone together too long, and all Roland's little habits had become irritations, like chewing too loud or not putting the toilet seat down.

Roland stared, one eyebrow lifted, and Jesse looked away.

The duo broke camp, packed the equipment sled and their backpacks, and bundled up for the day's climb. They were still two hard climbs from the summit, and Jesse needed to find two level spots where he could set up his

Arriflex 16mm motion picture camera and use the shotgun to trigger any potential avalanches. If he wanted the cover of Ski Magazine, he needed to catch Roland making his historic run.

Bile inched up his throat, anger growing in him like a storm. This was settled ground, he reminded himself. He'd lost by almost a second, a ski racing lifetime, and that second had made him the photographer and Roland the world champion. One second. A blink of an eye, a swallow, a breath of air.

"You ready?" Roland asked.

Jesse nodded, and the partners climbed from their comfortable stone and snow room, breaking through snowpack into bright sunlight. He pulled down his goggles and the world took on a yellow tint. He tightened his pack straps and knelt, grabbing the front of the equipment sled as Roland pushed it through the hole Jesse had made.

A line of snowshoe prints trailed down the mountain to the south. To the north, the sheer rockface was covered in a beard of ice with a cornice snow hat. Oceans of sparkling snow ran to the horizon to the west, a pristine coating of powder creating an immaculate carpet. Large boulders, like giant rotten teeth, pocked the western slope, but to Jesse's trained eye it looked to be the safer route.

If Jesse suggested they take the western face up to the lower horn, using the stones and ledges as support where they could put in safety lines, Roland would never go for it. It had to be Roland's idea. He finished putting on his snowshoes, and said, "If we slip over there, at least we'll hit a boulder before we plummet several thousand feet to our deaths."

Roland stopped stomping in his snowshoes and gazed at the western slope, then up the mountain face. To Jesse's surprise, he said, "Makes sense. Lead on up to the lower horn. I'll take a turn with the sled." All the supplies, skis, poles, climbing gear, cameras, and camping equipment were strapped to the sled. Clothes, personal gear, bedrolls and sleeping bags were stowed in their packs, which weighed thirty pounds each, not counting lengths or rope, ice axes, and water bottles which hung from the hikers like Christmas tree ornaments.

The sun glared down like an accusing eye and the polished snow became a desert, light refracting in a rainbow of colors. Jesse's skin and mouth were dry as bone, there being little moisture or humidity in the air despite the snow. Jesse pulled his bottle and drained its contents. The incline was steeper than he'd realized, and Roland was having trouble getting the sled up. He was stopped a hundred feet downslope, hands clawing into the snowpack.

Jesse continued, working his way toward a boulder that stuck from the snowpack like a raisin in flour. He pulled a piton from his climbing belt and tapped it into the stone with the flat tip of his ice axe. When he was done, he snapped in the carabiner at the end of his rope and dropped the free end down to Roland.

"I'll help you. Tie it off," Jesse said as he sat in the snow, bracing his legs, the rope running through his hands.

Roland fumbled with the rope for several minutes but was able to get it tied off. Completing any task with the heavy gloves on was a challenge, but with each step they took it got colder, the air harsher, the wind more bitter. He gave a thumbs up.

When they'd managed to get the sled up the slope, the companions shared the rest of Roland's water and lounged in the sun as they boiled snow, filling their bottles and drinking their fill of the hot liquid. They ate some dried fruit, stale bread, and dreamed it was steak and martinis.

Jesse was feeling good, light of spirit and mind, when Roland said, "Are you coming all the way to the peak?"

"Why wouldn't I?" Acid fought up his throat.

"I just . . . nothing. It's just, why make the climb only to climb back down?" Roland looked away.

The hatred Jesse felt for his old companion in that moment made a wave of shame crash over him. Only one person was going to ski down from the summit. "I'm bringing the still camera. I want a picture. For posterity."

"Like your carving?"

"Like my carving."

"Who's going to take the picture? The wind? The bear? Your monster?"

Jesse laughed to himself. Yeah, Roland, there's something else up here with us. They'd argued about the tracks in the snow, Jesse saying he didn't think it was wise to continue. Roland countered with Jesse wouldn't feel that way if he was to be the first to ski Abominable Peak. Jesse couldn't argue with that. The footprints in the snow had disappeared like whatever had made them flew away, though he knew it was just time and the wind blowing around snow.

Roland pushed to his feet. "You think we need an elevation marker?"

Jesse gazed up at the lower horn and judged it was a thousand feet above them. "Nah, we know the lower horn is around thirteen thousand feet, so that means we're at around twelve."

Roland nodded. "Okay." He looked at the sled.

"Yup, my turn," Jesse said.

The incline below the horn was less sheer, and they zigzagged up, Jesse having a much easier time pulling the sled than Roland had. They backtracked east as they climbed, abandoning the western slope as they rounded the lower horn, the upper horn hidden in swirling ice clouds.

The sun had long passed noon, and Jesse was sweating beneath several layers of long underwear. He hated the extreme cold, which led many to ask him, "Why skiing?" Most couldn't understand when he tried to explain the rush he got when he was riding, focusing on nothing but finding a line, nothing clouding his brain.

A roar, more of a pig cackling than a lion marking its territory, rolled over the mountainside like a toxic cloud. Roland froze, head jerking as he stared over his shoulder at Jesse.

It would be a lie to say Jesse didn't feel a twang of pleasure surge through him, seeing the fear in Roland's eyes, that look saying maybe Jesse was right. The wail faded away and the two men waited for a follow-up, or an answering cry, but nothing howled except the wind, the sand-like snow tinkling across the snowpack filling his head with static.

***

On the third day out from Fort Fortune, the duo called it a day at around 5 PM. They dug a large snow hole on the leeward side of a boulder, and even with the entrance uncovered it was warm inside the snow cocoon.

As Roland set up the tent, he said, "Not to say you were right, because . . . " The two men chuckled, but Jesse knew they were laughing at different things. Roland thought he was being self-deprecating, but Jesse thought he was being arrogant. No surprise there. "That didn't sound like a bear to me."

"Nope." The whoosh of the cookstove lighting sounded like the tent had caught fire.

"You're going to make me say it?" Roland said.

Yes, he was. "I'm supposed to read you—"

"The legend of the Metoh."

"Now, who's sounding crazy?"

Roland stared at the tent.

Jesse knew the legend well, his father told him the story many times when he was a young boy. There had been an Indian chief, Nefitti, who broke from the Ute people and started a splinter tribe. Chief Nefitti led his followers into the mountains before winter, and they all died, except the chief, whose heart turned to pure ice. It's said he walks the mountaintop searching for prey, a massive hairy thing with glowing red eyes.

"Most myths have some basis in fact." Roland sounded like he was trying to convince himself.

"What would you like to eat?" Jesse asked. "We're got stew, stew, and, oh, stew."

"Um, I'll take stew."

"Can you keep an eye while I go see where we're at?"

Roland nodded and accepted a metal spoon from Jesse.

Wind surged into the snow hole, tiny shards of ice biting Jesse's face. He untied the canvas covering the equipment sled and pulled free a wood box containing a theodolite—a device used to measure angles. Utilizing the basic formula of a triangle, and two pre-determined data points on the ground, he would be able to estimate their current height. The device didn't like the cold, and the lens began to fog immediately, so he picked up his pace.

Wind brushed over the slick mountainside, clouds of frozen mist filling the air, but Jesse was able to get a good reading. He'd checked their elevation enough times to know—based on the angle—they were exactly where he expected to be. They were at approximately fifteen thousand feet and had roughly two thousand feet to go.

Snow drifted off the huge cornice that crowned Abominable Peak like a fang. He searched the area, looking for a place to set up his camera. The plan was for Roland to ride the southern face, and lines formed in Jesse's head, drop-offs, boulders, and patches of chowder marking the landscape like obstacles on a miniature golf course.

"How we looking?" Roland joined him, sinking two feet into powder. "Stew is ready."

"Good," Jesse said. He opened his mouth to tell Roland about the lines he'd calculated, the perils he'd identified. It was all so clear, but Jesse said nothing.

"Get up early, play with the guns, hike up, and make the run at noonish when you've got sunlight at your back?" Roland said.

That was a reasonable suggestion, and would work, but

Jesse shook his head no. "There'll be too much glare." Jesse raised his arm and arced it over the southern horizon like a clock arm. He paused when he was pointing southwest. "3 PM. Then we rest under lower horn before we head down."

Roland looked confused. "So, how many stops do I need to make?"

"If all goes well, only once. Here," Jesse said. "You can pack up and send the sled down while I hike down and set up the camera atop lower horn. Where you stop after that is up to you."

Roland looked away. If he wanted, Roland could ski all the way back to Fort Fortune, but courtesy dictated he wait for Jesse, who planned to ride the equipment sled most of the way down. He didn't even want to strap on skis lest there be confusion about who the star of the day was.

Roland said, "Do you still plan to come to the peak?"

Jesse sighed but said nothing.

The partners crowded into the tent, ate, and the night passed without incident, the wind singing, rocks tapping, ice cracking, snow scurrying around like roaches. Jesse heard voices in the wind, as he always did. There were no signs of the bear—or whatever it was—but angst poked his nerves, and his stomach grumbled despite being full and warm.

Moonlight peeked into the snow hole, backlighting the side of the canvas tent, and as Jesse nodded off to sleep, he imagined he heard crunching footsteps on the snowpack outside their hole. When he focused, eliminating the sound of the wind and rushing snow and ice, there was nothing but cold silence, and the murmur of Roland's voice as he dreamt of what was to come.

The next morning, Jesse cleared a section of snowpack with a good view of the southern face. He'd be able to catch Roland as he came down the peak's cornice and ride down the face. It would be incredible footage if he made it, and even more incredible if he fell. Guilty tremors jangled his bones, knifed him in the back. The mind thinks evil things. He didn't want Roland to crash, but there was no denying he'd get more money for the footage that way, and more importantly, then it would be Jesse's turn and he'd have a shot at being the first person to ride Abominable Peak.

Jesse pushed the thoughts away, but they kept floating back to him like inappropriate fantasies. He didn't want it that way . . . and he didn't want Roland to get hurt. Whatever they were, Jesse didn't see them as enemies, though at times he hated his old partner more than he cared to admit.

He leveled his tripod and attached his Arriflex camera. He panned it up and down, then covered it so it didn't collect snow and ice from the wind. The lens and film were on the sled wrapped in blankets so they could be kept as warm as possible until needed. Frost could damage the lens, and film can go brittle in extreme cold. With his site scouted, he went to work with his German Leica M3 35mm rangefinder camera. It was already loaded with film, and he snapped pictures of the landscape, the blue-white horizons dotted with the snowcapped mountain peaks of Mount Elbert, Bull Hill, and Casco Peak.

Roland watched Jesse fumble with the still camera as he checked all his gear one last time. "So, you going to tell me how you're going to pull this picture off? There a third person up here I don't know about?"

Jesse held up a round metal device that looked like an old school round tire gauge.

"Am I supposed to know what that is?" Roland said.

"You'll see."

The partners broke out the shotguns and blasted away, firing at the slope above, tufts of white lifting from the snowpack with each shot. Spindrifts tumbled down the mountaintop, but no avalanches were triggered.

Jesse led the trek to the summit, which was a boring, anticlimactic slog up the final stretch of incline to the top of the peak's snow cornice.

"Stand over there," Jesse said, as he motioned west. He dug into the snowpack, building a small ice tower. He placed the camera's case atop the pillar of packed snow, then using it as a tripod, placed the still camera and focused it.

Roland watched him like he'd eaten a canary.

Jesse stood before the camera and turned his back on Roland so he couldn't see what he was doing. The Photoclip Recta was specially made for Leica M3 cameras and utilized a clockwork mechanism to time delay the opening of the shutter. He carefully attached the device to the camera using the bent bracket atop the device and set the countdown for thirty seconds by twisting the spring-loaded timer knob. Then, he hurried behind the camera, checked his shot one more time, and joined Roland.

Jesse looked at his watch and said, "Ten seconds." He counted silently in his head. When he reached eight, he smiled.

Roland threw his arm around his shoulders.

The device depressed the shutter button, and Jesse saw the lens aperture flash as it opened. The click of the camera echoed over the wind and Roland let his arm fall to his side.

Jesse looked at him and said, "Why'd you do that?"

Roland threw up his hands. "Trying to make it look like you want to be here." He stomped off, picking up his skis and knocking the snow off them.

Jesse started down to the movie camera without a word.

"How long do you want me to wait?"

Jesse stopped, turned, and said, "You've got eyes."

The trek down was easier than the climb up—gravity and all that rot—and he descended the roughly thousand feet of snowpack and chowder in less than an hour. He took his time, stopping to rest twice and drink water, knowing Roland waited anxiously above, most likely thinking about the compressing snow.

When he reached where the camera was set up, he

urinated, writing his name in the clean snow. Then, with a precision reserved for building ships in bottles, he packed away the still camera and broke out the canister of film and the Arriflex's lens.

A hush fell over the mountaintop, the wind a gentle murmur, tiny spindrifts dancing down the southern face like miniature frozen ballerinas. Jesse thought he heard his blood pumping through his veins, but realized the sound was water running deep beneath the heavy layer of snowpack.

He angled the camera down, snapped on the lens, then clicked the film canister into place, making sure the film fed in properly. Jesse grasped the stainless-steel pivot arm and angled the camera up as he peered at the viewfinder and adjusted the accordion-like light damper at the end of the lens housing.

The precise eye of the camera revealed white cotton candy with sprinkles of rock, and the image got sharper as he focused the unit. The camera's eye found Roland as Jesse panned slowly across the peak, but a dark shadow caught his eye, and he swung the camera away from Roland.

A massive shadow cut across the snowpack, working its way up the eastern slope of the peak's cornice.

11

January 29, 2018, Fort Fortune—Elevation 9,871 feet

THE LUCKY STRIKE saloon was one of the oldest buildings in Fort Fortune. In the early days of the mining operation, it had been administrative offices for the foreman and his support staff, payroll, shipping, and—at night—became a speakeasy where workers drank, told tall tales, and blew off steam. As mining operations expanded, and Fort Fortune grew and modernized, a suite of offices was created in the new dormitory building, which left the ramshackle structure free to be a booze oasis full time. Buried in the snow outside were makeshift tables made of every type of garbage known to man, and in summer, when the weather was more accommodating, people ate and drank outside. In the frigid months of ski season, the place was packed from the moment it opened until long after it officially closed.

Lucky's was a melting pot in which everyone had a common addiction. On any given night the saloon entertained rich and poor, posers and real deals, pros and wannabes, hangers-on and adrenaline addicts from all walks of life. If you had the money and the moxie, you could ride Abominable Peak if you waited your turn—or paid really big bucks.

Not that getting a spot was easy no matter how much cheese you had. Fort Fortune could only support 128 people at one time, and the snowcat only plodded up the mountain once a week with supplies and new visitors, taking back down those whose adventures had ended.

Then, there were the people like Chance—lifers. He'd be at Abominable Peak all season, slinging drinks, hiding from his sorrow, and taking rides when he could. His crew was scheduled to be on the peak for ten days—a lifetime for them—but when they left, he'd be alone again.

Chance and his crew sat at a table made from the lid of a shipping container. Lucky's was crowded but quiet, everyone watching Chance, but not watching him. He caught their sideways glances, their stares in the reflective surfaces. It was the calm before the show, the crowd's murmuring like an orchestra tuning. Everyone was waiting for Chance to spill his story.

Chance raised his whiskey. "To Jibber."

"To Jibber." They clashed glasses.

"Everything handled in that regard?" Chance asked. He didn't want to bring down the party, but one of the crew was dead. They'd wrapped him and brought his remains down off the mountain, and at some point soon someone—probably him—would have to call Jibber's sister and arrange to have his body shipped home.

Biggie nodded. "There's an unheated storage facility where the miners keep supplies and gear. He's in there, mostly . . . frozen." It sounded horrible, but it was for the best. There was no way to bury the body because of the frozen ground. There was an old graveyard in the hills outside of camp, where those who died in the early days of the mine were buried, but nobody had been interred there in over forty years.

Jibber's sister wouldn't be surprised by the call. Like the partners of police officers and soldiers, loved ones of extreme riders always walked the knife blade of worry, constantly wondering when the call would come, telling them their loved one had been buried under tons of snow, or had hit a tree, or one of the other million things that can kill you on the mountain.

Chance took a pull off his drink, the warm alcohol melting the ice cube in his stomach, but the sorrow remained. He felt the crowd around him, the anxious tremor that ran just below the festivities like ice water. His wound stung, and he saw the beast's angry face in his mind's eye.

"Oh, I almost forgot," said Tina as she dug into her jacket pocket. She pulled free Chance's Swiss Army knife, a thin smile cutting across her red, tear-stained face. She looked like an angry flower. As she handed Chance his knife, he felt heat simmer between them. "Meant to give it to you yesterday, but I forgot."

Chance stared at the knife as he accepted it. The last time he'd seen the blade it was sinking into powder, and he recalled thinking he'd never see it again. "I . . . don't know what to say." He gripped the closed knife in a tight fist.

"Thank you would work," she said.

"Thank you." He met the eye of each of his crew. "All of you, for everything."

"Forget it," Colin said.

"No," Chance said. "I don't intend to forget anything."

The grumble of the crowd, the gentle whistle of the wind, the rumble of generators, and the endless sound of snow pelting Lucky's filled the saloon.

"How do you feel?" Tina asked.

He sighed. "Much better now that I'm fed and have several of these in me." Chance held up his glass. He flexed his injured arm and winced. "Arm still hurts when I stretch the wound, but it'll be fine."

"What about?" Colin swirled his finger around his face.

Chance couldn't feel his cheeks because they were covered in a generous layer of topical burn cream. His cheeks were gray-black where the roots of frostbite had begun to take hold. The general opinion was that the burns would heal, but he'd be left with dirty clouds on both his cheeks like complimentary birthmarks.

“Are we going to talk about what happened to Jibber?” Bomber said. His beard was combed, but the nest of blonde hair atop his head looked like it hadn’t been brushed since he’d arrived at Fort Fortune.

Chance waited.

“Talk?” Colin said.

“About what?” Biggie said.

“We’re sure it was a bear?” Bomber asked. “I mean . . . ” He glanced at Chance, who lifted an eyebrow. “You all heard what Chance said.”

“You didn’t see Jibber’s body,” Tina said. “He was mauled . . . I’ve never seen a bear do anything like that.”

“Then you’re lucky,” Biggie said. “You ever see what happens to cars parked in national parks when food is left in the vehicle?”

Nobody answered.

“Doors torn off, windows smashed, claw marks that go through fenders and hoods,” Biggie said.

“Yeah, but do they . . . dine like they’re feasting. One of his arms and half a leg was missing,” Tina said.

“You said it yourself,” Colin said. “All the increased mining activity has the bears out and about when they shouldn’t be.”

“At sixteen thousand feet?” Chance asked. His tone had been harsher than he’d intended.

“What’s at sixteen thousand feet?” said a middle-aged woman wearing a blue one-piece snowsuit, her long jet-black hair tied back in a ponytail, glass of wine in hand. A younger man and woman stood behind her like medical interns.

“I’m sorry,” Tina said. “Do we know you?”

“Let me buy you a round of drinks and you will,” the woman said.

Everyone looked at Chance for his approval. Free drinks were a strong motivator, but they knew as well as Chance did that the woman most likely wanted Chance’s story. It was now common knowledge who his grandfather had been, but not how he'd died.

"Shelly," Chance called out.

The bartender popped up from where she was washing glasses behind the bar. "Yo!"

"Another round for us all, and charge it to—?" Chance said.

The harsh overhead lighting made the woman's hair look slick, and when she tossed her head, she looked like a model coming out of a swimming pool. "Reality Groove Films," she said.

Tina let a small gasp escape her lips, Bomber and Colin shifted in their seats, but Biggie made no sign. RG was one of the premier extreme sports film companies.

"I meant what is your name?" Chance said, trying to hide his attraction to the woman by not looking directly at her, but that made things even more awkward.

"Of course." She chuckled. "Tatiana Crow. It looks like you folks can drink, and I don't want to get stuck with the bill."

"So, this is business, then?" Biggie asked.

"Of a sort."

The murmur of the crowd seemed to rise and fall like waves crashing on the beach. Outside, the wind hollered, the perpetual buzz of generators like the buzz of flies.

"Can we pull up seats?" She motioned back at her two companions. "This here is Ju Ju. Boom and sound."

A petite young man who looked to be of South American descent waved.

"And that there is Maggie. She handles the camera."

The girl smiled, her eyes bored, dreadlock-like blonde hair spilling around her shoulders, bright against her black ski jacket.

"What is it you do?" Tina said, the sharpness of her tone only achievable when a woman is talking to another woman.

"I make it all happen." She lifted her eyebrows as she stared at Chance.

Chance nodded and the crew made space at the table.

Shelly came with the drinks, and an uncomfortable silence spread over the group. Chance was the one in charge, so he intended to make Ms. 'Make It Happen' fire the opening salvo.

"So, I'm sorry to hear about your mate," Tatiana said.

Chance nodded, pursed his lips, waited.

"You are Charles Hance, aren't you?"

"Call me Chance."

"Your grandad is a legend around here."

Chance nodded again but didn't speak.

"Saw his picture on the wall in the old barrack."

"That's what you want? To talk about how my grandad died here, just like my friend Jibber?" Chance's voice rose in volume and intensity with each word.

Tatiana looked bashfully at the wood floor, sipping her wine, but didn't deny the claim.

"That's it then?" Colin said.

Wine sloshed onto the table as Tatiana put her glass down, eyes blazing with mojo. "I'd be lying if I didn't want to get you on film talking about what happened to you up there. Tying it to your grandad just makes the whole story more compelling. But that's for later." She switched gears like she was driving a race car. "What I want to know is do you intend to ride tomorrow? Any of you?"

There it was. The proverbial elephant on the snowflake. The show must go on and sitting around drinking all day when they could be cutting lines on the face wasn't what Jibber would've wanted. He'd want his crew to ride and never look back, because that's what he would've done had it been any of them. They used to talk about it regularly—what they'd do if one of them died on the hill. The unanimous decision had been, go on to the next hill and celebrate the deceased's life with a victory.

Now, after everything that had happened, the initial

plan seemed insane, so naïve. Chance knew he could ride, bad wing and all, but he wasn't sure if he wanted to.

Everyone at the table looked at something other than Chance.

Biggie bailed him out. "Personally, I plan to honor Jibber's memory and ride." He looked at the others. Tina and Colin nodded, but Bomber didn't move as he stared at his beer, brow furrowed.

Tatiana cleared her throat but remained quiet.

To Chance, it appeared the chatter in the bar had dwindled away, his heart hammering in his chest like a marching band. The tension in the room was palpable, his skin crawling with angst and indecision. He leaned forward, drew himself up and straightened his back as he finished his whiskey, put down the empty glass, and picked up his fresh drink with his good arm. Still, he said nothing as he took a slow sip, commanding his audience. He lifted his wounded arm and said, "Probably not smart to ride."

No response. Everyone within earshot knew there was more coming.

"But I'm going back up the mountain," Chance said.

Tina tossed back her head.

Colin and Bomber's eyes grew wide, and Biggie said, "Wait . . . if you're not riding, what are you doing?"

Chance said nothing.

"Is it true what I've heard?" Tatiana asked.

Wind, blowing snow, glasses tinkling, a cough.

Tatiana sighed. "Not getting much for my money."

Chance made a show of tossing back his whiskey, then lifting his glass to signal Shelly for another. He was feeling no pain—not even in his arm—and his vision was getting hazy with sleep. He blurted, "You don't believe it?"

"Believe what?" Tatiana said. She nodded over her shoulder to Maggie as if to say, "Make sure you're listening to this."

Tina said, "Chance, do you really—?"

Chance shouted, "What do you think, Tina? Huh? That Jibber was killed and eaten by a bear? That what you believe?"

Tina said nothing and looked away.

"So, let's go get this thing on film," Tatiana said.

Chance's crew laughed, but he didn't. Confusion flooded him. Why did he even care? Jibber was gone, and they'd never know what happened to him. Whether it was a bear, a mountain lion, or some bizarre mutant, what difference did it make? Nobody was accusing him of lying. He had nothing to prove to anyone, so why did he feel like he did? He should simply forget the entire ordeal.

But he couldn't. Wouldn't. The creature had tried to kill him just as Abominable Peak had. Was that the fate his grandfather had met? Had he died bloodied and disemboweled in the snow, his skeleton lost within the snowpack?

"I'd agree to use nothing unless approved by you. All footage. No exceptions," Tatiana said.

"You'll sign a contract?" Colin asked, parroting what his agent always asked.

"Sure. No tricks. No sensationalism. I'm doing a piece on winter in Fort Fortune, and your grandad's story was going to be part of it whether you participated or not. Why not get your family's side of the story on the record?"

His family's side. Anger exploded in his head, ears ringing, vision going blurry red. He opened his mouth to attack, then closed it. Perhaps that was another reason to accept her offer? On the mountain, working on the documentary, perhaps he could put his grandfather to rest, let his ghost go.

The uncomfortable gap in the conversation stretched out like a fart in a restaurant. He wanted to find the beast . . . he'd come to that decision, at least. The desire to ride hadn't returned, which was unusual. After the accident, the focus of his depression had been not being able to compete, to ride. Like any injured professional athlete, the urge to ride usually surged above all others. Now, he wanted to hunt the beast. What that meant exactly he didn't know, but the tension drained from his neck with the realization that he was no longer a pro boarder, and unless something drastically changed in the next eight weeks, he was done on the pro tour, whether they wanted him or not.

"So, you're saying we chopper up to the collection point? Me, you, and Tweedledum and Tweedledee here?" Chance jerked a thumb toward Ju Ju and Maggie. "Then what? We ask the thing for its autograph?"

Tatiana said, "It found you with no trouble."

"And almost killed him," Tina said.

A slight over-exaggeration, but it certainly could've come to that.

"This time we'll be prepared," Tatiana said.

"Oh, really? You know how to be prepared for something . . . " Bomber looked to Chance for support. "Something we have very little information about."

Chance knew his crew believed his story or at least believed that he believed what he was saying was true, but he'd almost died on the mountain, which put his account and judgment in question.

"We'll bring protection," Ju Ju said. It was the first time the guy had spoken, and his voice was small and squeaky like a child's.

"Protection?"

Tatiana nodded.

Ju Ju squeaked, "According to Stormie, tomorrow is supposed to be perfect conditions, so Trevor is planning on going up four times."

"I'm in," Chance blurted.

Arguing wind pressed against the Lucky Strike, glasses tinkling, but the crowd had gone still, the entire room pretending not to listen to every word of Chance's conversation.

The table erupted all at once. Tina told him he needed to rest, Biggie went on about his arm wound and all his bumps and bruises, and Colin and Bomber said there was nothing to be gained by picking a scab. Thing was, Chance felt rested, his injuries were under control, and all he'd done for the last year was pick scabs.

"I need some air," Chance said. He downed his drink, pushed up from the table, and headed out into the frigid moonlit night.

12

THE COLD HIT him in the face like a splash of boiling water, the old wooden door's hinges creaking as it slapped closed behind him. He couldn't feel much of his damaged cheeks except the tingle of healing, and his other wounds ached with an alcohol dulled urgency. He checked zippers and drawstrings to ensure he was sealed up. Like an astronaut donning a spacesuit, every seal needed to be checked because the slightest leak would let his heat escape like oxygen. He climbed out the snowy foyer and made his way up onto the path that ran along the surface of the snowpack. Stars twinkled across the cloud-dusted sky, the imposing storm clouds in the east a distant reminder of the prior days' storm. Moonlight bounced off snow and verglas, icicles hanging from every vertical surface.

Fort Fortune sat in a shallow valley, where snow tended to accumulate, creating huge sand dune-like drifts. Paths were dug between the buildings that were in use, and as Chance walked, snowy retaining walls rose on both sides of the trail.

The camp was like a building that's been expanded many times and thus reflected multiple generations of building materials, technology, and mining techniques. Some of the buildings, like the old barrack and the original warehouse, looked much the same way they did in Chance's grandfather's pictures he'd taken the night he spent at Fort Fortune. The original barrack served as the "budget" accommodations, and the old warehouse stored the helicopter when not in use.

New buildings were scattered amongst these old structures like children, though many of them had no paths to their doors because they were off-limits and secured for the winter. Light spilled from the new building that housed the modern accommodations and the administrative offices of Fort Fortune Mining Corp. The place looked like a Holiday Inn and handled the food service where Chance got his three squares a day, and where heat and companionship were always plentiful.

He was staying in Cheapside, and hated not having his own bathroom, but there were worse things in life. He'd gotten a certain thrill when he'd sat by the old potbelly stove in the original barrack, sitting in the same spot his grandad had all those years ago. The place was old, dusty, and cold, but it was home.

Ice clinked and cracked, snow shifting and tinkling. The wind whistled and argued, brushing icy clouds off the snowdrifts like smoke from a chimney. A jingle on the wind . . . metal on metal . . . tapping.

He walked past the original barrack, climbing downslope in the moonlight to the southern overlook. To his left, mostly covered in snow, was the massive processing building. Formerly used to house the equipment needed for an open-pit mine and the raw gold and stone extracted, the structure had been converted to a processing facility that used chemicals to separate small amounts of gold and copper found all around the original gold vein, which had run dry twenty years ago.

Sculptures of twisted snow lined the path, interspersed with the tops of evergreen trees. Spindrifts twisted down the incline before him, puffs of frozen mist curling around the trees and statues of snow. Chance heard the snowy figures talking, arguing, debating. He heard his parents, his grandfather. Amy. They argued with the wind, which was on Chance's side. The wind wanted him to seek out the beast.

Time slipped away as the southern horizon opened before him. The moon hung low in the sky, tattered clouds fleeting across bright stars, snowcapped mountain peaks rolling into the night like giant snowballs.

Jingling and clinking echoed on the breeze.

A spray of icy crystals nipped Chance's nose, the wind gusting, reminding him of the last twenty-four hours and the dark line of clouds on the eastern horizon. He paused, staring at the path. There were slight indentations in the snow that looked like footprints filled with powder. The crunch of his feet told him he was walking again, following the prints.

His alcohol buzz was fading, pain growing in him like a tax debt, and he'd had enough crisp mountain air, and was considering heading back to the warmth of his rack, when his father's voice came on the wind, urging him forward.

A grunt carried on the breeze, then a growl—or cough? Chance couldn't be sure. Ice creaked, and wind cycled over the slope, humming and pounding.

He picked up his pace, the tracks getting deeper, fresher, but there was still no detail, no claw marks or crisscross patterns of boot prints. He was afraid the trail would disappear, and heat rose in him as he pictured himself standing alone in the snow. His arm chimed in with questions, his head throbbing in answer.

The wind shifted, as it often does at high elevations, pushing spirals of dancing snow over the incline. A cloud of frozen mist puffed over him, and for an instant Chance stood in a miniature whiteout, unable to see anything around him, the stars gone behind a blurry white curtain. Angst gnawed on his spine, the icy fingers of fear caressing his shoulders.

Snow spun in his face, the jingle of metal like the wind was sharpening a blade on a stone. A crackle . . . Energy zipped up his spine.

The whiteout cloud passed over him, crawling up the slope.

The stars returned, and Chance turned his attention back to the path, but didn't continue. His feet were affixed to the snowpack, eyes locked on a long shadow that fell across the path ahead. Moonlight reflected off snow and verglas, the world painted in harsh black and white, shadows blending into the night like water onto a shore.

Crunching in the snow as the shadow grew.

"Is someone there?" Came a voice on the wind.

The icy snake in Chance's throat wrapped around his vocal cords. The ping and jingle of metal had stopped.

A flashlight flicked on.

Chance was blinded, and he covered his face with his arm.

"Hello?" said the voice.

"Stefan?"

"Ja." The flashlight beam bounced to the ground, a cloud of light filling the area, the snowpack sparkling.

Chance released a breath he hadn't known he was holding.

Stefan Baumeister limped into the light, the keys in his jacket pocket jingling and clanging like riding spurs. Stefan was de facto winter Mayor of Fort Fortune. He ran Catching Clouds Adventure Tours, the company that had permits with the state of Colorado to conduct tours on Abominable Peak. The contract with the mining company gave CCAT exclusive rights to Fort Fortune's facilities during riding season, which started the first of the year and ended April first.

Stefan asked, "Why are you out here in the cold after what you've been through."

"Needed some air."

"Been a long day," Stefan said as he gazed at the southern star-filled horizon, wisps of frozen mist swirling and lifting from the snowpack like steam. The wind picked up, currents of freezing air pushing snow and gnat-sized shards of ice over the mountains.

The gale roared and howled and grunted. Chance stared at Stefan, trying to see if the German's expression revealed if he'd heard what Chance had . . .

He blurted, "Did you hear that?"

Stefan nodded. "The wind is a siren's song. It will tell you what you want to hear, help you see things that aren't there, and when you're in the right state of mind, it'll talk to you. Clear as day, like your ma was rattling in your ears."

Chance closed his eyes and did hear his mother's voice.

"Are you alright?" Stefan asked. "I don't need to call my lawyer, do I?" He was smiling.

Chance had signed a release, and while he could sue CCAT, it would be hard finding a judge or a jury that wouldn't think Chance had understood the risk he was taking when he got on a helicopter, rode to the top of the world, then jumped off.

He said, "I'll be fine. Crushed ego more than anything else."

"I heard."

"Good news travels fast."

"Ja."

They were friendly, not friends, but Stefan had given him his opportunity at Lucky's, and he felt he owed the man. "You ever see any strange shit up there?"

Stefan had retired from riding years prior, but he still went up the mountain for fun, and had ridden Abominable Peak many times in his youth. Now, he was bent and broken from years of hammering his knees and overstretching joints too many times over too many years.

Stefan shook his head no. "Thought I saw the Metoh once." He went silent.

"And?"

"Turned out to be ice hanging off a dead tree," Stefan said. "The shadow, it just ..." He stared at Chance, the whites of his eyes glowing in the moonlight. "The shadow didn't slash my arm, and no bear has ever attacked anyone up here except drunken miners trying to tip them like cows."

Chance laughed. "Thank you."

"For what?"

"Not thinking I'm crazy."

"These hills have eyes. And they see everyone in a different way."

Chance said nothing, snow shifting over verglas.

"What are you going to do next?" Stefan said.

"What's the deal with Tatiana and her film?"

Now Stefan laughed. "She's some piece of work, ja?"

"From the little I saw."

"I know she's legit because her company is. They paid full freight, and they're not riding," Stefan said.

"Should be good for business."

He shrugged. "Who knows. Too many people and . . . " He looked at the ground, then jerked up in defiance. "All I'm saying is if they open a Starbucks next to Lucky's, I'm done. Why do you care about Tatiana? Do you . . . um . . . like her?"

"She wants to hunt the beast with me. The legend of Chief Nefitti, his frozen heart, and the Metoh. Tie it to my grandad and Jibber," Chance said. It felt good to say it to someone.

Stefan remained silent.

"She said she'd only use what I approved."

Stefan stifled a laugh.

"What? She said she'd sign a paper."

"Come on, kid. You've been around."

Chance said nothing, worry stirring the worms in his gut.

"They'll use what they want and say, 'Sue us. See you in court.' Even if you have the money to fight them—which judging by you having to work as a bartender and all, I'm thinking you might not be so liquid at the moment—it wouldn't matter. The footage would be out, and the damage done."

He was liquid, alright. Air. He had nada. "Damage?"

"Let's just say that when stories are profit-driven, there tends to be a certain . . . theatrical element that may distort the story. Will you be okay with the clickbait headline 'Drug Addict Grandson Almost Dies on Same Mountain as Legendary Grandfather.'"

Chance flinched and hoped Stefan hadn't noticed.

He had. "Look, I'm sorry to be blunt. I get you want proof the creature exists. You're far from the first one, but you won't find anything up there but snow and death."

Yet, he had to go. Chance stood brooding, anger growing in him, but he didn't know why.

With father-like precision, Stefan said, "Sorry about Jibber. That why you need to go back up there?"

Chance nodded slowly. It was part of the reason, but it was really about him, Chance. He needed to see the beast with his own eyes again, know what he'd experienced up on the mountain was real, and that it all hadn't been a snow-blind delusion. And, yeah, if he got the chance, the creature would pay for Jibber. He'd accept the same currency his friend had paid: blood.

"Well, I can't let you go up there without a weapon. I've got a rifle I can spare, with a few shells. You ever hunt before?"

"Once, when I was very young, but I was more concerned with my handheld football game," Chance said. He'd recently bought a throwback version of the old game that had dots as players on a two-inch monochrome screen.

"So . . . you might want to get some bait. Like when you hunt deer you spray buck urine, or like chumming the water with nasty shit and blood when you go big game fishing," Stefan said.

"You're saying I should set a trap?"

Stefan sighed in frustration. "No. I mean put some type

of scent out there that might draw it to you, instead of you traipsing around the cold, dangerous mountainside exposed."

"Like meat?"

"Good luck with that. No, I was thinking garbage, and yeah . . . chicken bones or meat bones you might be able to dig out of the kitchen waste," Stefan said.

"Sounds like you want to come. We've got an extra seat."

Stefan massaged his leg like the injury was new, then rubbed his gloved hands together. "I gave up on that a long time ago. I'm at peace not knowing everything about this place."

Chance said nothing.

"See me in the AM," Stefan said.

Chance smiled.

"And be careful up there, Chance. That peak has a way about it, and whatever's up there is part of it. Don't add another obsession to your list."

Chance's head jerked back like he'd been punched.

"Easy, I know your type. I was your type. Sleep on it, and we'll talk in the morning."

Chance nodded.

13

January 30, 2018, Fort Fortune—Elevation 9,871 feet

CHANCE DIDN'T FEEL differently when he woke the next morning, refreshed and eager, the horrors of the past three days already receding into memory. If anything, he felt more certain that the answers he needed were on Abominable Peak. Harsh winter wind piped down the potbelly stove's chimney throat, chanting, and heat rolled off the old cast iron stove. He was lucky his billet was so close to the heat. At the far end of the wood structure by the front door, riders slept in bags designed for sub-zero temperatures. He'd yet to meet a rider that cared. It all made for better stories when they relived their adventure in bars, at family gatherings, and on job interviews.

He dressed, taking extra care to clean and wrap the gashes on his arm, then packed himself into his cocoon of polyester and polypropylene. Pain needling his arms, Chance hefted his pack, and pushed out into the early morning sunlight, his stomach screaming for breakfast.

Generators hummed and snowpack crunched beneath his feet, and powder blew and sifted as people moved about Fort Fortune. He headed for the dining hall, which was on the far end of the new living accommodations. Rooms in the new building were nothing fancy, but there was plumbing and normal water service and heat, and several rooms had private bathrooms if you had the scratch. The facility was nothing to look at, a squat cinderblock structure with a green metal roof. The building was labeled simply, Housing & Food, and there were a few windows, but fewer comforts.

Fort Fortune was very much like an island; if a rider didn't bring it there, the rider won't find it there.

"Yo!" someone yelled. The high-pitched scream of metal scraping over metal rang over the camp, and Chance veered onto the path that led to the copter hangar. Trevor should know the day's schedule and could let him know when Tatiana was scheduled to go up. He still needed to meet Stefan, and he wanted to see his crew off, but there was no sign of them. They were staying in the new building and would sleep until half an hour before their scheduled departure.

The two large double doors of the hangar stood open, and Chance saw the large pieces of mining equipment moving like ghosts through the doors. The hum of servos echoed over the snowpack as the helicopter platform slid into the morning brightness. Dimples of color refracted off the slick black bird, Trevor walking beside the moving platform, hands rolling in a 'keep it coming' gesture.

"Howdy," Trevor said as Chance approached. "How you doing?"

"Good," he said. "I'm heading up with Tatiana. When you taking them up?"

Trevor looked confused. "Tina and the others will be here in a minute." His gaze strayed to Chance's damaged wing, which he held protectively against his side. "Though, I guess you're not riding."

"Not from the top anyway."

"So, why are you heading up?"

"To see what there is to be seen."

Trevor shook his head. "That lady paid big bucks for me to bring you guys up to the collection site."

Usually, Trevor only landed at the collection site when riders chose not to take their ride all the way to the fort, which was rare. Some folks actually enjoyed staying at the collection site base camp. Made them feel like they'd done more than just ride the peak's surface. Under normal circumstances, Chance would have to ruck the two thousand feet up to the camp, but sometimes it paid to have rich friends . . . or at least someone who needed something from him and could afford to pay full freight for the bird.

Chance said, "Yeah, thanks. We last?"

"Nope." Trevor smiled. "Those rich . . . " he looked over his shoulder. "Those rich assholes from Dubai want to be picked up after their peak run. Supposedly, the rest of the run is 'boring', so I'll bring you up then. Figure 10:30ish."

"Tatiana aware?"

"Affirmative."

"See you later." Chance turned to leave, and Trevor reached out and snagged his coat sleeve.

"Be careful up there . . . I heard everything last night, and today everyone at the fort knows," Trevor said.

"And? What are the odds I don't make it back down?" Anger settled in Chance's chest like spoiled fish.

"Nobody's betting on that, mate."

"What then?"

"It's about fifty-fifty that you'll lose it up there. Never ride again." Trevor looked at the ground.

"Yo!" yelled Bomber as he slapped Chance on the back.

"You change your mind?" asked Biggie.

Colin and Tina smiled at them.

"Nope. I'm heading up later with the film crew to look around."

Wind gusted over Fort Fortune, snaking through the companions, and dusting them with snow.

There wasn't much else to say, and Chance stood back and watched his crew load their gear, snap their boards into their landing skid holders, and pile into the copter. The bird's rotors started to spin, and Chance waved, then turned his back on his crew and went to get food.

The hall was quiet, a few groups eating, getting ready

for the day's runs. Riding from the peak wasn't the only activity CCAT provided. There were numerous snowshoeing hikes, cross country ski trails, and if one was willing to make the effort, many less dangerous pristine runs that could be enjoyed by boarders and skiers alike. A standard trip came with two heli trips to the peak, and the remainder of a standard tourist's week was filled with these ancillary activities.

Chance dropped his pack, filled his plate with powdered eggs, sausage patties, and added a tall glass of water. He took his food to a corner table where he ate alone in silence.

When he was done, he brought his empty plate into the kitchen, where he found Gaston Lenôtre, a famous French chef on leave from a Paris restaurant who was paying his heli fees and lodging by cooking gourmet meals for the guests of Fort Fortune.

"Bonjour, mon ami," Gaston said as Chance glided through the swinging door into the immaculate kitchen.

"Bonjour," Chance said. He'd ridden all over the world and knew a few words of many languages, not counting curses.

"Was your meal not to your liking?" The chef's face was twisted with stress.

"No . . . no, the eggs were good. I'm wondering if . . . " His idea was nuts, and now that he had to say it out loud, he was doubting the entire plan.

"Qu'est-ce que c'est?"

Chance said nothing. No idea what his friend had said.

"Ah . . . " Gaston searched for the right words. "You spit it out?"

Chance said, "Where do you stow the garbage?"

Gaston's face scrunched like he'd downed a gallon of sour milk. "Garbage?" His accent made the word sound like a type of perfume.

"Yeah, like old food? Stuff people didn't eat."

"Sir, I assure you everything I serve—"

"Easy." Chance padded the air. "I need some nasty stuff for bait."

"Bait? Monsieur

Chance said nothing. He wasn't telling the guy he was going to search for the abominable snowman.

Gaston sighed and pointed to a blue sealed plastic barrel at the rear of the kitchen. "It's got today's kitchen waste in it. There are more in the back. They're stored and transported down the mountain in spring."

Chance had never thought about where their garbage went. He pointed to a white food container that sat on a stainless-steel worktable. "You wouldn't happen to have an empty one of those I could borrow, do you?"

Gaston pointed to a corner where a stack of pails—connected like nesting dolls—rose above a pile of boxes. "Take what you need."

"Merci," Chance said, but Gaston only grunted.

After considerable effort, he was able to pull an empty pail from the sleeve and pried off the blue container's rubberwear-like lid. The stench that assailed Chance made him gag, and his eggs and sausage almost reappeared. He realized he had no gloves, no way to get the crap into his bucket. He put the lid back on the barrel and fetched gloves from Gaston, then proceeded to pick through his chosen barrel, towel tied over his face. There was nasty raw chicken guts, rotting vegetables of all kinds, bones from spareribs, and a viscous goo that he scoped into the pail with his eyes closed because it smelled so bad.

He sealed the white food container when it was half-full, resealed the garbage pail, and leaned against the wall to catch his breath, tears streaming down his cheeks. The scent of rot hung in the air like body odor.

Next up was Stefan. His office was in his sleeping quarters because an office would mean he had one less room to rent. The offices of the mining company were sealed, and Chance wasn't even sure where they were.

Chance crunched through Fort Fortune, people bustling about, following the maze of stamped paths in the snowpack. Sun glinted off the peaks to the north, the pristine snow slick with a coating of thin ice, boulders, and the tops of trees sticking from the snowpack.

"Ahoy," said Stefan. He was walking toward Chance on the thin path.

"Was just coming to see you," Chance said.

"Figured. I'm heading to eat." Stefan pulled a rifle from his shoulder, letting it hang by the strap.

Chance didn't know much about guns, but he knew rifles were fairly basic weapons, yet he still hesitated. Could he shoot the creature? Kill it if need be? He had no doubts he could. He took the rifle and pulled back the bolt, checking to see if it was loaded. The rifle was a black semiautomatic Ruger .22 caliber long barrel.

"This is all I can spare, and there's only seven rounds in it," Stefan said as he handed Chance a ten-round rotary magazine.

Chance stared at it like a kid looking at a picture of a naked person for the first time.

Stefan leaned in and pointed. "Just snap it in behind the trigger guard when you need the weapon. Easy."

Chance thanked Stefan, stowed the clip, shouldered the rifle, and moved on, the helicopter thundering as it ferried riders up to the peak.

He arrived at the heli pickup to find Tatiana and her sidekicks waiting. They shifted on their feet and rubbed gloved hands together. Maggie kept reaching for her back pocket, presumedly looking for her phone, but finding nothing. Data transmission on the hill was very expensive, and sketchy on good days, so phones tended to get ditched.

Chance lifted the chum bucket. "We've got us some special sauce. Smells like dead ass."

"Great," Tatiana said and smiled, the black hair escaping from beneath her knitted cap shinning as if wet.

Chance dropped his pack, which was filled with essentials, though they intended to be back in Fort Fortune by dark. The pack had an ice axe strapped to its side and helmet perched on its top with goggles strung over to the front.

"I had Ju Ju grab you an old board, just in case you decide to ride down from the collection spot," Tatiana said. The board was a white Burton with blue stripes. Very passable.

"Thanks," Chance said. Then voicing his own fears, added, "You still sure you want to do this?"

She nodded. "You and your family story aside, if I can get footage of the thing you saw, it will launch my career into the stratosphere."

"True that," said Ju Ju.

The *womp-womp* of pounding rotors echoed over the mountain as Trevor wheeled the bird around and put her down next to the old warehouse in a cloud of snow and frozen mist. The rotors slowed, but the sound of thumping air didn't ease as Chance and the others loaded the copter with gear. With only four passengers, there was plenty of room for Maggie's silver camera cases, and Tatiana's container of emergency supplies.

Chance didn't care whether things went as planned or not. If things got dicey, he'd strap on his borrowed Burton and ride on home, broken wing and all.

The copter's engine cycled up, kicking up snow and clouds of freezing mist. His stomach fell as the copter lifted into the air, Fort Fortune disappearing in frozen clouds, dazzling light bouncing off the snowpack.

The sound of avalanche triggering explosions echoed over the mountain.

Chance chuckled. For all the good that'll do.

14

A TEAM OF BOARDERS and skiers waited for the copter, and Chance shook his head as Trevor put the bird on the ground. Clouds of swirling snow created a whiteout, sunlight bouncing off snowpack, rainbows of color knifing through the white. The rotors slowed and the powder settled, revealing five boarders in overly colorful gear leaning on their boards.

The whirlybird shuddered as Trevor landed on flat stone, the landing skids shrieking as they scraped over the rock. The craft settled and Ju Ju popped the side door and slid it back. Wind pushed into the cabin, the scent of smoke carrying faintly on the breeze, tattered clouds streaking across a slate blue sky.

Tatiana asked, "Why didn't those guys just ride the rest of the way down to Fort Fortune?"

Chance wasn't sure how to answer, so he hiked his shoulders. He'd decided to treat Tatiana like a reporter, and until he got to know her better, what he told her would be need-to-know.

"Real riders don't zoom the bunny hill," Maggie said.

Chance smirked. He couldn't help himself. The camerawoman was right. It took moxie and a certain level of insanity to want to ride Abominable Peak, let alone actually do it, but it also took money. Lots of it. And with money came ego, self-importance, and the ever-damaging assholism. Judging by their new, colorful gear, these posers—though, technically he had no right to call them that if they'd ridden the hill—part-time adventurers, were more concerned about the story, the selfies, than the ride.

The other crew didn't even say hello as they climbed silently into the chopper. Chance stood next to his team's pile of supplies, trying to meet each riders' eye as they walked past, but they didn't even glance his way. To them, he'd gotten off at the bottom of the escalator. Two years ago, they would've been asking for his autograph.

"Who else will be around here today?" Ju Ju asked.

"Nobody," Chance said. "Trevor has more drops at the top, but they're ride-throughs."

"So, that's good," Maggie said.

"Why's that?" Tatiana said.

"Last time I checked, silence was an important attribute of a hunter," Maggie said.

Snow pelted the companions, the wind arguing and singing.

"So, where do we start?" Tatiana asked.

Chance pointed at the food container. "We hike away from here. Up the mountain until we find tracks, or some sign, then we put out our bait and wait."

"Wait?" Tatiana said.

"Hunting is mostly sitting around doing nothing," Maggie said. She did that thing with her hands that photographers do when they're trying to frame a shot. "This light is going to be a bitch."

"You've got the big diffuser, right?" Tatiana asked.

Maggie nodded. "It's the contrast I'm worried about. Chance said the bea—this thing is white, and in case you haven't noticed, there's a lot of white up here."

"And it's maldito cold," Ju Ju said.

"Your Latin blood," Maggie joked.

Tatiana didn't take the lead, so Chance did. "You can store the supplies in that red tent there." Ju Ju moved the two supply crates as Maggie unfolded a small sled that held her silver camera gear cases perfectly. Tatiana stood watching, her long hair blowing in the breeze, Chance's face reflected in her large sunglasses. Chance had told the woman to wear goggles, but she'd resisted, and Chance saw that the glasses were already fogging. His watch said the current temperature was a tropical fourteen degrees and sweat was already running down his back.

Chance hefted his pack, slung the rifle over a shoulder, and grabbed his board and the bucket. There was a makeshift ski rack made from two dead evergreens stripped of their leaves and propped horizontally between two stones. Chance left his board there and headed for a thin path through the snowpack that headed upslope toward the overhang where he'd seen his grandfather's marker chiseled into the mountain.

Footsteps crunched behind him, but nobody questioned Chance or complained as he led the party steadily up the southern face, their passage causing tiny spindrifts to cascade over the powder. They'd been walking half an hour when the helicopter roared overhead, dropping in over the peak. Clouds of snow obscured the whirlybird, the *womp-womp* of the pounding rotors echoing off the mountains like thunder.

Seven minutes later they took a break and watched six boarders carve-up the southern face. Chance knew this crew well, friends of friends that were on the peak for the next two weeks. Their lines were crisp and professional, teams of two intertwining their rides, leaving a braided pattern in the sugary powder. The team zipped by to the east, and they didn't even see Chance, despite him waving his arms.

"They're in the zone," Chance said.

"Can we talk about that on camera?" Tatiana said.

He nodded. "You've got a good zoom lens, Maggie?"

"I can take a picture of an ant on a baby's ass from a hundred yards out," she said.

"So, we're looking for an area where you'd have a long view in all directions, yet still remain hidden?"

She nodded.

The only options he'd seen were boulders, but if they set up atop one of those they'd have nowhere to hide. If they set up behind a stone or deadfall, the creature would invariably come at them from the direction the camera eyes couldn't see.

"Let's get up a little higher up," Chance said. He dug into the snowpack with his heel and started forcing his way up the slope again.

The team came across a narrow crevasse, and Chance wondered if it connected to his tunnel, but concluded it didn't. Like this crack, his crevasse had run north to south, though there had been many side-shoots, so it wasn't impossible. The group gave the crack a wide berth, and Chance's stomach stung with angst as the memory of falling through the snowpack reasserted itself, elbowing its way back into his RAM.

A copse of evergreens clung to the hillside, mostly buried in snow, the tips of the trees barely poking through, which made the glade look like a young forest. Chance liked the cover of the trees, but they would limit the view, so he trudged through the treetops until he reached a sharp cliff face that rose two hundred feet and stretched into to whiteness to the east and west.

Chance stared up at the cliff, searching for a good spot for their stand. With the cliff to the north, their view was impeded, and Chance tried to overlay his current position over the path he'd taken down the mountain.

"How much further?" Tatiana asked.

Chance turned, and was surprised to see the woman's face red, her glasses at the end of her nose, her jacket unzipped.

"I would zip up," he said.

"I'm sweating to death," she said.

"Unless you want to freeze to death, I suggest you zip it," Chance said.

Tatian's eyes blazed, but she zipped up.

"I think we need to get up there," Chance said as he pointed up the cliff face.

Tatiana and Maggie laughed, and Ju Ju harrumphed.

"Look, mountain man, there's no way we can climb that. What about—?"

Chance held up a hand, and when she stopped talking, he started walking again, following the line of the cliff face to the east.

"Are you going to fill us in?" Tatiana said.

"Do I have to?"

She sighed. Loudly.

"There's a series of seracs on the eastern slope, and this cliff face diminishes and breaks up as it cuts east, so we should be able to hike up there. Plus," he said, pausing and turning for effect. "We'll be closer to where I saw the creature."

That ended the complaining, but it took another ninety minutes to find a spot where Chance was comfortable threading through a field of boulders, steadily climbing up to the jagged ridgeline.

"I still don't see what this buys us," Ju Ju said.

"Sorry?" Chance said.

"If I'm remembering right from when we were shooting B-roll, the slope above the cliff is steep, no cracks or stone, no boulders. There's no place to hide. They'll be able to see us from Fort Fortune."

"No, they won't see us. Nothing will."

Chance headed west along the ridge, looking for a snowdrift that wasn't coated with ice, and he found the perfect spot along the cliff's edge. He dropped his pack and started to dig.

The movie people watched, mouths hanging open in confusion.

Tatiana said, "A hole? That's the idea?"

"I think I see what he's doing," Maggie said, and started digging.

Ju Ju shrugged and joined in, but Tatiana stood back, her dark eyes wet with cold.

It took half an hour, but when Chance and the crew were done, they'd made a ten by ten- foot snow hole five feet deep and it was obvious what Chance planned to do.

Tatiana said, "Don't go any deeper. Actually, you've already gone too deep."

"Why's that?" Chance said.

"The height of the tripod," she said.

Chance made a pile of snow in the center of the hole and Ju Ju and Maggie stomped it down. After a few minutes of work, there was a solid snow table in the center of their foxhole.

"You want us to set up?" Maggie said. She was looking at Chance, but when she realized her mistake, her head jerked toward Tatiana, who shrugged.

"Ju Ju, you come with me. We'll spread some . . . bait, while Maggie set's up, and Tatiana . . . " Chance paused and smiled at her. "While Tatiana makes it all happen."

Even in the cold, she managed an icy stare, cheeks going red.

The pop and snap of camera cases opening echoed over the peak as Chance and Ju Ju headed back east along the ridgeline. To the south, mountains rolled like massive snowdrifts, sunlight arcing through the cloud cover like heavenly rays. A layer of thin mist hung at about ten thousand feet, making it look like Fort Fortune sat atop a cloud.

"You have a spot in mind?" Ju Ju said.

Chance nodded. "We'll bait three locations, one in each direction, minus south."

"We should have baited down there as we climbed," Ju Ju said.

Chance shook his head. "Thought of that, but I don't want to draw whatever we're hunting to the collection site."

Ju Ju nodded.

They passed the spot where they'd climbed onto the ridge, and Chance headed upslope into a patch of underbrush sticking from snowpack behind a large boulder.

"Might want to cover your nose," he said, peeling the lid off the special sauce.

The lowest tide, rotting flesh . . .

Ju Ju hung tough for a few seconds; forehead knitted as he covered his nose with his hand. Then, he was coughing, a steady stream of cloudy liquid speckled yellow with egg and brown with sausage splattering the powder.

Chance dumped some of the oozing trash onto the snowpack, then backed away, letting drips of the nasty brown goo splatter the snow every few feet. He laid a trail west until he was a hundred yards from the snow hole, then he veered north, up the sheer slope.

The climbing was hard, and he had to break the coating of ice with his heel before each step.

When he had three trails laid, he put the top back on the bucket and returned to the snow hole. As he approached, all he saw above the snowpack was the camera atop its tripod. Chance reached the edge of the hole, and Tatiana and Maggie sat at ease, staring at the camera screen.

"Good to go?" Chance said.

Tatiana nodded. "You?"

Chance gave a thumbs up, and jumped into the hole, followed by Ju Ju.

The sun arced past noon, and the party ate sandwiches as they stripped off hats and gloves. They were enjoying the heat rolling off the snowpack when a wail echoed on the wind.

Chance's head jerked toward Tatiana, but the woman didn't appear to have heard the cry. Ju Ju and Maggie also didn't react.

Time rolled by, and several times Chance thought he heard grunts and sniffing on the breeze, but as the day waned, there'd been no definitive sign of the creature.

Chance looked at his watch, and said, “What time is Trevor coming to grab us?”

“5:30ish, right before dark,” Tatiana said.

“It’s going to take us at least an hour to get back to the collection site. I don’t want to keep Trevor waiting and I’d rather not be caught up here overnight. Again,” Chance said.

“Give it another hour?” Maggie said.

Chance nodded as he nestled into himself, the cold starting to penetrate his snow pants and shell. His ass was an ice cube but sweat dripped down his back.

As the sun dropped in the west, treetops, boulders, cornices, snowdrifts, and thin seracs cast dark undulating shadows across the ocean of white. At 4 PM, they packed up and left.

Of the Metoh, there had been no sign.

15

February 1, 2018, Fort Fortune—Elevation 9,871 feet

THE THIRD DAY of hunting the mountainside for the creature ran late. Chance stopped by the barrack, dropped his pack, cleaned up and changed clothes, then double-timed it to the Lucky Strike. He was late for his shift, and he already owed hours because of his lost time on the mountain and his injury. He'd wasted another day, found nothing, and Chance was starting to think the Metoh might be messing with him. He'd left stinking trash and rotting flesh all over the mountain, and he hadn't found so much as a track.

The saloon crowd was subdued, but the joint was full, and his crew was at the bar. Jibber's death hung over Fort Fortune like a solitary black cloud. It didn't matter to the riders how he'd died. Everyone in the Lucky Strike was nursing their own obsessions, thinking about how it could've been them that was killed. Part of the thrill of riding extreme peaks was knowing that at any moment it could be all over, kaput, and that blinding excitement is more powerful than any drug Chance had ever tried.

Shelly tossed a towel at him as he slipped behind the bar. "You're late. Again."

"I ever tell you how smart and talented you are? What're you doing up here?" Chance flirted. In the real-world Shelly was a corporate attorney that was so good at her job, the partners of her firm let her disappear for two months every year. She didn't need to sling drinks, but it killed time when she wasn't on the mountain, and she'd bartended in college and enjoyed the work and conversation.

She tossed her blonde ponytail dramatically and said, "Baby, I'm out of your league and you know it."

He did. Chance chuckled as he started wiping down the bar.

Tina whistled. "Damn. You're a smoking ruin."

Bomber, Colin, and Biggie laughed, but Chance frowned when he noticed Jibber's sharp cackle was missing from the sycophantic chorus.

Chance said, "Even when I was on the circuit, I didn't have game, you know that."

During the brief change of shifts a line had formed at the end of the bar. The Lucky Strike didn't have table service, and Chance slung drinks as he caught up with folks—shaking martinis, pouring beers, mixing rum and cokes. Even blending a margarita didn't knock him out of rhythm as he answered questions about his experience on the mountain, what he thought happened to Jibber, and what he planned to do next. He chatted politely as he worked, one of a bartender's primary skills. Walk and chew gum at the same time. Talk and mix.

When Chance was caught up, he wiped down the bar and topped-off his crew.

Tiny shards of ice pelted the old wood building, and wind whistled and sang through every crack and pinhole. In a corner, a large kerosene heater puffed and belched.

Bomber said, "See anything today? Boring as hell here. They need more stuff to do on non-ride days."

Chance shook his head. "Nothing but snow, ice, and stone."

"No signs at all?" Tina said.

"Not so much as a footprint. It's almost like the thing is hiding from us," Chance said.

Biggie laughed. "It's a big mountain, mate."

"It didn't have any problem finding me the first time."

"Maybe because there's four of you in the crew? Maybe it's scared of so many people?" Colin said.

"Or you need to go higher up?" Bomber said.

Chance's memory soared back to the massive shadow, the claw that had raked his arm. "Maybe."

Tina said, "I contacted Jibber's family. Talked to his mom."

Chance didn't ask how it went. He knew Mrs. Taldo, and she'd told Chance more than once she felt like Jibber was a police officer, or a soldier, and she'd fully expected to one day get a call saying her son had died some horrible death. That wouldn't have made the news any easier to take, and Jibber was all the woman had left.

"Thank you," Chance said. "You tell her I'll come see her when I can? Bring Jibber home?"

She nodded as she took a pull off her rum and coke, a tear leaking down her face.

"You heading back up tomorrow? We're supposed to ride, and the weather looks like it's going to cooperate, though there's another storm moving in," Tina said.

Chance poured scotch and Drambuie into a tumbler filled with ice as he said, "I don't know. Sure seems like I'm wasting my time."

"At least you're doing something," Colin said as he looked up from his whiskey. He was clearly several deep judging by his bloodshot eyes.

"Yeah, what am I doing?" Chance set up a row of five shot glasses and filled them with tequila. He lifted one and nodded at the others, who collected their shots. "To Jibber." He lifted his glass.

The companions saluted and drank, the five empty glasses hitting the bar at almost the same moment.

"We miss you up there, brother," Biggie said.

"Yeah," Colin said, stirred from his daze.

"You up to heading out with us tomorrow?" Tina asked.

Chance stared at the empty shot glasses and waited. His arm was far from healed, but he'd didn't want to use that as an excuse.

"Got to get back on the horse," Biggie said.

"I do? Why?" Chance said. "I'm not feeling it."

Snow scoured wood, wind howled and argued, the tinkle of glasses and chatter echoed through the Lucky Strike.

Chance's chest went cold. What he'd just said was sacrilege. Riders didn't understand, or care to understand, people who no longer felt the urge to ride. It was like quitting the military or ratting out your coworkers. Certain sins were unforgivable and meant immediate and permanent exile.

"That's a bit extreme, Bro," Biggie said.

"It's in your blood. Give it some time," Tina said.

His crew knew, as did Chance, that if he quit riding his friends would leave him behind like they had when he'd gotten hurt and built an addiction bigger than a stadium. The difference this time was he would never see them again. Out on tour, he'd be spoken of as if he'd passed away, memories of his greatness and moxie, and sorrow for his breakdown. He understood, knew if it had been one of the others, he'd probably do the same thing. What did he expect? That they should give up their lives, their careers and dreams, for him?

A hush fell over the crowd as the saloon door slapped back on its hinges, snow billowing through the opening around a person clad in all black ski gear. The person's hands were moving frantically, but mumbling was all that could be heard through the person's face wrap.

A patron Chance didn't know got up and went to the door, where there was a brief exchange as the newcomer uncovered his face, revealing a dark beard below two wide eyes.

Chance inched out from behind the bar, threading

through the crowd. He was in charge of the place at the moment. He looked around for Stefan but didn't see him.

"You've got to come with me," ranted the bearded man. "Lima is gone. Hurt."

"Calm down," Chance said as he approached.

A crowd had formed at the entrance, but it parted like the Red Sea when Moses arrived, everyone staring at Chance as he worked his way through the throng. Nobody wanted to deal with a problem. Toasting and drinking to a dead boarder you didn't know was one thing, having the party put on hold was something altogether different, and was never well received.

Chance put a hand on the man's shoulder. "What's your name?"

"Terry. Terry Haplin."

"Well, Terry Haplin," Chance lightly grasped the man's arm and guided him toward a seat. "Why don't you sit down. I'll get you a drink of water and you can—"

The guy jerked his arm from Chance's grasp. "No! You must listen. Come with me. My wife. Lima. She's been taken. Hurt."

That was the first time Chance had heard the word "taken" used, and his mind was reeling with scenarios that made bile creep up his throat and pain blossom in his lower back. Chance patted the air. "Easy. What do you mean taken?"

The Lucky Strike had gone silent.

Between sputtering breaths, Terry said, "We were on our way here from the dormitory. I left her for one minute to duck inside and take a leak. I left her alone for five minutes."

Chance looked around at the other patrons as if verifying Terry's wife wasn't in the crowd. "How do you know she didn't go back to the dorm? The ladies' room? Maybe she forgot something in your room?"

Terry shook his head. "There's . . . there's blood in the

snow. At least, I think it's blood. I called for her. Yelled at the top of my lungs. Nothing."

Even Mother Nature appeared interested, and the whistle and howl of the wind and churning snow eased.

Chance didn't know what to say. He stared into the man's frantic eyes and believed him.

One of the riders from Dubai, whom Chance had seen earlier at the pickup spot, stepped forward, face twisted. "What else did you see?" He gave Chance an accusing glance.

"Saw? Nothing . . . I . . . "

"Show us," the man said.

Terry nodded and headed for the door.

The saloon filled with the sounds of chairs scraping on the old wood floor, glasses hitting tables, and jackets being zipped.

"Wait," Chance said. "Not everyone needs to—"

The crowd began funneling out of the Lucky Strike, Terry leading the way into darkness.

"Shit." Chance spun on his heel and found his crew staring at him, holding his coat. "Thanks," he said as he pulled on his jacket, hat, and gloves.

The cold night air took the breath from Chance's lungs as he rushed out into the night. Stars blinked through tissue paper clouds, the waning quarter moon hanging low on the horizon like a postcard, the round snowdrift-like peaks of the Sawatch Mountains glinting in the moonlight.

A line formed on the thin path pounded into the snowpack as people followed Terry across Fort Fortune, toward the new dormitory building. Snowdrifts rose on both sides of the trail, miniature spindrifts rolling onto the path.

Tina and the others fell in behind Chance, who joined the line that was now moving slower than those at the Department of Motor Vehicles. Cold bit at every patch of exposed skin, and a chill crawled up his pants and down his shirt sleeves like icy snakes. He only had one layer of clothes on because he'd expected to be inside all night.

There was a bottleneck ahead, and the line stopped moving. People stood still in the howling wind, their breath clouds billowing around their heads.

Chance waited a couple of minutes, then said, “Screw this.” He climbed the snowdrift next to the path, sinking knee-deep into fresh power. Like cars going around a wreck on the highway, folks followed Chance’s lead, climbing up onto the loose snowpack and struggling through the snow.

He was panting and sucking for air when he arrived at the throng standing next to the dormitory. Biggie was behind him, but Tina, Colin, and Bomber had hung back, waiting in line.

Terry was at the center of the crowd, and everyone was staring down at something Chance couldn’t see. He heard Stefan’s voice over the murmur of the crowd and the shriek of the wind. “That could be many things.”

A primal urge of aggression ran through Chase, and he edged through the crowd, sliding down the snowbank and pushing his way onto the thin stomped path that ran around the outside of the dormitory.

A black dot, smaller than a quarter but bigger than a nickel marred the snow path. Several smaller dots trailed down the path into darkness. The line of connect-the-dots stood out on the whiteness like a cockroach on a birthday cake. It was impossible to see individual footprints on the path with all the conflicting boot prints.

“She was out here,” Terry wailed. There was no sign of Lima.

Chance slipped his way to the center of the crowd, people making way when they saw who it was. All of Fort Fortune knew about Jibber, had heard Chance’s tale of survival.

The slick black dots could be blood, though Chance was searching for any explanation other than that. It could be from a hole in someone’s food carton. Someone who’d had a bit too much cheer spilling their drink as they took an evening stroll in the frigidness atop the world. The possibilities were endless, yet no matter how he tried to spin things, his brain kept coming back to the same thing.

Metoh.

Terry lurched forward, following the trail of dots in the snow, and Stefan and the others fell in line behind him.

Chance followed. As the group trudged around the corner of the new dormitory, a scream echoed above the wind and shifting snow. Chance froze, and the person behind him bumped into him.

Terry was wailing and crying, screaming his wife's name.

The crowd surged forward again, and the stomped path petered out. Chance climbed onto the snowpack, the black dots getting larger, more frequent.

Stefan dropped to one knee, Terry crying and floundering over his shoulder.

Chance worked his way forward, the tequila shot churning and bubbling in his stomach.

Submerged an inch in the powdery snow was a white ear, pink with cold, a tiny gold hoop earring hanging from the bloodied lobe.

Terry screamed, and Stefan hugged and tried to calm him. "It's true. It got her. Oh my God. It—" Terry saw Chance. "You!"

Chance looked over his shoulder, certain the man's anger wasn't directed at him, but found everyone's eyes locked on him. He grew hot, the cold rushing from him as guilt, worry, and fear fought for control of his emotions. He knew what was coming.

"You said the creature you saw was emboldened to protect its territory. That right?" Terry snapped.

"Terry, look, I don't think—" Stefan said.

"I don't care what anyone thinks. If what he said is true . . . " Terry pointed his gloved finger at Chance. "If you're telling the truth, whatever the thing is, then you led it down here and now it's taken my wife!"

A brief instant of screaming wind before many people started talking at once. “The animals have the same right to the mountain as we do. We’re in their territory. The new mine stirred them up.”

On and on, and as Chance stared into the deepening night, he knew what he needed to do.

16

February 2, 2019, Abominable Peak, southern slope—Elevation 10,476 feet

COLD IS A KILLER. A monster. An enemy. It sucks the life from body and mind, numbing the senses, twisting reality, making death a mercy as it chokes and kills with its arctic breath. Stars blinked through thickening clouds, the wind cutting through Chance, making his bones pulse, stealing his breath, and giving his pain a name. The gashes on his arm throbbed and shouted, his knees ached, cramps tightened his back and neck. Stefan's rifle was slung over a shoulder, and it brought some comfort, but it was useless against the cold. Squalls and drifts of sparkling white rolled down the mountain face—rocks and cliffs dark marks in the starlight. Shadows danced and reflected in the verglas, glistening in the night. He hugged himself, drawing in a deep breath. He was used to the elevation, but not the cold's wicked wrath.

Flashlight beams bounced around the mountainside as the team of nine trekked single file, following the beaten trail that led up the southern slope toward the collection point. The snowpack was cracked and torn up everywhere the trail of blood led, nasty chowder, like something massive had lumbered up the mountain. Chance's watch glowed green, reading 1:37 AM. They'd been hiking for three hours and had ascended more than a thousand feet, yet other than the thinning trail of presumed blood, there'd been no sign of Lima.

Kimberly led. She was a pro boarder wannabe who'd served as a medic in the Army, and she covered part of her heli fees and lodging by doing double duty as a field medicine professional and rescue support specialist. Chance was next in line, followed by Biggie and Tatiana and her film crew. Then came Terry, Joe, and Dave—Terry's mates.

Chance hadn't asked for permission, didn't speak to Stefan, or even his crew. He'd hightailed back to the barrack, put on two layers of long underwear, grabbed his stuff, and headed out to follow the trail. His entire crew had wanted to join him, but it was decided a small party could move faster. The team hadn't expected to go far, and Chance placated most would-be followers by promising to report back soon. That hadn't been acceptable to Tatiana, and since Stefan was involved—making money—from the documentary, Chance didn't push the issue.

Kimberly reached a narrow crevasse that ran diagonally across the slope, an icy trap waiting to snatch any living thing that ventured too close. Kimberly shone her light around the incline, then side to side as she examined her position.

She yelled back to the group, "So, what do you think? We're not equipped for an overnight. Didn't think we'd be out here this long."

Chance wasn't interested in spending the night in a snow hole, but if he had to, he could. He said nothing.

"You're suggesting we turn back?" Terry yelled above the howling wind and shifting snow.

"We've got noth—We haven't found Lima," Tatiana said.

Kimberly leaned right so she could see Tatiana, and said, "Why are you here again?"

"Because you don't own the mountain," Tatiana said.

"And," Maggie said, blazing her boss with a "take it easy" look. "We're the free press."

The debate to allow Tatiana and her crew had become contentious. There were other, more qualified people that wanted to help, but Tatiana had refused to stay behind, saying, "How will you stop me from following?"

"So, what are we doing?" Kimberly said.

"Keep going a bit further. We're not that far from the collection site, and there's supplies there," Terry said.

"Hate to be the voice of negativity but we've got at least another thousand feet of steep hiking and climbing before we get there. It's dark, the snowpack is loose, the rock covered in verglas," said Biggie.

Chance stared west. Even in the deep of night, the dark clouds could be seen marching across the horizon, slowly billowing east like stuffing leaking from a dirty pillow. The wind cajoled and argued, whispering, telling Chance all was good. Keep going. Don't worry about the cold. You'll be fine.

The party's reflections swayed and shifted in the ice that covered everything, the flashlight beams refracting like laser beams. Ice cracked and popped, and images of the mountainside coming alive, all the peaks of the Sawatch range battling like stone giants, tossing pieces of the mountain, filled his drifting mind.

He stared up into darkness, envisioning the collection spot, thinking of the marker chiseled in stone. He wished Grandad would make an appearance and give him advice, help him understand what was happening. In that moment, Chance felt alone, abandoned, despite Kimberly being two feet in front of him and Biggie two feet behind. A deep sense of foreboding and unease crept through him, pushing out the cold and pain and angst.

"This is nuts. We're never going to find . . . " Kimberly's voice sank beneath the sounds of footfalls crunching in snow, and the ever-present battle of the wind.

Terry yelled, "You have something to say?"

The line of hikers came to a shuddering halt and the group tightened. Everyone inched forward like school children trying to hear their teacher scold another student.

Kimberly shouted, "I know this is personal for you, and

I'm sorry, but that's why you shouldn't be out here searching. You're too close to this." She shook her head, and the thin covering of snow atop her helmet slid down onto her face shield. She wiped it away. "I'm thinking of everyone's safety."

Biggie added, "Maybe we should head back. Come back out at first light. Trevor can go up. We're wandering around in the dark out here and soon—"

"Head back!" Terry threw up his hands, then deflated as he calmed. People who rode Abominable Peak might be unhinged, but they didn't panic. "Listen up, everyone. One of two things is going to happen. One, I find my wife or proof she's dead. Two, I die trying to accomplish item one. Does that settle things?"

Kimberly couldn't look at Terry, but she said, "I'm sorry. I'm not dying or losing someone up here because of desperation. There's been no sign of your wife. No sign of anything except what might be blood, and even if it's blood, we've got no idea where it came from, and—"

A primal shriek pierced the moonlit gloom, echoing off stone, reverberating as it faded away, clouds of snow swirling like ghosts. The wind answered, screaming over peaks and cutting through narrow crevasses.

The wind serenaded, coaxed, whispered.

Kimberly was the first to shake herself free of the reverie. "Unfortunately, I think Biggie is right. We've got a ways to go before we reach the collection spot."

Terry's two mates hadn't said a word, but they stared expectantly at Terry, their eyes shining behind their snow goggles.

Terry said, "I'm not going anywhere." His tone softened, though he still had to yell to be heard above the gale. "I understand if you all want to head back. Really. You owe me nothing." He turned to Joe and Dave. "Same goes for you guys."

"I'm not going anywhere," Dave said.

Joe looked less convinced, and Terry appeared to read the man's mind, and said, "You're thinking of your kids, Joe. I get it. Go back. There's nothing you can do here that I can't. Please. The last thing Lima would want is your kids growing up without a father."

Joe nodded.

Biggie said, "I'm with Chance."

His friend was an open book, and Chance could tell by the tone of his voice he wanted to head back. Chance said, "I'm going on, but you're not."

Biggie's helmeted head jerked back like he'd been punched. "What? Why? What did I—?"

Chance held up his gloved hand. "You've done all that can be expected. I agree with Terry. Only two of us need to continue on, and we've got three."

The bearded man shook his head. "Not happening. I . . . abandoned you once. Ain't happening again."

Chance nodded as warmth spread through him, pushing away the ever-present cold.

"We're coming." Tatiana eased around Maggie, who held up her camera, documenting the debate.

"Turn that damn thing off," Terry yelled. "This isn't a fucking circus. Shit!" he yelled.

Maggie lowered the camera.

Kimberly said, "You guys aren't even riders . . . " She looked around, apparently noticing her slight. "What I mean is, you have less mountain experience than they do, and all they do is cause avalanches and search for the safest, fastest lines." She winced and shook her head. "Sorry, Chance. Maybe I should just shut up."

"No worries. There's no moratorium on the word avalanche," he said. He addressed Tatiana. "Kimberly is trying to protect you. It's not safe out here, and it's got little to do with whatever it is we're tracking."

"And if we do find her," Terry said. "You're not filming her."

Tatiana sighed, a cloud of frosty mist momentarily obscuring her face. “I would never do that. You know what I want to film.” In many places around the world, the faces of corpses were regularly seen on TV news, but Americans weren’t fans of seeing dead bodies.

“What about you, Kimberly?” Tatiana said. “You’re paid to help and protect us, right?”

Kimberly’s eyes grew wide behind her goggles, the harsh light of the flashlight’s beam making her face milky, her eyes a deeper blue. “I’m paid . . . ” She chuckled. “To support rescue efforts of boarders and skiers who get lost or hurt on the hill, and to deal with superficial medical issues. I’m not paid—” She shook her head. “—to put my life on the line when I don’t see a positive outcome or have any real evidence.”

“So, you’re saying she’s dead?” Terry yelled.

“I’m saying . . . odds are odds, and I’m not willing to die to find out.” She pushed past Chance, Biggie, and the others as she headed back down the incline.

Joe said his goodbyes, and after a brief debate, Maggie handed the camera over to Tatiana, and she and Ju Ju headed back with the others.

When they were gone, Terry said, “They’re bailing, and we didn’t even talk about what I’m most afraid of. What if there’s more than one creature? Rabid bear, whatever. That would make sense, right?”

The thought had crossed Chance’s mind and was quickly dismissed. That was a possibility he couldn’t contemplate at the moment. He had to concentrate on putting one foot in front of the other, finding Lima. Nothing else mattered.

The team trudged on in silence. There was nothing left to say, and when they found a chunk of red fabric from Lima’s jacket with a chunk of flesh glued to it via ice and dried blood, no words were necessary. They simply went on, flashlights cutting through the blackness and dancing off the verglas like piles of jewels.

Crunch with his boot heel, step, lift, repeat.

Chance had been leading for an hour when he called a halt to rest. "Someone else is going to have to take the lead. I'm shot." The lead person created the steps by which all those who trailed after used, and for Chance it had been like taking two steps for every one.

"Looks like we're almost there," Chance said.

Above a cornice of snow jutted from the mountainside like a broken tooth, dark spindrifts wheeling down its face like tiny comets caught in flashlight beams. Shadows danced behind every drift and stone, the verglas reflecting the moon and mountain peaks to the south like a surreal painting.

Terry pushed to his feet and took the lead, blazing a trail up the slope, the crunch, pop, and slide of his steps piercing the veil of wind.

Chance and Biggie waited as Tatiana and Dave fell in behind Terry. Dave looked miserable, and Tatiana was less disheveled but appeared equally despondent as she held the camera at the ready.

When their companions were out of earshot, Biggie said, "We're beyond the point of no return."

"Yup," Chance said. "We were before, though I didn't list it as a reason because I wanted to get rid of some of our dead weight so we could move faster."

"Had a feeling," Biggie said. "We've got another hour or two, at least." He turned his back on Chance and followed the others.

"Hey," Chance said.

Biggie stopped and turned.

"Isn't the new vein of gold they've been mining east of here?"

Biggie nodded.

Terry and the others were already a hundred feet above, cutting across the incline.

Biggie cupped his hands to his mouth. "Hold up." He

turned to Chance. "It will take us out of our way and the trail doesn't go that way."

"How far is it, you think?"

"A ways. It's on the cusp of the eastern face, seracs, and crevasses all over the place. Chowder on every incline, as you know. No way we can hike it in the dark. Probably not in the light without setting lines and using climbing gear, and even then, it would be a nightmare."

Chance nodded.

Biggie yelled, "You can go on."

Chance's thoughts scattered like leaves in an autumn gale; he was back in the bar at Fort Fortune, up on the peak with his crew. Red eyes appraised him as a crevasse slowly closed. Darkness pressed in on him, cold burrowing in his flesh like maggots, his vision blurring with sleep. Frozen mist rose from the snowpack, spinning and swirling like miniature cyclones. He inched up his jacket sleeve, the glow of his watch face sending daggers of green light bending and shifting over the glassy snowpack. He looked down the mountainside again, searching for Fort Fortune, any sign that told him he wasn't one of five people left alive in the world. Cold rattled his teeth and he hugged himself as he stepped carefully into Terry's steps, and everyone in front of him had strengthened.

Stars wheeled overhead and time became counting steps. Ten and start again. Ten and start again. Sleep crept in around the edges of his vision, the night working with the cold to bring him down, and he was dozing as he trudged.

Terry screamed, and the laughing and shrieking wind, the harsh night and the unforgiving mountain ignored him. Snow swirled and the trail of blood, and the tracks, faded to a flat white nothingness.

17

DARKNESS IS THE ally of cold, and together they make a formidable pair. The cold works on your body, draining heat and energy, which creates stress and fear and death. Darkness sits in the background, letting cold take the lead, always shifting, changing, concealing, and whispering of what could be hiding in the veiled blackness. With combined force, cold and darkness had worn Chance's nerves to the nub. He wasn't used to any of this, not even the mountain, really. When he boarded, he got dropped off or hauled up on a lift, and he rode. Normally the only other parts of the mountain he saw were the bar and locker room, and the rational portion of his mind kept screaming that he was out of his league. That idea angered him, though he couldn't ignore it. He knew that much. The mountains, the ocean—nature, can't be underestimated or it would kill you for your disrespect.

When cold and darkness joined forces with time, there was little that could defeat them. Time devours all things—people, animals, buildings, and civilizations. It breaks steel, withers wood, and grinds mountains to dust. There is nothing that can defeat time, and Chance felt its constant pressure, always reminding him that its two partners, cold and darkness, were waiting to take him.

The team of five blundered up the slope, and Chance thought he saw sealed cracks in the verglas to the east, spidery dark lines stretching across the starlit glow of snowpack like magic marker. Chance was no longer concerned with finding the creature. The gear shift of his brain had slid to survival mode. His hands and feet were ice, his throat so dry it hurt when he took a deep breath, and a faint tremor ran through his legs. He couldn't go much farther, but he didn't think he had to.

They reached a cliff face that disappeared into the darkness.

"We're here," Biggie said.

"Not quite," Chance said.

At the top of the cliff was the flat stone area that was the collection point, and landing pad. Food, shelter, warmth . . . it all waited for him in a sealed emergency container above in the blackness. All he had to do was get to it.

The cliff face was unclimbable in the dark, even with crampons and proper climbing gear, but even if he had such gear, and it was the brightest day of the year, Chance wouldn't try an ascent. None of them, except for Biggie who'd done some serious climbing, were skilled enough to make the attempt.

"We have to go around," Terry said.

"Which way?" Dave asked.

"Here!" Tatiana shouted, and everyone's head jerked in her direction. She faced northwest, her back to the party, one foot planted before her, her other behind as she braced herself on the mountainside, her face lit by the camera's viewscreen.

The cliff face was covered in verglas and icicles, and it reflected the moon, dark circles marking craters, stars blinking like tiny eyes in the background. He wondered when the first person would ride the titan dunes on the moon. It would happen. People had been surfing and riding sand dunes and grassy hillsides for years. It was only a matter of time before some crazy bastard rode the face of Mons Huygens in a spacesuit, but it wouldn't be him.

Chance couldn't see what Tatiana was looking at and he

didn't understand how she was getting any useful footage in the dark. The light mounted atop her camera splashed a fifteen-foot column of light in the direction she pointed the camera, but she was too far away from the rock face and the glow faded into blackness before it reached the wall.

Terry said, "I don't see anything."

"Look," she said. The camera's light arced to the ground, and Chance and the others surged forward, crowding around Tatiana.

A trail of blood and tracks, side by side footprints partly filled with sugary snow, led toward a sheet of vertical ice clinging to the cliff face. Icicles hung from a ledge above the mirror of ice, huge spears that were easily a foot thick and ten feet long.

Chance stared at the party's reflection in the verglas, the moon in the backdrop watching like a cyclopean eye.

The tracks trailed behind the slab of ice, under the rack of icicles, both of which hid the maw of a cave.

A rancid smell wafted from the cavern—rot, filth, and the sharp scent of . . . Chance couldn't put a finger on it. Sage, maybe? Evergreen? If the scent that flowed from the cave had a voice, it would say, "Go away. Now. Get off my snowpack."

The cave entrance was encrusted with snow and ice, shards of multicolored stone sticking from the white. A massive snowdrift spilled from the mouth, and a cornice overhung the entrance.

"End of the line," Biggie said.

"Screw that," Terry surged forward, climbing up the snowdrift toward the black hole that marked the cave's entry.

Chance grabbed his arm. "Wait." He let the rifle fall from his shoulder into his hands. "Things just got real."

"I don't give a shit," Terry said. He and Dave climbed, spindrifts of snow cascading down onto Chance and the others.

Terry and Dave were five feet from the hole when a scream echoed off the walls of ice and stone. A wail so shrill and filled with pain it sent the little mice scurrying down Chance's spine.

"That was . . . human," Tatiana said. She checked her camera and fell in behind Terry, who stared into the black maw of the cavern, his breaths puffing white, frozen mist rising from his shoulders. Harsh LED light filled the space, painting everything in dazzling black and white, the ice wall hiding the cave entrance sparkling with mineral specs encased in the runoff.

The party waited. Biggie coughed, and Dave watched Terry, who hadn't taken his eyes off the cave entrance, jagged shards of stone filling the edges of the hole like crooked teeth, the dark tunnel, like the throat of an immense beast.

Without warning, Terry surged forward, frantically climbing the snowdrift, slipping and sliding, pushing torrents of snow toward Chance and the others.

"Wait," Chance said, but nobody heard him as his words were drowned out by the whistling wind funneling around the wall of ice, reverberating off the cliff face and piping through the icicles like organ tubes.

As Terry disappeared into the hole he said, "Just me. Everyone else wait."

Dave ignored him and slid into the cave behind him.

Tatiana turned the camera's steady eye on Chance, and he looked away. She scrambled up to the cave and went inside, the camera's light bouncing off the walls.

Chance's nerves danced on a wire. He understood the emotions, the motivations. Tatiana was on her own. Her motivation was money. Fame. Dave's was friendship and loyalty. He could respect that. Same as Biggie. He would follow Chance. Terry had made it clear he was taking this to its conclusion, whatever that meant.

So that left him.

Chance's primal side wanted to go forward, help, protect, settle things with the beast. Close out an obsession. The rational side of his mind reminded him that it might not be possible, and the payment for a mistake could very well be death. He asked himself what he had to gain. There was much to lose.

He'd decided to sit tight, wait it out, help if called upon, but when crying and wailing blew from the cave like trumpet blasts he changed his mind.

"Any way I can get you to wait here?" Chance asked.

Biggie shook his head.

Chance nodded, and the two companions started their way up the incline.

More crying and wailing. It sounded like Terry. Who else would it be? White light poured from the cave mouth like there was an artificial sun within, and Chance was thankful for his goggles.

The drips of blood grew, large footprints with clawed tips pressed deep into the snowpack. On the floor inside the cave mouth there was a puddle of blood and a stone depression. Now there could be little doubt.

"That change things?" Biggie said, looking over his shoulder out the cave entrance.

"Not for me," Chance said.

Biggie nodded.

Chance covered his nose with his gloved hand to mute the noxious smell infiltrating his nose, but it didn't help much. The cave was an ancient pocket in limestone, a common feature in the Rocky Mountains. He was no scientist, but Chance knew the Rockies were underwater seventy million years ago when the Earth went through dramatic changes. The seas that covered the region were home to all kinds of creatures, and when they died their shells accumulated on the sea floor. Over millions of years, the shells were compacted, forming rock known as limestone. As the seas retreated, and the Rocky Mountains forced their way up like dandelions, and as rainwater mixed with carbon dioxide, weak carbonic acid was formed, and it slowly ate away at the limestone, creating pockets that, over a very long period, formed passageways and caverns.

Stalactites ending in icicles dripped water, and draperies of clear ice magnified the rough multicolored walls. Chance shone his light up and saw that the walls of the cave leaned inward and came together thirty feet above, a knot of ice and clear swords hanging from the stony gable roof. Boulders, gravel, and ice littered the ground.

Here and there bones littered the floor, which sloped upward at a twenty-degree angle.

In the blackness ahead, Tatiana's camera lit the cavern like a subway tunnel, and Chance shut down his torch. Terry and the others were inching forward, bracing themselves as the icy slope got steeper and more treacherous. Large bones appeared in the gloom along the cave walls, the well-worn path meandering around boulders.

"No!" Terry wailed.

The wind answered, a vicious howl that chanted as it died away.

Relief flooded through Chance. It was over. They'd found her and could head up to the collection spot and camp for the night. It would only take an hour to walk around the cliff face. Heat spread through him, that precursor to fear. He looked back the way they'd come, but there was nothing but stone and the humming wind. Shadows danced on the walls, the harsh camera light washing out the color.

Terry was on his knees, head in his hands, Dave over his shoulder. Tatiana held her camera before her, staring at the viewscreen.

Chance eased up the slick incline, and when he arrived at Tatiana's side, all the concerns and misgivings he'd had came rushing back like an avalanche. An arm wrapped in a black coat sleeve, severed at the elbow and missing two fingers on its hand, rested amidst a puddle of blood. Crimson splatters covered the floor, chunks of fat and globs of fleshy gristle dotted the area around the arm like spilt red ice cream.

"Dear God," Biggie said.

"I don't think He can help," Chance said.

Terry started to cry, slowly at first, then picking up speed as tears rolled down his cheeks and he stripped off his goggles, helmet, and hat.

"Don't do that, Terry. I know you feel warm because we were climbing and—"

"What does it matter? She's gone. Has to be," Terry wailed and cried, his grief spilling out.

Dave put an arm around his shoulders.

"She could still be alive," Chance said, hardly believing the words he'd uttered.

Terry wailed and said, "Look! Look!"

Then, Chance got logical, the rational side of his brain asking what the hell was the other side up to. Where did he hope this went? Chance said, "Let's take a look at why the animal took Lima in the first place. If it meant to kill her, why drag her all the way up here? No, reality is more disturbing, but also hopeful."

"Explain," Terry said. He'd stopped crying, but anger spread over his face. It was the look of a man who had come to terms with something very difficult, only for someone to offer another option that put his closure in doubt.

Chance wanted to clam up, keep quiet, instead he said, "Look." Chance took a deep breath. "This might be hard to hear, but the creature may be keeping her alive as food . . . maybe for its offspring."

"Fresh meat?" Terry said, his face distorted in surprise and anger.

"You think we should go on?" Dave said, unable to keep the disbelief from his voice.

"All I'm saying is neither of Terry's two criteria has been met."

Terry looked at Dave, who shrugged. Terry got to his feet, dusting himself off. He said, “Okay. Okay.”

As if on cue, a guttural roar echoed through the cavern, but the cry wasn’t what turned Chance’s stomach to ice and sent pain running up his back and to the tips of his fingers and toes.

The roar had come from behind the searchers, from where they’d come.

18

THE SNOW AND ICE faded as the companions burrowed deeper into the mountain. The drips of blood had become small puddles, and the more Chance saw, the more he was convinced he'd spun some serious bullshit. Lima was dead, and when they found her—*if* they found her—it would break Terry. Chance rolled his shoulders and cracked his neck. He was twelve thousand feet up in the blackness and cold with no supplies, and somehow, he was chasing another ghost.

Without snow and ice clinging to every surface, the tunnel got wider and taller, and cracks and pockets filled the walls above like windows. The group hadn't come across a side passage on their level, but above . . . in the darkness. Splatters of white bird droppings marked the floor, and Chance wondered if bats also called the cave home. He'd seen no guano and didn't think bats liked high elevations.

Going back wasn't an option after his speech, no matter what they all thought they'd heard on the wind. Chance knew the scream hadn't been the wind, but denial is an amazing partner.

Patches of icicles hung from fissures in the stone like modern art, their long, sleek beauty sparkling under the flashlight beams that bounced around the cavern.

"Wow," said Terry. He was in the lead and had jerked to a halt.

A white frozen spiderweb that would've rivaled anything

made by Shelob blocked the tunnel. Thick strands, like frozen saliva, crisscrossed the walls in an intricate pattern and was torn open at its center. The webbing tinkled like miniature wind chimes as the cut threads swayed in the gentle breeze pushing up through the tunnel. Squeaking and scratching echoed off stone, and Terry hesitated, leaning in through the hole in the web like Sam Gamgee.

"You ever see a web this big?" Tatiana asked. She was documenting the scene with her camera, the frozen silk glittering in a myriad of colors.

"Sometimes you'll see big wolf spiders up here because of all the small mammals that run around in the warmer months, but they typically like open spaces and don't spin webs," Biggie said. He hadn't spoken in some time, and his runny nose created snot icicles in his mustache and beard.

"A spider that doesn't spin webs?" Dave said.

"Yeah," Biggie said. "Wolf spiders hunt and ambush prey. Old school, like a tiger."

A stab of heat ran through Chance and perspiration rolled down his forehead and back.

"So . . . what the hell is this?" Tatiana asked as she panned the camera, the eye-like lens finding Biggie.

The large man shrugged. "There's many species of spiders in these mountains, but most are on the smaller side. I'm thinking the strands look much bigger than they are because of the frost coating them."

That appeared to appease Terry, because he nodded and continued on, pushing through the frozen strands into darkness.

Tatiana went next, the camera documenting everything.

One by one, they stepped through the webbing, the trail of blood leading deeper into the mountain. The tunnel itself hadn't changed much, aside from wider and more frequent cracks appearing in the walls above. The black scars stood out under the hard artificial light, and the breeze sang an unintelligible chanting dirge.

Grunts, snorts, and the sound of flesh being ripped and pulled from bone echoed faintly down the tunnel.

Chance gripped the rifle so tightly, his hands hurt. He slowly slid back the bolt, eyed the shell as it popped into the firing chamber, then quietly eased it back, the faint click fading into the murmuring wind.

"Lights out," whispered Terry.

The flashlights blinked out until the camera was the only light.

"You going to turn that off?" Terry said, his tone a monument of restraint.

"You hear that. We're almost there and you want me to stop filming?" Tatiana said.

Chance pulled the camera from her hand. "You're putting us in danger." He snapped the viewscreen closed.

The camera's light went out and the cavern was plunged into impenetrable darkness.

Darkness . . . Cold . . . And they were running out of time.

He handed Tatiana her camera. "You can turn it on when I say. Do you understand?"

Tatiana didn't respond.

"I need to hear you say you agree, or you can head back," Chance said.

Still, Tatiana didn't answer. He knew what she was thinking. People like her weren't used to being talked to like that, and she was calculating various outcomes depending on the level of aggression in her response. Several long heartbeats slipped away before she said, "Fine."

The rescuers muddled along, darkness pressing in on them, whispering and asking questions Chance didn't have the answers to. Boulders blocked their path, and the tunnel took several turns.

A deep gurgling growl rumbled through the cavern like grinding stone.

When riding extreme slopes, thinking can be an enemy.

Pause to think and death could be the price. Chance was trained to act, to process what he saw fast and react accordingly. Muscle memory. Instinct. He brought up the gun, aiming into the darkness ahead.

"Light'em up," Chance yelled.

Harsh light splashed over the cave.

Tatiana gasped as she jerked the camera downward.

Lima lay sprawled in a large puddle of fresh blood, her legs twisted at odd angles, both arms severed at the elbows. Her hat and coat were missing, her face smashed and broken, her right eye gone, white bone glinting in the socket.

Massive footprints with claw marks at the end of each of the four digits trailed deeper into the cavern.

A roar floated up the tunnel from the direction they'd come, and this time it was much louder and closer.

Terry dropped to the ground next to his wife's corpse, blood splashing his snow pants. He caressed her face, pushed back her hair as he closed her remaining eye. His face twisted and tightened as it barreled through the stages of grief. His eyes went wide with shock and denial, but soon his face shifted to red-cheeked anger. He looked at the floor and wept as he clenched his fists.

"It's not fair. It's not fair," he moaned repeatedly.

Dave dropped his pack, dug out his sleeping bag, and spread it over Lima's body.

Chance made the sign of the cross because that's what he was supposed to do.

A pig-bark thundered through the cave, and Tatiana swung the camera around, light dancing off the walls.

Chance spun and brought up the gun, but he was pushed aside by a powerful blow that knocked him from his feet and sent him sprawling. Two red eyes stared down at him, and when the camera's light found the creature, the image of its face would forever be imprinted in the bedrock of his mind. The beast's apelike face was smeared with blood, and dirt slashed across distended cheeks. Thick bloody fangs hung over red lips, which were peeled back in a snarl. The white fur around its neck and head hung like dirty dreadlocks, the beast's chest dark with dried blood.

The creature howled, and the echo rang through the tunnel like a bell. The camera's light cut through the blackness, the beast's shadow growing. It stood ten feet tall, and its shadow filled the cave as it lunged toward Terry. The monster swatted the grieving husband like he was an annoying gnat, and Terry was thrown aside as the beast defended its food.

Chance aimed and fired, the shot sounding like an explosion in the confined space.

The creature stomped on Terry like he was on fire and the beast was trying to put out the flames.

Terry squealed as he tried to escape, but the thing continued to beat him until he fell still.

Tatiana ran and managed to slip past the creature's outstretched arm. As the beast reached for her, Chance saw no wound on either hand, which confirmed their worst fears. Whatever the animal was, there was more than one.

The light from Tatiana's camera had faded, and shadows writhed and danced. He gripped the gun, curled his finger around the trigger, but he couldn't get a bead on the thing. The beast was like smoke, slipping and slithering in the shadows, and with Biggie and Dave in the area he was concerned about missing again and the possibility of a ricochet. He'd been lucky the first time.

Biggie saved Chance from further deliberation and grabbed him by the shoulders, jerking him to his feet. "Dave!" Biggie yelled louder than Chance had ever heard the man scream.

Dave stood next to Terry's fallen body, his silhouette barely visible in the darkness.

"Dave!" Biggie yelled again, but Dave was somewhere else, lost in his shock.

The beast growled and came on, rushing at Chance and

Biggie as they slipped and slid down the tunnel. The beast's claws as they scraped the stone floor were like rending metal, its harsh breathing and trembling growl like a chugging engine.

Chance doubled his pace. He hadn't left Dave behind—he and Biggie had drawn the beast away, at least that was what he was selling and both sides of his brain were buying. Then he remembered there could be another creature waiting at the entrance or bounding down the tunnel and coming right at them.

Biggie flicked on his flashlight, and Chance did the same. No need for secrecy and stealth any longer. It was a race now, and when Chance glanced over his shoulder and didn't see two glowing red dots trailing after, a gentle wave of relief flooded him.

Snow and ice appeared on the floor and walls, and the duo climbed through the hole in the spider web, the square of pale light that marked the exit appearing in the distance. He saw Tatiana ahead, her footfalls echoing through the tunnel accompanied by the constant sound of dripping water, cracking ice, and the singing of the wind.

Biggie and Chance both lost their footing and slid down the snow-covered incline to the tunnel mouth. Biggie jumped into the snow pile, followed by Chance and the companions rolled down the snowdrift to the floor. The ice wall hiding the cave glowed blue with the light from Tatiana's camera. Chance's reflection wavered, his head lengthening as if he was in a funhouse.

The three companions sat in the loose snow for several minutes, catching their breath, and listening for the beast, and Terry and Dave. No sounds came from the cave except the whistling wind. Tatiana didn't open the camera's viewscreen.

"Now what?" Biggie said.

Chance didn't know. They'd found Lima and the price had been her husband's life. Dave hadn't appeared, and

Chance's thoughts strayed to Fort Fortune. Talk about a buzzkill. His mind started working on logistics, sorting out issues. They needed to get both bodies down the slope, but that task seemed problematic with the creature lurking about. He needed to retreat and come back with reinforcements, more weapons and knowledge, somebody who was a better shot than him.

Dave plunged through the cave mouth and tumbled down the snowdrift, coming to a stop next to Biggie, Chance, and Tatiana. Tears streaked his face, running through dirt, creating thin mud rivers down his cheeks.

Chance felt compelled to say something, to try and put the man at ease, but what do you say to someone who's seen their friend ripped apart by a ten-foot monster with fangs and razor-sharp claws? "None of this is your fault. None of it," he said.

Dave nodded. "Doesn't matter, you know that."

Chance was confused and his brow knitted.

Dave looked away. "I know both of their parents, siblings. I'm going to have to tell them."

Biggie glanced up at the cave entry, then at Chance as he lifted his eyebrows.

Chance didn't know what to do so he bought himself some time. "What was the situation in there when you left?"

"It ran after you guys and I didn't see it again," Dave said.

"Not at all?"

He shook his head. "This might go down as the shortest season in Abominable Peak history. No way can folks stay in Fort Fortune. We need to call the authorities. Make them aware," Dave said.

Biggie looked at the ground. "Tatiana . . . Odd question given the circumstances . . . but did you get all that?" he asked.

"Much of it," she said.

So, they had proof. "Let's hike up to the collection spot

and get some shut eye. We'll take turns standing guard with the rifle, then head down in the morning," Chance said.

"We're not going to—" Dave looked at the cave entrance.

"They're gone," Chance said. "I'm sorry for that. Sorrier than I've been in a long time, but we're alive. There's nothing to be gained by heading back in there without the proper support."

Biggie added, "Big risk for no reward."

In a rare show of humanity, Tatiana said, "But they'll be . . . "

"There will already be closed casket funerals for them, but let's see if we can keep the body count to three," Chance said. He was surprised by the rage in his voice, Jibber's face filling his mind, heat bubbling in his stomach. Anger had replaced fear and worry, beating back the cold and darkness. But time . . .

He pushed to his feet, looked up at the cave mouth one last time, and slipped past the curtain of icicles.

19

January 16th, 1951, Abominable Peak—Elevation 16,971 feet

ROLAND TRIED TO enjoy his time alone on the summit, but each minute was like an hour, his heart racing like a rabbit's, anticipation, fear, and doubt twisting his stomach with pre-run jitters. The wind shrieked, the cold finding every gap in his poplin and wool cocoon. He straightened his goggles, checked zippers, and pulled up his gloves as he took in the unobstructed view. The vast cloud-streaked sky stretched in every direction like a carpet, the rolling peaks of the Sawatch Range poking through the fluffy cloud layer.

He closed his eyes and took a deep breath, remembering everything it had taken to get to this moment, all the sacrifices and pain. He opened his eyes as he slowly exhaled, his breath puffing in the air as he let go of some of the stress and worry that made riding vertical peaks so thrilling. Sunlight sparkled off the snow and ice, the southern face slick and dimpled with color, his mind tracing a line, avoiding boulders and large patches of chowder. Jesse was taking his time hiking down to the camera site. There was no rush, but Roland was ready to go, and waiting was torture. He frowned, thinking of how Jesse must feel. He'd made the trip, dealt with the same adversities, but there can be only one first, and adding more people to the expedition would've complicated things beyond their ability to fund the adventure.

When Jesse reached his camera, Roland shook the snow off his skis and inspected them. His planks were cutting-edge laminated wood, with ash on the top and bottom, and birch sandwiched between. This new design made the skis much lighter and stronger than traditional solid wood skis, but the glue often failed, causing warping and splitting along the edges as they delaminated. This could happen very fast, especially in extreme temperatures, and a ragged edge could mean death.

The skis looked good, no bubbling or cracks, and he placed them in the snow at his feet. Roland's boots clicked into place as he snapped into his Saf-ski bindings. He eyed the bear trap-like bindings with suspicion. They were also new, the first emergency bindings that released the ski from the boot in a fall. They'd saved many broken bones, and though Roland was still wary his skis might fall off at an inopportune moment, the positives outweighed the potential problems. He fed his hands through the safety straps on his poles and stomped his skis, jumping and leaning back, lifting the ski tips, trying to knock the planks off his feet, but the bindings held.

He was ready.

Jesse stood behind the Arriflex, a small dark figure. All was good to go.

He looked straight down, the incline like the face of a frozen tidal wave. Wind howled and argued, sugary snow shifting over the peak's overhanging cornice. There was nothing left to do but go.

Roland inched forward, sliding his skis, and the cloud-filled horizon grew as he slipped over the edge.

A rush of wind assailed him as he flew down the southern face of Abominable Peak. A hill no person had ever ridden.

Instantly, he was moving too fast, nothing but blinding white glare spreading to the blue cotton candy-streaked horizon. He jumped and pivoted, bringing his skis horizontal, powder spraying like flames. He was engulfed in snow, the edges of his planks sliding, finding nothing but sugar, no leverage, his stomach sinking.

Roland leaped again, swinging his skis around a hundred and eighty degrees, putting on the breaks like he was picking his way through moguls. Powder flowed like water, but his knees shook, the stress of resistance climbing up his legs as the planks flexed and caught an edge.

The jolt almost toppled him, and Roland hopped again, bringing the skis around, chopping into the snowpack, spraying powder. Back in control, he cut a narrow line diagonally across the mountainside, slipping under the overhang of the cornice as he launched off a boulder.

He landed in a drift of powder built-up before the stone, and went under, white filling his vision as he bounced off his butt. He shifted, scissoring down the slope in a controlled slide. Roland connected dots as he filtered out boulders, crevasses, and a field of chowder with thick chunks of ice sticking from the snowpack like teeth on a saw blade. Roland broke left, carving a wide arc and bolting toward two sharp-edged stones that stuck from the snowpack, blue sky between them.

He jumped and cut, slowing as he knifed between the stones. Blinding sunlight danced off snow, biting cold and howling wind funneling through the boulders. He was knocked off his line as the ground buckled and lifted, dirty white hair and red eyes forming from the mountainside.

A primal cry, what Roland imagined an angry dinosaur would sound like, echoed over the mountain. Pain cut through him as knife-like claws tore across his back, over his shoulder, and down his left side. Bloody heat ran down his leg, filling his boot, and he flinched when another roar pierced the day.

The left side of his body went on strike and Roland's knees came unhinged. He went down, hearing rather than feeling his right knee flex and snap, the pop louder than the rushing snow. The fancy new bindings worked, and Roland's skis released as he cartwheeled through the cold white maelstrom. He hit stone, and his arm cracked and broke like a chicken bone, but he didn't feel any pain.

Air rushed from his lungs as he hit the snowpack and slid down the incline toward Jesse. His leg and arm dangled like broken wings, blood poured down his side, and dizziness spun him like a top, vision blurry, the cold wrapping him in its embrace as the wind consoled him.

With a great effort, he flipped onto his stomach, desperately clawing at the loose snowpack with his good hand. It was no use. It felt like he was trying to find leverage in water, and as he flailed and struggled his goggles tore off and he lost his hat. Snow filled his ears, his field of vision. Roland pressed his eyes closed, pink-white lightning exploding in his head as he came to a halt, face pressed against rock, pain finally surging through him.

A gurgle-bark, and a low howl, almost like a whistle, pierced the chaos, then faded in a choppy echo that joined with the angry wind.

Sugar poured down the southern face, massive spindrifts cascading over Roland where he lay twisted, sticking from the snowpack like a piece of trash. Warmth spread through him as he tried to move his legs, but they were packed beneath the snow. He dug with his good arm, but it was no good, and soon he was buried to his shoulders, snow driving into his face. Roland tossed his head back and forth as snow covered his head, creating a pocket of breathing space.

Everything went still. Cold soaked into him, the heat from the blood caked in his clothes fighting back, but it was a losing battle. Cold and darkness, together again, and in a few minutes, he'd run out of air. And time.

His thoughts drifted, and he concluded it was appropriate that it end this way. On a mountain, in the snow like a relic buried in the desert. When the snow melted and the summer hikers came, they'd find his frozen corpse, his skis and poles. His family would probably put his equipment on display somewhere. One of those dusty spots in the back corner of a ski lodge, where a brass plaque would name him as one of the best skiers ever, and how he'd given it all up for one epic ride.

Starbursts exploded at the edges of his vision, his body straining for oxygen and finding only carbon dioxide. Crimson eyes stared at him through the blackness of fading consciousness, an angry apelike face, straggled knots of filthy white hair, the scent of rot and blood. He heard his grandfather chanting in his head, but he couldn't understand what he was saying. Story of Roland's life, and with that thought, he let it all go.

***

Jesse jerked back from the camera like it had tried to bite him, his gaze shifting from the viewfinder to the white cloud lifting from the slope above like the fallout from an explosion. Spindrifts cascaded down the incline, and he held his breath, waiting for Roland to burst from the avalanche like a superhero.

Seconds ticked away and the snow stopped flowing, and there was no sign of Roland.

He leaned in and looked through the viewfinder as he arced the camera's eye across the slope. The Arriflex tapped and clicked, the film rolling. He'd gotten it all. The entire horrific crash, the blur of white, the shadow.

Jesse lurched into motion. Whatever had passed between him and Roland, no matter how cheated he felt, he couldn't just leave him to die. He stomped through the snow to the sled and peeled open the leather bag holding one of the shotguns. The cold steel of the old gun stung his hands, and Jesse took out his gloves and pulled them on. He broke the gun, stuffed shells into both barrels, and snapped the shotgun closed with a flick of his wrist.

Then, he shouldered the weapon and climbed, heat

piping through him, a single-minded focus consuming him. Crack, step, push up, repeat. Snow slid downslope behind him, and twice he almost got caught in the flow and dragged back down, but both times he swam in the powder, head down, and managed to stem the tide.

Ten minutes passed, and he was halfway to the dissipating cloud of frozen mist that hovered over the accident site, when he saw one of Roland's skis sticking from the snow like a narrow curved grave marker. He doubled his efforts, heart thumping, Roland's blue frozen face filling his mind. He'd thought of Roland crashing many times on those cold nights in the tent when envy cajoled. He pushed the thoughts away. He'd never meant for it to actually happen. Skiing wasn't that important.

Jesse realized he was yelling, calling out Roland's name, his voice cracking and shrill. He fell quiet, tuning out the wind, the crunch and shift of the snow, and beneath it all . . .

"Help! Help!" Like the coo of a dove.

He searched the slope, leveling the shotgun, swinging it back and forth as he continued his frantic climb. There'd been no sign of the massive shadow, the dark figure that materialized from the snowpack like a wraith. The feeling that he was being watched, weighed and measured, filled him like the knowledge of something forgotten.

There was a depression in the mound of loose snow ahead, and the calls for help got louder. Jesse stuck the butt of the shotgun into the snow, dropped to his knees, and dug, tossing snow aside in a madding rush. Frozen strands of hair appeared in the snowpack like green grass through frost. Jesse slowed, digging and clearing away powder like an archeologist brushing away a million years of dirt from an ancient artifact.

Roland spit and sucked in air, his head sticking from the snowpack like he been buried in beach sand by children.

"Thank you," Roland sputtered. His face was deep red, his lips blue, but he was alive.

Jesse fell back onto his butt, exhausted, panting and sucking for air. "Thought . . . I . . . lost you."

"Me, too," Roland said. "And you still might."

Jesse went back to work, and in minutes there was enough space for him to drag Roland out of the hole and up onto the snowpack.

Roland wailed in pain, his broken leg dangling from the knee, arm split at the elbow, the left side of his jacket and snow pants in tatters, four large gashes raking across his back and down his left side.

Jesse iced and cleaned the wounds, then wrapped them the best he could with scarves. The bleeding had stopped, but his friend was white as flour, the fire in his eyes fading.

"We need to get off the mountain," Roland said. "I've lost . . . a lot of blood."

Jesse nodded as he stared up at Roland's line, which swerved and cut across the pristine snowpack, then ended like Roland had disappeared. He hadn't even made it to camera site one. After everything they'd gone through—the hike, the trek through the Sawatch Range in the Jeep, the preparation, expense, and sacrifice. It had all been for nothing. Except . . . the footage.

"I could give it a go," Jesse said, and his head jerked back like he couldn't believe the words had come out of his mouth. "I mean . . . " he stammered, but like a fart in church, what he'd said was out there, and he couldn't put the stench back in the bottle.

Roland's brow knitted, eyes glassy, face red with cold and pasty with lack of blood.

"Crazy, I know . . . "

"It's too . . . " Roland coughed hard and spit up blood. "Dangerous, and I'm in . . . " He shook his head. "Everything is loose up there. The same thing would happen to you. Look at me!"

"Yeah," Jesse said. "I was just thinking out loud . . . Wishing, really." Jesse rolled his shoulders, looked down the slope, and pulled the gun from the snow. "I'm going down to get the sled. We'll strap you to it and bring you down. As soon as I get things stabilized, I'll boil some snow and we can—"

A loud crack, followed by a pop, reverberated over the peak, and the ground shifted.

Roland and Jesse slid down the incline atop a cookie of snow. The chunk of snowpack sliced through powder like a boat, spraying snow on both sides, the blue cloud-filled horizon rushing toward them, the camera spot looming ahead, the drop-off beyond.

Jesse flipped and tossed in the wave of snow, lashing out with the shotgun, using it as a spike as he tried to stop his slide. The gun bounced from his hand and disappeared in the raging torrent of snow.

Roland screamed, and Jesse's jacket was yanked up over his head as something snagged his collar. He slowed, Roland screaming. Through the powder and clouds of snow dust, Jesse saw Roland wedged against a stone, his body bent around the rock as he held onto Jesse's jacket with his good arm.

For three heartbeats, Roland held on, and Jesse slowed, powder pouring over him as he dug in his heels, sinking under the wave of white. He came to a grinding, snow-snapping stop.

Jesse inched up the incline a foot, digging in and taking his weight off Roland's arm. The duo panted and caught their breath, tiny spindrifts rolling over them, spittle leaking from Jesse's mouth and freezing on his tight beard.

Roland cried, shifting his position, trying to take the pressure off his back, but he moved too far and slipped around the stone, grabbed vainly at the sliding ice and snow, and slid down the incline.

"Argh," Jesse wailed as he lunged forward, falling onto his side as he grabbed Roland's wounded arm. The duo spun down the incline like a pinwheel.

Roland cried out in pain, leaving a red trail of blood in the clean snow as the pair plummeted toward the drop-off. Now it was Jesse's turn, and he held tightly onto Roland as he angled his legs down, trying to find leverage, his feet bouncing off rocks and buried vegetation.

They hit a boulder and the duo went airborne, sailing through the air and landing hard on the snowpack. Jesse was able to stop their slide, but now their positions were reversed. Roland stared up at Jesse as he held onto his partner's hand, blue sky filling the background.

Jesse felt the urge to let him go, but he held on tight. If Roland went over the edge, he'd go over the edge. That's just how it had to be.

The pair slipped farther, and they spun, clawing for purchase, changing positions as Roland's body sank deeper into the snowpack and he used himself as a break to stop their slide.

Jesse hung onto Roland's hand, feet struggling to find anything but powder. He looked downslope but there was nothing but blue sky. They'd careened past the camera and were clinging to the snowpack that overhung the drop-off, twenty feet from slipping over the edge into oblivion. He stared up at Roland, who was red-faced from strain. When their eyes met, Roland looked away, and Jesse's stomach sank.

Roland screamed, the hollow thump of his arm popping from its socket piercing the day. He struggled to stay wedged in the snowpack, but he was slipping in the loose powder.

"I can't . . ."

With a chilling certainty that brought an odd comfort, Jesse realized what was about to happen.

"I'm sorry," Roland said, and let him go.

Wind and snow lashed Jesse's face as he slid toward the precipice. He scratched and fought, trying to find anything to grab onto in the sea of white, but there was nothing, and as his stomach dropped the sense of falling consumed him, and Jesse regretted nothing. He didn't even blame Roland. He'd done his best, and what good would it have done if they'd both gone over the cliff and plummeted to their deaths?

Jesse Hance didn't cry out as he fell, didn't curse anyone's name or scream to God. He simply faded into the tumult of blinding whiteness.

20

February 2, 2018, Abominable Peak, south slope—Elevation 10,171 feet

DUSK INCHED OVER the mountain, leaking under every cornice, and burrowing into every dell and crevasse. Chance pushed out with his feet, his board's bindings creaking under the stress. His own board was long gone, and the bindings on his loaner didn't fit his boots right. Biggie was in Chance's wake, hair flowing in the breeze, his shell glowing in the half-light. They cut a wide swath, running along the service road that was the closest thing Abominable Peak had to a groomed trail. He pressed his injured wing against his side as he cycled his legs back and forth, cutting a nice line through powder.

The night in the tent hadn't been horrible. He'd had food and water, a sleeping bag, and Chance managed to stay relatively warm, and other than his throbbing arm and the nudge and poke of his many bumps and bruises, he'd managed to get some sleep and felt refreshed. The team had left the collection spot at noon, and Tatiana and Dave decided to hike down to Fort Fortune via the most direct footpath.

Chance cut east, launching off a snowbank and riding the rail of an exposed section of stone. He heard Biggie cheer, and for the briefest of instants Chance felt the urge to open it up and tear down the mountain, but he held back, his arm ridiculing and scolding.

Biggie slid up beside him, arms out, crouched low as he slalomed back and forth in a tight pattern. “You go off the trail on purpose?” his friend asked.

Chance nodded and banked hard right, shooting over a narrow gap filled with ice water, and pulling his board horizontal to his body, pushing snow and slush like a plow as he came to a halt.

Biggie slid to a stop beside him. “Everything okay?” he asked.

Chance nodded. “Isn’t the original mine entrance around here somewhere?”

Biggie’s face twisted with consternation. “Are you bloomin’ nuts, mate? I’ve just got to ask.”

“I want to see if there’s anything to be seen.”

Biggie harrumphed. “I love you, Chance, but I don’t care if there’s a trail of gold coins. No way am I going in there, even if we can find it.”

Chance said nothing.

“Everything will be buried.”

“We’ll find it.” Chance adjusted his goggles and pushed off, sliding east toward a large bowl filled with boulders. The pair launched off the edge of a depression, Chance tucking his injured arm protectively as he crashed into the snowpack.

Biggie arced right, and the two friends shot in and out of the field of boulders with a precision that looked practiced, snow flying, frozen clouds of mist filling the air.

“Chance! Hold up,” Biggie yelled.

Chance spared a glance over his shoulder and saw that Biggie had stopped, so he cut hard right, turning up the slope, slowing his momentum until he was sliding backwards. He hopped, spun himself around, and glided down to where Biggie stared at the ground.

The pristine white was splattered crimson, entrails and sinew running through the blood like snot. Pieces of meat and fat splashed outward, away from the mountain lion’s carcass, its chest flayed open, insides gone. It was a large male, and the beast's frosted eyes stared up into the growing darkness, its brown coat dark with dried blood. The snowpack was stomped and disturbed all around the dead creature, indicating a struggle. Four large gashes marred the dead lion's hindquarter, and Chance hugged himself, pulling his arm in tighter to his side.

The wind howled and screamed in warning. Leave. Run. Ride with all swiftness, the wind argued and warned. Sugary snow sifted over the snowpack, all the exposed rock wet with melted verglas. Anything that could find, catch, and kill an adult male mountain lion was something better left alone.

Biggie looked around and said, "I wish you hadn't given the rifle to Tatiana and Dave."

Chance's nerves walked the tightrope of his spine, head pounding in rhythm with his heart. He searched the area, looking for large, clawed footprints in the snow, but he saw nothing apart from the confused prints of the fight.

The duo left the lion's corpse behind and turned downslope. The entrance to the original Lucky Strike Number One gold mine was below, on the cusp between the tall, sharp Abominable Peak, and the rolling hills that surrounded the narrow valley containing Fort Fortune.

As he rode, Chance's thoughts dogged and distracted him. Riding had always been his release as well as his obsession, and clearing his mind was one of the reasons he loved boarding. While he was riding, there could be nothing else, but as he cut a straight line south, his head filled with images of the mountain lion, the blood and entrails.

Patches of dark blue appeared in the mounds of snow ahead, like windows on another world. Chance cycled his feet back and forth, slowing as he came around a snowdrift topped with a deep blue peak. Equipment and supplies covered with blue tarps and snow flanked both sides of the mine entrance. An old wooden sign, left up for posterity and history, identified the iced-up hole leading into the mountain as Lucky Strike Number One.

Chance snapped out of his board and Biggie did the same. A wall of icicles covered the mine entrance, which was boarded up and labeled as closed and dangerous.

"Well, that settles that," Chance said.

Huge four digit footprints trailed in and out of the mine, a large section of the icicle wall broken away. Drips of blood marred the whiteness, but they were black and dried, not from the fresh kill they'd just seen.

"This mine meets up with Lucky Strike Two. That's how they found the second vein," Biggie said.

Chance's skin squirmed like he was covered in tiny spiders, and he pawed at the pill vial in his jacket as he stared at the dark maw where something had broken itself an entrance. The wind whistled, snow swirling in the air. He took a step forward and Biggie grabbed his elbow.

"No," the big man said.

Chance nodded and tugged himself free, inching forward and sticking his head into the dark opening.

The musty scent of rot, waste, and spoiled fish floated on the air, the cavern filled with thick blackness. An old-style track with two steel rails and wood supports trailed away into darkness, but he saw no mining carts. Red eyes didn't pierce the darkness, and he heard no grunts or moans. He backed out, examining the deep claw marks around the edges of the ice hole.

"Seen enough?" Biggie said.

"These . . . things are using the mine system to move around at lower elevations," Chance said.

Biggie looked downslope in the direction of Fort Fortune. "That means they can get to camp."

Chance nodded, recalling the old mine entrance he'd seen next to the warehouse. In the old days, miners would use the tunnel to get to the vein, but over the years it was determined that the passage wasn't safe, and could cave-in, so it was abandoned.

They snapped back into their bindings and went south. Deepening dusk seeped over the land, the western horizon a dark purple-orange. A chill iced Chance's bones, his stomach protesting the lack of lunch. He needed a drink as well. His nerves were thrumming like piano wires, and he couldn't get the images of Lima and Terry out of his head. The way they'd been torn open and thrown aside like garbage. Then, he heard the hippie lady's shrill voice screaming about how the animals of the mountain had just as much right—more, in fact—to be there than they did, and as much as that complicated the ethics of the situation, it was the truth. They had no business being up here for thrills. Gold? Maybe. But to take joy rides? He just wasn't so sure anymore, and he wondered if his grandfather would've agreed.

The duo smelled the fire long before they saw it. The faint scent of smoke wafted up the slope, tiny gray specks of ash floating in the air like snow. Dusk pressed in on the mountain, an orange glow spilling from the valley and Fort Fortune.

"That can't be good," Biggie said, and he straightened out, bombing downhill, the fastest way between two points and all that rot. He got low, his gloved hand trailing in the snowpack as he cut a line through powder.

Chance fell in behind him, ash hitting his face and leaving tiny black specks of soot on his jacket and goggles. Wind tore at his shell, its sleeves flapping in the breeze. He bent his knees, staying low as he zipped down the slope, minimizing wind resistance. Shards of pain knifed through his injured arm as he shifted and balanced, the movement pulling on the delicate scabs that had formed over each gash. Blood leaked into his long underwear, but it didn't feel like much.

The partners arrived home to find Fort Fortune churning like a beehive that's been smacked with a stick. Black smoke poured over base camp, obscuring most of the half-buried buildings. The warehouse that contained the helicopter and mining equipment was on fire, tall flames reflecting off the snow and ice. Heat rolled toward Chance in waves as he dropped onto a well-worn trail and headed for the warehouse.

A fire brigade was holding a hose connected to a water tank, but there appeared to be a frozen line or some other issue because no water flowed from the hose. Stefan was at the head of the line, the hose control nozzle in his hands. He was cursing and screaming in German, his voice rising above to complaining wind. He dropped the hose and stalked around in the firelight, throwing up his hands as he disappeared and reappeared in the rolling clouds of smoke. People fled before him, lines of onlookers fleeing the commotion and heading for the dormitories or the Lucky Strike.

Stefan put his hands on his hips, gazing at the fire like a child. Chance had an idea of what the moment meant to him. It was the end of his business running tours in the Sawatch, and the end to riding Abominable Peak. Without the copter and a place to protect it from the elements, there could be no rides, and Chance figured the insurance policies and permits would fail soon after.

The rumble of snowmobiles firing up echoed over Fort Fortune, and Stefan hobbled away, knifing through the line of people like a nail, yelling and screaming.

Chance and Biggie came to a stop just outside the fire's glow and snapped out of their bindings.

Trevor stood off to the side, watching his bird burn.

"I'm going to talk to Trevor. Go find the crew and see what the hell is going on," Chance said.

Biggie nodded and trudged toward the Lucky Strike through the knee-deep powder because the packed footpaths were stopped up.

Chance sunk to his waist as he avoided the path and cut the line, snow running up under his shell and divebombing down his butt-crack.

"Yo," he said when he arrived at Trevor's side.

Trevor's head fell to the side like a skull nudged by the wind, his eyes ablaze with the reflection of the fire. Intense heat rolled off the collapsing warehouse, snow and ice hissing as it melted, thin rivulets of water running beneath the snowpack. Trevor returned his gaze to the remnants of his chopper.

"What the hell happened?" Chance asked.

Trevor remained silent.

Chance put a hand on the man's shoulder and said, "Trevor?"

The warehouse's main support beam gave up its ghost and the metal roof came crashing down, sending firework-like streamers into the night sky, the concussion *womp* breaking icicles, dumping overhung snowdrifts, and cracking ice. The fire blazed white-orange, black and orange fireballs rolling over the snowpack, the intense heat melting the roof, the scent of heated metal like sniffing the inside of an old tin can.

"Trevor?" Chance said louder.

The man's head jerked toward Chance, eyes burning. "What!"

"What the hell happened here?"

"You've got eyes."

"How did it start?"

Trevor hiked his shoulders.

The warehouse was far from the other buildings, and there was enough of a snowpack that Chance didn't think the fire spreading was a concern. Stefan had regained control and was setting up a perimeter around the burning building. If any debris missiled across Fort Fortune, someone would be there to douse it.

"We were drinking, just hanging out, when it happened again." Trevor stared at the flames, eyes focused as he stood rigid, snow, smoke and ash swirling around him.

"Another person dead, blood all over, and this time it

happened inside the snowmobile shed. Somewhere we thought was safe. Her face smashed—"

An ache, like a knife being twisted into his chest, took the air from his lungs. Chance knew without asking what had happened, what had killed the woman, but he needed to hear someone else say it to help him rationalize his sanity.

"How did she die?"

He laughed, a manic, unhinged cackle that sent the mice scurrying down Chance's spine. "Your beast. Your Metoh."

21

THE SCENE OF Francesca Ranoldi's murder was the worst yet. The shed's doors had deep claw marks running across them, the hinge holding the lock torn away, the old curved forged steel handle hanging by one screw. Francesca hung upside down like a piece of meat in a freezer, her ankles trussed, a thick puddle of congealed blood on the floor, her bloody blonde hair hanging in frosty strands like red icicles. Her chest cavity was open, ribs broken away, and her innards had been removed. Chance thought of the mountain lion as he examined the drips of blood and globs of gristle and fat that clung to the walls and surrounding snowmobiles. The snow rider's engine covers were up, their wiring torn out. Bloody claw marks marred the walls and supply cabinets as if the creature had been looking for something.

Perhaps the most disturbing part of the scene was Francesca's crushed face. Her tongue lolled out, and both of her eyes had been removed. Many cultures believed that removing the eyes of the dead hindered them in the next world, blinded the person in their next life, and was considered a punishment for sins while on Earth. A steady thrum of unease vibrated through Chance, and he tossed his head side to side, trying to shake the angst, but couldn't. These beasts weren't mindless carnivores instinctively protecting their turf.

This was something more. The fire at the warehouse,

where they kept the machine that roared up the mountain and dropped invaders. Was it a coincidence that building was the one that caught fire? Why not the new dormitory where there were kitchens, fireplaces? The Lucky Strike, or the snowmobile shed where there was gas, a blow torch?

He tried to crack his neck and failed again. A deep sense of worry and sorrow crept over him. He needed to do something now, fast.

"She was in here, getting the snow riders ready for the morning," Stefan said.

"She was alone?" Chance asked.

Stefan nodded. "As far as we know, but we really don't know shit."

"I don't think anyone should go anywhere alone until we figure out . . . " What? Chance had no clue. "Have you notified the staties? The cops? Called down mountain?"

"Yeah," Stefan said. "Already done. Staties said we're not a priority because we don't have anyone requiring major medical attention." He glanced at Francesca's swinging corpse. "They said they could get a chopper here at the end of the day tomorrow. That was if something more important didn't come up."

"Should I . . . ?" He pointed at Francesca Ranoldi's corpse where it spun slowly in the breeze, blood dripping from her hanging hair.

"We were preparing to deal with her when the fire started," Stefan said. "I got—"

A faint roar echoed over Fort Fortune as if arguing with the wind, and it was answered by a second call that was closer and more guttural.

Stefan and Chance stared at one another in the dimly lit room, snow eddying in through the open door, cold and darkness taking a foothold, preparing the battlefield for the arrival of time. Chance glanced at the green glow of his watch. It was 9:19 PM. A long time until sunup.

"I've got people coming to take care of her. They'll put

her with the others," Stefan said. "Let's cut her down." He flicked open his utility knife.

As Chance waited, Stefan sawed away at the rope. The knot was complex, like a rat king.

As he worked, Stefan said, "I saw you lost a couple of folks."

Chance didn't respond. After Jibber's death he'd been numb, and he'd barely had time to think about Terry and Lima.

"I take it they're not returning?"

Chance spilled what had happened; their pursuit of the beast, the trail, what they'd seen, the cave. "You can watch some of it. That reminds me, have you seen Tatiana or Dave?"

"Haven't been in the Lucky Strike yet tonight, and I've been busy trying to keep Fort Fortune from coming apart at the seams, but . . . " He shook his head. "But I failed."

It was impossible to avoid the puddle of blood beneath the corpse, and when the partners were done cutting Francesca down and laying her out on a clean section of floor, there were bloody boot prints everywhere.

The grisly scene had an air of serial killer nonchalance about it as if those who'd dealt with the situation hadn't cared if they got blood splatters on their clean shoes. The entire thing made Chance sick to his stomach—the coppery scent of blood, the tang of meat, and the faint onset of decomposing flesh making bile surge up his throat as his stomach snarled and twisted.

Two men arrived and took Francesca Ranoldi away to what Chance thought of as the Fort Fortune morgue, and all that was left were her bodily fluids and the smell of death and shit.

"Can these be fixed?" he asked, indicating the snowmobiles.

Stefan hiked his shoulders. "Might be able to cobble together one or two from what's left of all six. I just don't know, and it would take time." He sat on the black pleather seat of a yellow Polaris, and pulled off his skull cap, lifted his fogged goggles, then let out a long, lazy breath. "You got my gun?"

"Sorry," Chance said. "Tatiana and Dave have it."

Stefan sighed.

Chance left Stefan with his thoughts and went in search of his crew. People bustled about. The fire was out, but black smoke still rolled off the glowing charred remains of wood and twisted metal. Some folks weren't waiting until morning. The emergency snowcat was powered up and folks were loading gear, several snowmobiles lined up behind it. He didn't see any of his crew, but he knew where he'd find them.

The Lucky Strike was packed, and Chance found Biggie and the others huddled around a table in the rear of the establishment, a half-full pitcher of martini at the center of the table.

"Yo," he said.

All heads turned his way, then his friends were vaulting from their seats, clapping him on the back, shoveling platitudes and trumped-up concern. Tina even gave him a peck on the cheek.

"We were worried, man," Colin said.

"Yeah, Biggie told us . . . You okay?" Tina asked.

Chance nodded, and Bomber slapped him on the back so hard he lurched forward. He was guided to a chair, and a full martini was placed before him. Medicine first. He lifted the worn glass, scratches and bubbles running through it. He took a long pull, relishing the burn of the vodka, the warmth spreading through his stomach, then on through his body, awakening the scratches on his arm. He closed his eyes and took a deep breath, but the glazed death-darkened eyes of Jibber, Terry, Lima, and Francesca Ranoldi stared at him in the blackness. He hadn't known the women, yet a nagging feeling of failure dogged him, asking if he'd done everything he could have, helped in every way possible. Those questions, if they could ever be answered satisfactorily, were for another time.

The crew drank and munched on snacks in silence, the events of the last two days draining from Chance only to be replaced with fuzzy weariness.

He pushed his half-empty glass away and said, "We need to plan. Get supplies." He looked around the bar as if expecting to see the crowd listening in on their conversation, but everyone was lost in their own confusion, worry, and fear, sipping drinks and pretending to pay him no mind. "I bet the kitchens are being raided as we speak. There's going to be nothing left."

"Can't we—?" Colin started.

"No," Chance snapped. "We can't sit here and get drunk. These things are coming. Can't you see that? We need to figure out where we're spending the night. We need weapons, and we'll have to take turns standing guard." He pushed up from the table, the shriek of his chair drawing the attention of the surrounding tables.

Tina finished her drink and said, "Sorry. You're right. We just thought . . . " She looked at the table.

Chance eyed each of his crew. He understood what they were going through. He'd gone through the same thing, the realization that the party was over—maybe for good—and it was time to pull on the big boy snow pants and deal with the problem at hand, and that didn't involve boarding, talking about boarding, or partying. A buzzkill for sure.

Colin said, "So, what were you thinking?"

He sighed. "These creatures . . . " What to say? He didn't know anything, had nothing but vague ideas based on a very loose list of facts. "Whatever we're dealing with knows this mountain better than us—much better. Its senses are fine-tuned, so we have to hide. Completely, and it's clear it . . . *they*, don't want us here."

"They?" Bomber said.

"Weren't you paying attention?" Tina said. "The beast that killed Lima and Terry couldn't have been the same creature that murdered Francesca. Not unless it has super healing powers as well as a direct tunnel that allowed it to get here before Chance and Biggie, who were riding."

Bomber stared at her blankly.

"The one that killed Terry and Lima didn't have a hand wound," Chance added.

Bomber nodded.

"Anyone seen Tatiana?" Chance asked.

A chorus of no and shaking heads.

"Why do you care all of sudden?" Colin asked.

"She's got proof, pictures of the thing. Not that proof is needed at this point," Biggie said.

"I guess we can't worry about that now," Chance said. "Where's the best place to hunker down, catch some rest, and wait out the night?"

"Too many people at the new dormitory," Tina said. "If you want to blend in, disappear, that's not the spot."

"The old barrack is made of wood, has solid doors, the old potbelly," Bomber said.

"We can't have a fire, but . . . " Chance looked at Biggie who nodded. "It might work. What about weapons?"

"What happened to Stefan's gun?" Colin said.

"Tatiana or Dave has it," he said. "Any other ideas?"

"I've got a hunting knife in my locker," Colin said.

"I can beat that," said Bomber. "There's an old shotgun in the display case at the barrack. Shells are another story."

"Anything else?" Chance said.

If there were weapons to be had in Fort Fortune, they were most likely already spoken for.

Chance said, "I bet Stefan has shells, but that's for later."

"There's a bunch of tools in the snowmobile shed," Tina said.

"Let's get set up before we worry about that. The barrack makes sense. All our personal stuff that's not been taken by the gods of the mountain is there, and we've even got a small supply of food and water."

"That's if people haven't pillaged it," Biggie said.

Chance looked around the bar. People drank, laughed, hid from a reality that was staring them in the face. Denial isn't just a voluntary refusal but a necessity, because stopping the party was an unforgivable sin and nobody wanted to be left without a seat when the music stopped. He lifted his martini glass and spun it between his forefinger and thumb, then brought it to his lips and downed the contents.

The burn tweaked his senses.

"Let's get to it then."

"Maybe we should leave in twos, so we're not noticed," Bomber said.

And there it was. Chance knew it was only a matter of time before the people left at Fort Fortune were consumed with worry and fear, and soon they'd start seeing shadows and enemies in everyone. Then, they were only a couple of misunderstandings away from a mob.

"Yeah," Chance said. He pushed up from the table and put his hand on Biggie's shoulder. "You're with me. Let's get set up and we can worry about what's next."

Biggie finished his drink and got up.

"You all be careful," Chance said. He eyed Shelly as she bustled behind the bar. "There are cases of water in the back, pretzels, chips and stuff. I'll grab some on our way out. I can slip out the backdoor."

The conspirators nodded, eyes drifting to the table.

Chance blended into the crowd and waited until Shelly was swamped, then he slipped behind the bar and went into the backroom like he owned the place. Meanwhile, Biggie went out the front door and around back to wait for him. He made up a box of water and bags of chips, nuts, and popcorn, then pushed open the rear door and handed it off to Biggie. He glanced back over a shoulder, and the storeroom was empty and dark. He slipped out into the night and closed the door gently behind him.

Fort Fortune had settled down and few people walked the beaten paths. The wind had picked up, and it roared and yelled, pushing around powder and smoke, assisting the cold. The line of approaching storm clouds filled the western horizon. Rectangles of light glowed in the darkness as people hid in their rooms—some hiding from the truth, others probably having similar conversations to the one he and his crew just had. The snowcat and line of snowmobiles were gone, and the unnatural rumble of power generators rose above the gale.

The pair arrived back at the barrack to find it locked, and mostly empty. Twelve people sat around the potbelly stove, and all their heads jerked in Chance's direction like a flock of birds when he and Biggie pushed through the door and strolled down the center aisle, all eyes going wide, chatter ceasing. Nobody argued when Chance insisted the fire be put out, not after he explained why. They killed the lights as well, leaving only red daggers of light from newly installed exit signs and fire detectors glowing in the blackness.

When the entire crew arrived, they secured the front door and huddled in the rear of the building with the others. Colin broke out the water and ripped open a bag of pretzels. They passed the food around. The crinkle of the bag, the snap and crack of breaking pretzels, and the chewing of the companions was cathartic.

The stove grew cold, the air crisp, and Chance hugged himself and stared up at the outline of his grandfather's picture mounted on the vanity wall at the rear of the barrack. He couldn't see the image in the darkness, but knew it was surrounded by initials carved into the wood, names painted on, written on with marker and pen. People who had come to the mountain to ride and follow in the footsteps of Roland Harvey and Jesse Hance. The cabinet with the old double barrel shotgun and other Abominable Peak artifacts was a dark box below the picture.

Chance looked away, worry burrowing into him like maggots, heat bubbling in his chest, anger and frustration taking hold. A gust of wind surged through every crack and pinhole, playing the building like a broken flute, the faint chatter of the other travelers fading into the torturous night.

22

TIME STRETCHED OUT, minutes like hours, the wind singing and probing every crack. It was cold with the stove off, and most of the travelers had migrated to their racks and were bundled in their sleeping bags. A big guy named Devero stood guard in the rear of the building, and Chance and a woman who called herself Rai sat by the front entrance. Chance had an ice axe he'd pillaged from the snowmobile shed, and Rai had a hammer strapped to the end of a broomstick like a spear to give her some reach. They were an early warning system, nothing more, one several of the folks holed up in the barrack didn't think was necessary. As the night had stretched on, the complaints about the no fire rule grew, but Chance held his ground with the support of his crew.

Chance couldn't stop referring to "the creature" in the singular. His mind refused to accept that there could be an army of ten-foot abominable snowmen forming outside, preparing to attack, red eyes locked on the barrack like they could see through walls. The beasts had shown a remarkable level of ingenuity, and they were angry, perhaps even hungry and felt threatened. All bad things regardless of the type of animal.

"You ever play spin the bottle?" Rai said.

Chance saw her white teeth in the darkness as she smiled. He felt as dapper as a pisshole in the snow, and he fingered the pill vial in the pocket of his jacket. Rai was attractive—but making out was the last thing on his mind and more proof folks weren't taking the situation as seriously as they should. Yet . . . it had been a long time since he'd even been on a date. "Not with just two people," he said. "And not since high school."

"Too bad," she said.

Chance sat with his back pressed to a cabinet. To his right was a wooden table, atop which was the food, flashlights, an unlit oil lantern, and old cups, bowls, and plates. A coffee maker that looked like it was from the 1950's—all big shiny chrome—glinted in the thin daggers of moonlight that penetrated the frost and ice encrusted building. A mound of packs and gear sat at the ready just in case they had to leave in a hurry.

A pop snapped through the barrack, like a small caliber handgun firing a solitary shot.

Chance and Rai froze in the darkness, listening, but there was nothing but the angry wind.

"What the hell was that?" Rai asked.

Chance pointed up into the darkness and said, "Those wood beams up there. Even though they're very old, they still shrink and expand based on the temperature and moisture."

"Okay."

"When you were a kid, you don't remember being scared of the sounds your house made?" Chance said.

"I lived in an apartment," she said. "But there was this one sound, whenever it rained, a ticking like two pieces of wood scraping together."

"Same thing," Chance said. "Cold and dry conditions make the wood shrink, and heat or moisture expands it."

She said nothing, the whites of her eyes striving through the darkness.

Chance was mansplaining. "Sorry for the lecture."

"No worries," she said. "Are you—?"

A muffled scratching sound at the door.

Chance peered down the passage that ran through the center of the barrack, and Devero's silhouette could be seen at the end of the aisle, the whites of his eyes staring toward the front door. He'd heard the sound, along with the gentle snores and murmurs of dreamy adventures that sang in chorus with the wind, which was always underneath it all like a splinter in Chance's brain.

The scraping got louder and more intense, like someone was raking a knife blade over wood. The wind puffed and yelled, and beneath it . . . grunting? Heavy breathing or gurgling.

A wood beam popped, and Chance jumped.

There was a distant banging outside as if some part of a building had partially torn away and was hanging on as the wind fought to tear it away.

"Did you hear that?" Chance said. He needed to hear someone else say they had.

"What do you mean, the wind?"

Squeaks and clinks made Rai and Chance jerk their heads toward the row of bunks. Biggie's large, dark form dropped from his bed into his boots, and he shuffled to Chance's side. He said, "My shift."

Rai didn't hesitate, she vaulted to her feet and disappeared into the darkness toward her bunk.

"Guess that's what happens when a pretty girl asks you to play spin the bottle and you say no," Biggie said.

"You heard that?"

"Every pitiful second of it," Biggie said. "Go get some sleep. I'll wake Greg. We've got thi—"

A long, drawn-out scrape echoed through the building, accompanied by a perfectly timed crack of wood tightening.

Biggie went to the door and Chance got to his feet.

Wind hissed and yelled, ice and snow tinkling, the perpetual rumble of generators in the background.

"I've got this," Biggie said. "Get some shut-eye."

Chance didn't think he could sleep, but he nodded and

left Biggie alone. He walked down the center aisle, people sleeping and shifting in their bunks, talking to people that weren't there, coughing, farting, and gurgling.

A thump on the roof and Chance glanced up into the blackness. Another thump, very faint . . . the wind.

Tina, and three other people Chance didn't know, sat in a circle in front of the silent potbelly stove, passing around a flask of whiskey. He took a seat next to Tina and held out his hand, and a big man with a bushy beard handed him the flask. He couldn't see the man's face in the blackness, but Chance smelled his rancid alcohol-stained breath, the scent of body odor palpable.

Chance took a long pull, feeling the burn, relishing the glow of fuzzy peace. He passed the flask to Tina. Time dripped away, and when the flask was empty the other travelers retreated to their bunks one by one until only Tina and Chance were left.

"Didn't you just have guard duty?" Tina said.

He nodded, then realized she couldn't see him and said, "Yeah, but there's no way I can sleep."

"You should try."

"I will."

She coughed. "This place is something, huh?"

Chance said nothing because he knew what was coming, and he felt his grandfather staring down at him from his picture on the back wall.

"They say this place hasn't changed much since . . . your grandad was here."

People were always uncomfortable mentioning his grandfather as if they knew something of his fate Chance didn't. He brushed away the surge of frustration and anger. "Hence the lovely amenities."

She laughed, and said, "I chose to stay here, all the history, the old . . . It's like being back there. Don't you ever wonder what it was like that night your grandad and Roland Harvey got here? There was nothing. They were truly alone."

"Yup," Chance said. He didn't tell her about the scratches they'd found on the door, the tracks in the snow . . . It had all been there in his grandfather's diary that Roland had brought back with him.

A crack and the sound of shattering glass as an array of icicles broke from the overhang.

Tina jumped and Chance put a hand on her arm. "It's okay. Just falling icicles." He saw her head rotate as if searching.

Another thump on the roof . . . or was it sliding snow?

"You don't like to talk about your grandad, huh?" she said.

"It not that . . . it's just . . . do you know how it feels to live in another person's shadow?"

"He was just . . . Wasn't he in charge of the camera?"

Chance chuckled. "Yeah, because he lost to Roland by one second. He was a champion skier in his own right, some said better than Roland."

She waited.

"See that picture up on the—of course you can't—but you know it, right?"

"Yes."

"I've seen that picture of my grandad and Roland on the summit of Abominable for as long as I can remember. My dad had a copy. You see his face in the picture, the arm Roland has around his shoulders? It was all for show."

Still, Tina said nothing.

"Then, he makes a mistake and dies," Chance said. "Some stupid fall while he was focused on the camera. Roland says he arrived to find my grandfather and the camera gone—along with the proof of his run. A chunk of snowpack was gone, and Roland figured his partner had plummeted to his death."

"But I—"

"Then, he falls and almost kills himself on the lower run? The easy section? Whereupon he uses the equipment sled to get himself back to Fort Fortune?" Chance said.

"You sound like you don't believe it?"

Chance sighed. "It's just . . . it doesn't make sense. Grandad was a professional. He knew what he was doing, and it's hard to believe he would've set up his camera in a spot without checking its stability."

"What other possibility is there?"

Chance stared up at the outline of his grandfather's picture. Rage burned his stomach, blurred his vision, and sent daggers of pain through his head. He breathed, calming himself. Tina didn't know she'd just stepped on a live wire.

"Tina, I've got so many things in life I don't deserve . . . I don't know what I think. I really don't, but the whole story never sat right with me. And this—" Chance got to his feet, arms out as he worked his way through the darkness to the back wall. He lifted the picture from the nail on which it hung, turned it over so the old brown paper and worn metal hanging cord faced out, and he replaced the picture on the nail by its frame.

"It's time I leave it all behind. All of it. Maybe even riding. Definitely pro boarding, there are other things I can—"

Two loud pops as wood beams flexed and moved in the darkness. A systematic thumping and crunching, like heavy feet trudging through the snowpack on the roof. The wind whispered and sighed, shrieking and yelling in warning.

The stove pipe rattled and belched, the metal shaking and bending, chant-like puffing sounds pushing around the gaps of the potbelly's lid. The thumping on the roof stopped, and the stovepipe vibrated harder and faster, the hum spreading over the barrack.

People woke, rubbed sleep from their eyes, some dropping into boots and venturing toward the rear of the building to see what all the commotion was about. Others rolled over and went back to sleep, content in their safety. A crowd formed around Tina and Chance, and someone flicked on a flashlight.

The beam of light started on the cold stove, puffs of soot leaking from the unit's cover, then moved up the shaking stovepipe to where it penetrated the roof. Tiny icicles clung to the pipe where it went through the roof, and they sparkled in the flashlight beam.

The wind howled and screamed.

Thump. Thump. Thump.

The stove pipe shook violently as if the wind were trying to jerk it from the roof like a splinter, then fell still. The flashlight shut off, and the wind howled and chanted.

Folks strayed back to their bunks, the night deepening.

The green glow of Chance's watch told him it was 3:19 AM.

Tina said, "Whatever you decide, about riding I mean . . . whatever you decide to do, I'll support you and help any way I can."

Chance nodded.

"I mean it."

"Thanks."

"You need to get some sleep," Tina said. "If everything goes well, tomorrow is going to be a very long day. Go lay down for a bit. I've got—" The dark silhouette of her head leaned back as she looked up at the stovepipe hidden in the blackness. "I've got this, and you can be sure I'll wake you if I need you."

Chance ass-inched until his back was against the rear wall. The wood was cold, and he wedged a blanket between himself and the wall. "I'm good right here," he said. "I'm not leaving you alone." His eyelids dipped immediately, the alcohol doing its work well, the fuzziness of sleep working its way forward. He blinked and closed his eyes.

Jibber's face waited there, Terry, all the others. None of the visions had eyes, their dark sockets empty voids. Then, his grandfather was there, arguing with his dad, thereafter with Amy, the three of them debating what to do about him. It was a fantasy, a dream he'd had when he was at his lowest point. There would be an intervention, led by his grandfather, father, and Amy. They'd explain things, make him understand what he needed to do. They would save him.

Amy's milky white image shifted and swayed. He heard faint screaming, the wails of someone in great pain, a woman.

He fought from sleep, his senses slowly coming back online as he hovered between slumber and waking, the netherworld of misconception, dreams, and mental errors. He rubbed his eyes, eased off the wall, pushed to his feet, and dusted himself off.

The screaming persisted. He hadn't been dreaming. Flashlight beams snapped on, the barrack filling with harsh light. People leapt from their bunks, donned boots, and gathered like a flock of birds that didn't know which way was south.

The woman's voice he'd heard in his dreams cried and gurgled, her screams rising above the wind like an out of tune violin.

A mighty roar thundered over the mountain, the wind laughing, the crack and pop of ice breaking like an irregular drumbeat. Ice clinging to the rafters cracked and popped, spraying cold shards across the room like shrapnel.

A tiny mosquito of ice caught Chance on the cheek, and he drew back.

People murmured questions.

"We need to do something."

"You're not opening that door."

Shadows danced as bile crept up Chance's throat, his stomach sour.

Thumps on the roof, flashing lights bouncing around, tiny snowflakes drifting down as frost and ice shook free.

"Help me," shrieked the woman.

Gagging, coughing, and then nothing but the raging wind and the faint rumble of generators.

23

February 3, 2018, Fort Fortune—Elevation 9,871 feet

CHANCE PUSHED THROUGH the crowd to the front of the barrack, Biggie's voice rising above the tumult of fighting and pleading. The wind laughed and shrieked, the scent of body odor and disinfectant fighting the ageless musty smell of the old building. Frightened faces eyed Chance as he walked. Flashlight beams bounced around the room, shadows writhing and fighting, reaching into the light.

"Move or I'll move you!" Chance didn't know the voice.

"You and what army?" Biggie said.

Chance arrived at the front door to find people huddled around Biggie and an older man with thinning hair and a hawklike nose. Two younger men stood behind him, clearly backup.

"Someone needs help out there. What kind of man are you?" some dude said.

That last comment contorted Biggie's face and he took a step away from the door, fists clinched.

The two young strangers stepped forward to greet him.

"Okay," Chance said as stepped between Biggie and the two young men, palms out in a calming gesture. "Easy. There's no enemies behind the walls."

Biggie's shoulders slumped and he flexed his hands and rolled his shoulders.

"I'm not—"

A thin wail, then a long gurgle pierced the night.

The old guy at the front of the crowd said, “It’s killing her!”

“What’s your name?” Chance asked.

“We don’t have ti—”

“What is your name? Simple question.”

“Raftford. Brand Raftford. And these are my two youngest sons, Brad and Rob. Happy? We’re running out of time.”

“For what exactly?” Chance said. He needed to take things down a notch, his concern from earlier inserting itself in the temporal lobe of his brain. One misunderstanding could lead to a mob.

Snow tinkled on wood, the wind cajoling and whistling. Someone sniffled.

“What do you mean?” Brand said.

“I see you’ve got an ice axe taped to a stick. You think that’s . . . sufficient?” Chance asked.

Biggie chuckled like Chance had scored a point.

“Yeah . . . it’s . . . sufficient. Now, get the hell out of the way and let my boys do their thing.”

Another wail flooded over Chance like a splash of freezing water, pain burning his chest.

Brad and Rob surged forward without warning, driving Biggie backward until he was pressed against the door. Biggie lashed out with a massive left hook that caught Brad square on the jaw. An earsplitting crack echoed through the barrack, Brad’s head snapping back like a PEZ dispenser. The guy went down, holding his jaw and wailing like a teenager who’d just been grounded for the weekend.

Chance lunged to help Biggie, but Brand’s leg shot out and tripped him. Chance tumbled forward, arms outstretched, and he hit the floor in a tangle.

Biggie wasn’t having much better luck. His jaw-shattering blow had cost him valuable time, and in that split second Rob bowled into him and wrapped him up, driving him into the door repeatedly. Biggie's head bounced off the old wood, the hollow thud like a bass drum.

Brand leaped over Chance, trying to join the fray, but he wasn't nimble enough.

Chance grabbed the man's ankle as he flew by, and he was able to hold onto it just long enough to disturb Brand's balance. The guy toppled forward, smacked his head on the table next to the door, and fell. He didn't move.

The fight at the door was over, and with one final colossal push, Biggie was slammed into the doorframe. When Rob released him, Biggie slumped to the floor.

Rob unlatched the door and swung it open. Cold and snow charged into the barrack.

Chance's vision blurred and time slowed. He was sleep deprived, his nerves tap dancing on his spine, his eyes jiggling in their sockets, legs trembling.

Biggie moaned, but he was sitting up, head in his hands, blood dripping through his fingers.

Rob bolted through the open door, but only got two feet.

A white-haired arm ending in a massive hand swatted him back, three-inch claws raking across his face and upper body. A roar thundered through the night, blackness and cold leading the attack.

Blood splattered the snowpack outside the barrack's door, and Rob was propelled backward like he'd shot from a cannon, slamming into the doorjamb with a bone rattling crunch.

A large shadow, a flash of dirty white hair.

Rob crawled over the barrack's threshold, one arm hanging, the other clawing the floor. Dark patches appeared on his jacket, the tattered fabric around the gashes soaked with blood. He whimpered and cried as he dragged himself into the room.

Wind gusted and a flurry of snow and frozen mist billowed through the open door. Two red eyes cut through the white, and the doorway went dark as a shadow blocked the moonlight.

Rob was jerked back, and he screamed, clawing at the floor as he was pulled out the door.

As if they'd been frozen in time, and an alarm had sounded, everyone in the barrack started moving and talking at once. Frantic cries, panic, people packing, though he had no idea where they'd go. Chance tried to peer through the two boarded up windows at the front of the barrack, but they were caked with ice and snow.

"Close the door," someone yelled.

That felt all wrong and very right at the same time. What could they do for Rob? Nothing. But they could save themselves.

Brad was getting to his feet, holding his jaw, eyes on fire. He stumbled toward the open door and was met by a wall of dirty white hair. He bounced off the beast like he was in a cartoon, careening backward and tripping over his father who was still out cold. He hit the floor, his head bounced off the wood, a loud *pop* reverberating through the chaos.

Chance's frost-bitten cheeks stung, arm wound singing, his knees wobbling as he stood nailed to the floor.

Biggie had managed to get to one knee, but he was still out of the game.

Rob's decapitated corpse flew into the room, bouncing off the floor and flying into the crowd. Like a wet dog shaking off water, blood splatter painted the crowd, floor, bunks. The corpse slid across the floor like a slab of meat; gristle, blood, and backbone sticking from Rob's tattered neck.

Someone shrieked, and like a troop of monkeys, the scream was answered with others—crying, wailing, and panic filling the room as everyone ran for the rear of the barrack.

A growl, and Chance's head snapped around.

The creature stooped, filling the open doorway, red eyes panning back and forth like Sauron's eye. Fangs hung over blood-stained lips, the white hair on the creature's chest matted with dried blood. The stench of rot and decay wafted through the room, the beast's harsh breathing like the chug of a truck's exhaust. The creature was at least eight feet tall, and as it bent and squeezed through the doorway, it almost got stuck. It growled and hissed, drawing itself up to its full height, bloodshot eyes searching, jaws opening in a toothy grin.

Chance started when he saw the wound on the beast's hand, and slipped his hand into a jacket pocket, gripping his grandfather's knife, the metal bringing comfort and confidence.

The creature stood still for a heartbeat, its long apelike arms hanging by its sides, dark three-inch talons at the end of each finger three feet from the floor. Snow hissed as it melted, steam lifting from the beast's dirty strands of knotted hair, pain cutting across the creature's leathery face. It hunched over, clearly uncomfortable in the confined space, and let loose with a deafening cry.

Riding skills, like video games or any precision expertise, requires years of training and experience to hone and build. The building of muscle memory that knows what's better for its host than its boss, the brain. Bank right or left? The brain worked too slowly to provide an answer in ride time, so boarders were taught to go with their instinct, to look ahead for potential pitfalls long before said decision needs to be made, then react accordingly. This was rarely a rational process, and split-second decision making sometimes led to unintended consequences.

Chance grabbed the oil lamp from the table next to the door, stabbed the ignitor button until a tiny blue-white flame rose from the wick, and threw the lantern at the beast.

It hit the creature in the chest and fell to the floor, splattering paraffin.

The beast paused, patting itself with its dirty hands, then bringing them to its nose, sniffing.

The lantern's wick was still burning, fuel leaking over the floor, beneath the creature's feet.

Womp.

Flames exploded from the broken lamp, crawling across the floor, and climbing up the screaming beast. Heat rolled off the creature as its hair caught fire, the beast stomping and wailing, waving its arms as it tried in vain to put out the flames.

Fire ran up the barrack's walls, rushing over the old ceiling joists, sparks and ash falling like snow. The fire alarm wailed, red daggers of light knifing through the darkness.

The monster took a step and threw back its head, white hair gone, its blackened leathery face melting away. The beast stumbled forward, reaching, and sprawled over Brad's corpse, but didn't fall.

"The gear!" It was Biggie. His friend was back on his feet, and he'd positioned himself between the creature and their pile of backpacks.

Heat rolled through the barrack in waves, the ceiling and walls on fire, flames advancing, crawling, licking the bunks. Everyone who was able had crowded into the rear of the building, and Chance heard chopping and cracking wood as someone pried open the rear door. The back entrance wasn't maintained and usually wasn't shoveled, despite fire code requiring two exits. The alarm chimed in a steady beat, filling Chance's head.

The creature stopped flailing, its red eyes going dark as it stumbled forward, the scent of burning flesh filling Chance's nostrils.

"Hurry!" Biggie frantically tossed backpacks up the center aisle.

Stifling heat like a blazing furnace blasted Chance in the face, the fire sucking the air from the room, smoke stinging his eyes, frost-bitten cheeks burning. He pulled up his shirt, covering his nose, but it didn't help. The front of the barrack was fully engulfed in flames, and Chance stumbled through the smoke, arm out like a blind man, mind spinning as fumes filled his lungs.

"Come on," he said when he reached Biggie, who was still jerking and tossing bags like he worked on a luggage team at an airport. When he didn't stop working, Chance grabbed his arm. "That's enough!"

That broke the trance, and Biggie paused, staring through the smoke at Chance. Then, the two men were moving, hopping over backpacks, pulling and dragging them away from the flames, toward the rear of the barrack.

A loud thumping and cracking and splintering echoed through the room as someone hacked at the rear door, the wood yelling and complaining.

The beast straightened, flames covering the creature's entire body. Burnt hair, smoke, cooking flesh . . . Chance choked as the creature drove forward, reaching for Chance and Biggie as they retreated. The creature bumped into bunks on both sides of the aisle, and flames crawled over the beds, blankets, and thin mattresses. The fiery figure raged one last time, a cry that faded to a gurgle as the beast fell face first, a shower of sparks and smoke billowing around it. The fire alarm shrieked, wood cracking and popping.

"What about Brand?" Biggie yelled.

Cracking wood and a mountainous crash as the front wall gave way and collapsed, sending sparks, balls of fire and smoke, and wooden shards scattering across what remained of the barrack. Wind and swirling snow poured in through the gaping hole, pushing back the flames as Chance and Biggie retreated, dragging backpacks. Several people saw what they were doing and helped, a ragged chain forming as the realization that their level of screwed went up exponentially if they didn't have their gear.

A scream of joy pierced the chaos. "Got it!"

The line before the rear door was clogged, and Chance and Biggie could go no farther. The top half of the door had been cut away, and people were climbing out through the hole onto the thick snowpack. Bags were passed through the hole, folks lifted and pulled. Everyone who rode extreme peaks was in good shape for the most part, and it only took a couple of minutes for the barrack to clear out.

Chance was the last person out, the heat within the barrack unbearable. Flames consumed everything. As he climbed from the burning building, the main support beam cracked. Chance dropped his pack and ran.

The barrack came down in a glorious display of fiery shooting stars, balls of flame and smoke. Shards of fire licked the darkness; sparks flew like fireflies. The melting snow hissed. The fire alarm squeaked and stuttered, then fell silent with a final awkward shriek that sounded like a robot dying.

"Everyone okay?" Biggie asked.

Murmurs and wagging heads as the group stood around like a group of teenagers at a high school dance. Heat rolled off the fire in waves. A deep sorrow washed over Chance, a feeling of failure so great he wanted to give up. Right there. Just sit in the snow and let darkness and cold wait for time to do its thing. He plopped onto his ass, staring at the flames, thinking of marshmallows, ghost stories, and good times long gone.

Biggie put a hand on his shoulder. "You alright?"

Chance said nothing. Brand and his dead sons' faces filling his mind.

"Where's your pack?" his friend asked.

"Where is everyone?" Chance said from his daze.

"Right here," Tina said. "All present and accounted for." She stood with Colin and Bomber behind Biggie.

Biggie persisted. "Your pack?"

Chance pointed back toward the fire, and Biggie retrieved the bag. It had a few burn holes in it from ash and flying debris, but the flame-retardant material worked well, and his belongings, including his sleeping bag, personals, and four power bars were safe—though, he figured the bars were melted.

The five companions said no more as they watched the barrack burn. It had been an original building, part of Fort Fortune since its inception. Melting snow hissed like voices, steamy ghosts writhing above the flames, puffing, and chanting, Chance's grandfather among them.

A gust of wind stirred the flames, and the specters dissipated.

24

FORT FORTUNE WAS aglow with the dying fire, ash falling like snow, sparks filling the air, the wind dancing with smoke. Chance rubbed his eyes, head pounding, his muscles like wet noodles as the adrenaline receded. The commotion had died down, and most folks had retreated to the dormitory to find a spot for the night. The fire was under control and on its way out, though the embers would be hot for days. The rumble of generators filled the night, beating back the howl of the wind. Pools of light leaked from beneath the Lucky Strike's entrance and around boarded-up windows. The glowing windows of the dormitory stood out like eyes in the darkness, the black patch of nothingness marking the destroyed warehouse in the backdrop. Tattered clouds ran overhead, the storm in the west a wall of dark cotton against the star-filled horizon, the snow-covered Sawatch Range shimmering in the moonlight. The scent of charred meat blended with the smoke, and Chance's sleep deprived mind thought of hamburgers, then Brand and his sons.

Tina coughed, and Chance heard the crunch of snow as his crew shifted on their feet behind him. They stood before the fire, Chance still lost in the flames, mind not fully back online, various red warning lights in the control center of his brain singing. His crew was waiting for him to tell them what to do next. Somehow, he'd become the leader. Funny how that happens. He didn't feel like a leader. Quite the opposite. He was a failure, and as the body count rose, and hysteria took hold, his guilt over Jibber and the others grew. His friends had come to Abominable Peak because of him.

The fire and blackened area surrounding the destroyed barrack was like a bloody wound on baby flesh. Flames fifteen feet tall still licked the darkness, sparks swirling like miniature cyclones, the mound of embers and heated metal ten feet high. Snow hissed and screamed as it melted, and around the edges of the charred area the snow had fully thawed, leaving a ring of mud and a series of puddles. Beyond the mud, slush grew in thickness as it rose up to the snowpack. The pristine powder of Fort Fortune was gray with soot; roofs, paths, every vertical surface stained with the remains of the hangar, and the barracks and its dead.

Biggie said, “What are you thinking?”

Chance turned, his arm reminding him he had four deep gashes barely healed. He held in a squeak of pain and said nothing.

Biggie looked into the flames.

Chance could only imagine what he must look like. Dirty, panic-stricken, covered in soot and dried blood, eyes bloodshot and frantic. He was in no condition to make this decision, but as he surveyed his friends he realized if he didn’t take charge nobody would. At their core, these were pampered professional snowboarders who were used to being fawned over, getting everything they wanted the second they wanted it. They were lost without handlers guiding them, telling them what to do. His crew might be able to ride the gnarliest hills, face immense dangers without so much as a moment’s thought, yet here, amongst the desolation and despair, they had no frame of reference. Chance had to get knocked on his ass before he truly began to understand life, the way the world works, but his buddies had yet to take their falls.

“We go find our boards or skis, and we get the hell out of here. Now,” Tina said. “That requires discussion?”

"In the dark? It's still hours until daylight, and you want to go sliding in zero-degree weather, with a storm coming, in the dark, with . . . those things . . . out there." Biggie threw up his hands.

Colin said, "What's your plan then? Hide out? That didn't work very well."

"No, it didn't," said Chance. His voice was just audible above the shrieking wind, the pop and crack of the fire, and the hum and hiss of melting ice and snow.

"I say we head to the dormitory," Biggie said. "Strength in numbers. There's got to be at least fifty people in there. You're telling me you think these things can take out fifty of us?"

"No," Chance said, turning to face his crew. "But they can take out some . . . you want that to be you?"

"And you know how that always works out. We'll end up taking on strays," Tina said, but she looked away, embarrassed.

"The way I see it, we've got two options," Colin said.

"So, which is it?" added Bomber.

"May I suggest a third option?" came a voice from the darkness just outside the fire's light.

Shadows writhed and gyrated, falling across Chance and his crew as three newcomers emerged from the smoky haze.

A short rat-like man held out a hand. "Wes Grant." Behind him, a woman and man who looked like fraternal twins flanked him on both sides.

"I've heard of you," Biggie said. "You're that agent. The guy with an ad in RIDE 'Zine."

"That's me," he said. "Up here, recruiting." He shot Chance a sideways glance.

Chance chuckled to himself. The guy certainly wasn't a rider, not with his water-stained alligator boots, jeans, silk shirt, and shearling jacket. "Care to share this third possibility?"

"Do nothing," Wes said.

Snow hissed, generators buzzed, wood popped and crackled, and the wind sang a mournful tune.

"Well, isn't that brilliant," Tina said. "That how you sell your clients? See, we just sit and do nothing, and all kinds of good things will just happen. Like magic."

Colin piled on, "Always works well."

"That's why I'm not recruiting either of you. No vision," Wes said, a snake-smirk spreading over his milky face, beady shards of shining onyx appraising Tina and crew like they were bugs not worthy of a swatting. He didn't look Chance's way.

Chance had nothing left; his patience had long ago fled, his body was in full revolt, and while the cold had been beaten back, darkness and time continued their attack. The deepest weariness he'd never experienced soaked him, his limbs filled with cement, his head a pool of confusion and throbbing pain. "Just spit it out, will you?" he said.

"Or go away," Biggie said.

"Really? You need me to explain this to you?" Wes looked over his shoulder at his partners. "We've got light, heat, a wide-open perimeter right here." He spread his arms, indicating the large open area surrounding the charred wound where the barrack had been. "We set up camp right here at the edge of the firelight, post a few guards and wait it out until morning."

"Hide in plain sight?" Chance said.

"We'll be able to see the things coming if they attack," Wes said.

"What do we need you for?" Colin asked.

"You don't need me, but this might be useful." Wes produced a Heckler & Koch VP9 pistol.

"Who are your partners?" Bomber asked.

"Minka and Mina. Brother and sister board team from Norway. Just missed the Olympics last year. You may have heard."

Chance hadn't.

Tina said, "Yeah, I remember. Minka, you placed third at Steven's Pass last year, yeah?"

The large Norwegian nodded.

"They're a family of few words," Wes said. "So, what do you say? We dig some snow holes and hunker down?" He held up the gun. "I can stand first watch."

"This isn't up to me, though the more I think about it, the more it makes sense ," Chance said. "Biggie?"

"I'll get digging," the big man said, and he dropped his pack in the mud.

Tina sighed and looked to Colin and Bomber, who were staring into the fire. "Fine," she said.

The new team of eight got to work, and within an hour there were four large snow holes dug like Hobbit holes into the slope of the snowpack around the charred zone. The heat had caused melting as far away as fifty feet, and the compacting snow was excellent for making snow structures. Fort Fortune had fallen still, the rumble of generators, shifting sugary snow, and the never-ending harassment of the wind the only sounds.

Light still spilled from the Lucky Strike and the dormitory, folks burning the midnight oil and keeping watch like Chance and his troop. He couldn't help feeling they'd be better off inside the cinderblock walls of the dorm, but the primal side of his brain made a stronger argument—sometimes being part of the masses made you a target. He liked this half measure, and they could run more easily . . . then he realized that wasn't true. They'd lost their boards in the fire, so unless they intended to hike all the way down to Gordan Gulch, they needed to find some old boards, and he knew exactly where there'd be some.

He turned from the fire, the entrances to the four snow holes glowing with lights that spilled out onto the snowpack. As the fire died, the melted snow refroze, forming a thick coating of verglas on the fringe of the burn site. Beyond their snowy Hobbiton, the dormitory, destroyed warehouse, still puffing smoke, glowed in the starlight.

Chance called, “Biggie, you awake?”

“No,” Biggie said.

“Get out here.”

Grunts, curses, then Biggie emerged, jacket open, hat askew, boots untied. “What is it?”

Chance waved him off and called to Wes, who was walking around the fire like a prison guard, the H&K at the ready.

“Be right back,” he called out, and Wes raised his hand.

“Come on,” Chance said. He had his knife, and the ice axe. Biggie had the club he’d made from a table leg.

“The shed?” Biggie guessed, and Chance nodded.

The duo walked the beaten path, going behind the dormitory, coming around the smoldering ruins of the warehouse, and passing behind a large snowdrift that was excavation equipment covered in tarps and snow. The shed was secured, and Chance paused before the closed doors, his memory somersaulting back to Francesca.

“You alright?” Biggie asked.

Chance’s arm throbbed, yelling, screaming, reminding . . . He hadn’t described the scene inside the shed to his crew in detail. He said, “You might want to wait out here.”

Biggie harrumphed, undid the door latch, and pulled open door to the snowmobile shack.

The rank stench of death hung in the air, that coppery rot smell that sticks to clothes and burrows deep into noses and lungs. Biggie flicked on his torch and the LED light cast wavering light across the blood-splattered shed.

Francesca’s body had been removed, but the black puddle of dried blood, and the dark footprints made Chance’s stomach turn.

Biggie stepped inside the shed, hugging the wall so he didn’t step in the carnage. “You weren’t kidding.” He stopped when the flashlight beam fell on the snow riders. “I assume none of them work?”

"Wires are torn out."

Biggie turned to look at Chance, squinting, forehead wrinkled.

Chance hiked his shoulders. "Come on."

The storage shed had been picked through, and there wasn't much to be found, but the old wooden box made from dismantled supply pallets had several boards, skis, but no poles—ski poles made good spears. Most of the boards were damaged, but several were ridable.

Chance picked through the bin of misfit boards and solo planks, thinking about how they'd been discarded like trash. His Burton Reaper had served him well.

A pink GNU runner with blue sunflowers and a busted nose caught his eye, and Chance pulled it free.

"Woot!" Biggie said. "That sunflower's kissed wood."

"Or a rock. I like it." The rounded nose of the board was splintered, but with a little work, Chance could dull the ragged edge. If he was counting on the nose of the board for help, he was in trouble anyway.

"There's not much here, but we're only gliding. We'll be taking it slow," Biggie said as he plucked out more boards for the crew.

The pair also found a bent ski pole, and a broken hammer, the old metal head and broken handle of little use in its current state. They packed everything onto the biggest snowboard, and pushed out into the darkness, closing the door behind them.

Chance felt better breathing in the cold night air, Francesca's blood, and her eyeless face in the rearview.

He and Biggie were halfway back to camp—Biggie pulling the snowboard sled with their plunder tied to it—when the dormitory's generator sputtered, coughed, and stalled. The building went dark, the dull glow of battery powered emergency lights leaking from windows and under doors going out, the faint murmur of music silenced.

The wind died away, sugary snow shifting over ice, the

front edge of the storm obscuring the moon, shadows and darkness filling every empty space. A faint clicking rose above the breeze, a tap of wood, or the rattle of bones, or the mashing of powerful jaws. Warmth spread through Chance's chest like he'd taken a shot of whiskey, his heart fighting to escape.

Biggie nudged Chance forward, and the pair slogged the last few hundred feet to camp.

The fire had mostly died away, white flames dancing above orange-white embers, thin wisps of black smoke drifting off what was left of the burnt wood and melted metal.

Biggie pulled the snowboard sled in front of his snow hole, dropped the lead line, and disappeared back into his hole without a word.

Wes arrived, gun at his side. "All good?"

Chance nodded. "I'll take watch. No way I'm sleeping." His gaze drifted toward the dark dormitory.

Wes looked at his feet, then at his gun, and nodded. He held out the H&K but drew it back slightly when Chance reached out to take it. "You know how to work one of these, right?"

"Point and pull the trigger?"

Wes sighed. "Close enough. The VP9 has the trigger safety latch . . . here." He pointed. "Also has a standard firing pin block like any striker-fired pistol, but what you really need to pay attention to is right here." He thumbed up the release and depressed the trigger safety. "See that?" His index finger marked a small red dot located on the rear of the slide. "That there is the cocking indicator, when you see that red dot, you're good to go."

"Got it."

"I'll send Minka out to relieve you in an hour."

"There's no—"

"One hour."

Wes handed Chance the gun, and he nodded.

Chance's mind drifted as he walked around the glowing heap of charred wood and metal, shapes forming in the embers as they cooled. A crampon, a metal water container, shriveled and crunched, black plastic sculptures of unknown origin, and . . .

The H&K felt heavy in his hand as he stared into the fire.

Beneath a twisted section of metal springs that had once been the innards of an old mattress, a black human skull stared up out from the embers, its two empty eye sockets filled with flames.

25

THE DOLDRUMS BEFORE dawn provide many advantages to those in tune with the rhythms of the night, the cycle of the Earth, and its creatures. There's a reason law enforcement shift changes happen in early morning and late evening when the world was in slumber. Circadian rhythms were different for every creature, but even in New York's hippest clubs, things winded down by 3:30 AM. Animals have their own, often foreign sleep patterns, their own ideas about when they felt most in control, in power. Chance's nerves danced at the thought. Dawn was only a couple of hours off, and he knew—not guessed, but knew—the creatures would either act before the sun came up, or not at all.

Chance and Biggie rested in a snow hole atop a platform of snowpack covered in mylar blankets, wrapped in their bags, fully clothed, except for boots. Moonlight angled in the hole, and every two minutes Minka would walk past the tent as he patrolled around the glowing remains of the barrack. Chance and his buddy couldn't sleep. They were too pumped-up, at the end of a run but unable to finish. It was like tarps being pulled over a ballfield when it rains. He itched to move forward, his palms stinging. He reached up to his breast and felt his single pain pill in the protective cylinder.

"Where you heading from here?" Biggie asked.

"Don't know." Chance chuckled. "I'd planned on

spending the season at Fort Fortune, then head home for the summer to decide if I wanted to try and make the circuit next year, but now . . . ”

“You'll be back on the circuit whenever you want. It doesn't . . . You're a legacy.”

“And I'll sell ads at the X-Games,” Chance said.

“That too. I can see the profile film now.”

The warble of a fire alarm pierced the night.

“Here we go,” Biggie said as he pushed off his icy platform into his boots.

Chance slipped into his boots and zipped up as he and Biggie headed out into the night, his arm wound stinging with cold as it reminded him it was still there.

The new dormitory was emptying from every exit, folks in night clothes bundled in their riding gear, boots untied, hats on and arms crossed in both frustration and for heat containment. People were yelling, and Stefan burst from the front entrance, guiding guests out. He was in long underwear, no jacket or hat. There was no sign of a fire.

Minka spun like a ballerina on crack, turning around, arms outstretched, the VP9 held in a double-handed grip, eyes frantic as he searched the darkness.

Wes, Tina, and the others emerged from their snowy holes, rubbing sleep from crusty eyes, and pulling on jackets and hats.

“What is it?” Tina said.

“It came at me . . . but . . . ” Minka's face twisted as he swung the gun around.

A snarl from the darkness to the south, the fire alarm wailing.

Minka spun and fired, the crack and pop of the H&K echoing over Fort Fortune. The bullet zipped through the air, then faded. Minka stood rigid, gun out, peering down its sight.

The fire alarm stopped screaming.

“What are you shooting at?” Chance said.

"It's out there. Right now. Watching us. Waiting. I saw its shadow," Minka said.

Folks were funneling back into the dormitory, and Stefan called over, "All good over there? We've got rooms for you all. Come inside."

Minka let the gun fall to his side. "Screw this." He started toward the dormitory, Mina in tow, their forms becoming silhouettes as they walked away from the embers' glow.

Wes flicked on a flashlight and trained it on the Norwegian like a laser. "Not with the gun you're not."

A streak of white, a massive dirty mop materializing from the darkness, emerging from the snowpack like a wraith. The beast roared as it charged Minka.

The Norwegian brought up the Heckler & Kock and fired, no hesitation and smooth as silk. He kept firing as the massive creature wrapped him up and drove him backward. The VP9 barked, 9mm rounds knifing through the creature and hitting the smoldering ruins of the barrack.

The H&K clicked empty, and the beast drove forward, legs churning, muscles rippling with the last of its strength as the beast wrapped Minka up and drove him backward.

The Norwegian slipped in the mud, and the empty VP9 fell from his hand as he clawed at the beast's face, struggling, and screaming.

Minka and the creature tumbled onto the glowing embers, the beast's hair catching fire as it lay atop the Norwegian, who screamed in horror and pain as his clothes caught fire and his skin and muscles burned from his bones.

A *womp* echoed over the remains of Fort Fortune and screaming and chaos erupted from the people trailing back into the dorm. A fireball landed amidst one of the lines, and people scattered like seagulls, clawing up snowdrifts. Screaming and yelling silenced the wind as people fled in every direction, climbing onto the snowpack, and running blindly into the night.

Minka screamed as flames consumed him, the beast's charred remains atop him melting around him. The rank scent of burning flesh wafted over the scene, the wind stirring and shaping the smoke, sparks like escaping fireflies. Minka gurgled, cried out for Mina, then went quiet.

Mina screamed, her rage and sorrow boiling over.

A creature appeared at the edge of the embers' glow, creeping around the pile of blazing debris that had been the barracks, the beast's long shadow falling over the mud and slush.

Womp. Womp. More fireballs landing like bombs.

The beast stepped into the light, and Colin and Bomber gasped in unison.

It was easily ten feet tall, covered in dirty strands of natty white hair, its red bloody eyes locked on Chance and company. Steam lifted from its shoulders as snow and ice knotted in its tangled coat melted, dirty water dripping from long icicle-like strands. Its face was contorted with rage, distended cheeks puffing in and out, steam blowing from the creature's flat nose like a train stack. It took a slow step forward and growled.

"Screw this," Bomber said as he ran.

A sharp scream of pain as Bomber went down, shadows dancing, a massive white carpet slamming him to the ground.

"No!" yelled Biggie, and he threw himself toward the fray, swinging his club as he screamed in fury, but Bomber was too far away, and he was too late.

The wind howled and screamed, smoke filling the air. The beast was on Bomber, who scratched and clawed at the monster as it held him in the mud, slashing at his face and neck with its three-inch claws. Blood splattered the snow, Bomber floundering and fighting until his body went limp.

The beast stopped pounding the corpse an instant before Biggie's club struck home, and it brought up an arm to partially block the blow. The creature wailed, a guttural yell of hatred and warning and victory.

The sound of breaking glass filled the night as dormitory windows shattered. The alarm wailed again, and this time smoke billowed from windows and open doors.

Biggie pulled back and swung for the fences again, the club swinging in a wide arc, the bat connecting with the side of the beast's head.

Two more creatures appeared, blocking the northern and southern escape routes. With the barrack's red-hot embers to the west, and the steep incline to the east with their Hobbit holes in its side, there were no options.

Chance pulled his grandfather's knife, flipped it in his hand, blade out in fighting position, though he had no illusions. If one of the things got hold of him, it was game over.

Biggie was knocked aside by a powerful strike from his enemy's baseball mitt-sized hand, and he went flying and landed in the slush and mud. He got to his knees, shaking his head, but he stayed there for three heartbeats catching his breath, and that saved his life.

His opponent lashed out, anticipating Biggie driving to his feet, but instead, its massive four fingered hand passed directly over Biggie's head, and Chance's friend rolled to the side and avoided the blow.

Tina, Wes, and the rest had their backs to the Hobbit holes, staring at the bedlam, eyes wide. They held primitive weapons at their sides and didn't look eager to join the fight.

People screamed, the wind laughed, and Chance's crew stared at him, waiting for guidance.

Biggie vaulted to his feet and swung his club, a colossal blow that connected with the creature's face. Blood spewed from the monster's flat apelike nose, its blood-stained eyes rolling in opposite directions.

Biggie swung again and again and again. Connecting each time, horrible thuds echoing over Fort Fortune.

The beast fell to its knees, prayed there for an instant, then fell face forward into the mud.

Biggie dropped to a knee, the club falling from his hands.

The creatures looking on howled, primal, guttural screams of frustration and pain. As if controlled by one mind, they threw their heads back and charged, powerful legs pumping, mud and slush flying.

Biggie fell in next to Chance.

Fight or flight. Chance surveyed his options one last time, but with the creatures coming at him from the north and south, and a mound of glowing rubble to the west, that left east. He ran in that direction, heading for where his crew, Wes, and Mina stood planted in the mud.

Chance heard Biggie's footfalls splashing behind him, and he didn't slow when he reached the slope with the snow holes burrowed into its side. He jumped, boots digging into the sugary snow as he tried to drive his momentum forward and up. His knees quaked, and for a fluttering heartbeat, Chance thought he was going to fall backward. Instead, he overcorrected and fell forward into the snow. His legs churned as he clawed at the incline, sliding in the loose snow, his hands cramping with cold.

Everyone followed, there were no words needed, and as the companions climbed for their lives, Chance had a brief jolt of hope.

It didn't last long.

Tina slipped, her feet sliding in the slush, and she skidded to the bottom of the slope where she landed in the mud and slush.

Chance stopped climbing.

Colin started back down, but time had won this race, and when the smaller of the two creatures arrived at the base of the incline, it grabbed Tina's foot and dragged her to the ground. She screamed and fought, twisting over onto her back, kicking and fighting with everything she had.

The beast gurgled, and it sounded too much like a laugh to Chance. Anger bloomed in him like a stinkweed. He flipped his blade in his hand and launched it at the beast's face.

The throw was successful, and not.

The knife hit the creature square between the eyes with the handle end. The knife fell away, and the monster reared back, Tina's foot slipping from its grasp.

She righted herself and scrambled up the incline, frantic, spindrifts and chunks of ice cascading down the slope behind her.

Colin planted his feet and waited, hand out.

Tina's climb was agonizingly slow, like a glacier moving, and Chance felt the hated mice traipsing up his spine. She reached Colin, and he helped her up the incline, his hand on her back, pushing and guiding as he braced himself after each step.

Chance continued his climb, panting hard, his stomach a knot of pain, acid creeping up his throat.

Biggie was the first to reach the snowpack above, and he held a hand out for Mina who was directly behind him, Wes behind her.

Chance struggled and fought. The incline was only twenty feet high, but it was like trying to climb in water. For each foot he advanced, he slipped back two. His tank was empty, muscles running on fumes. His knees buckled, and he slipped down the incline toward the beasts, who stood waiting patiently, shifting from foot to foot, staring up as they waited for a starling to fall from its nest.

Colin grabbed Chance's arm and stopped his slide.

Chance cried out in pain, the scabs on his wounded arm breaking free, hot blood dripping down his sleeve. Colin yanked him up, and Chance was able to dig in his toes and propel himself up the slope. He looked down the incline, and the two beasts were gone. Shadows danced in the slick mud puddles around the remains of the barrack, the glow of the dead fire reflecting off verglas and powder.

Biggie screamed.

26

UNDERESTIMATING ONE'S OPPONENT is a fundamental sin. At a minimum, said transgression creates unnecessary work and needless losses. At worst, it kills.

Chance's stomach sank, the realization that he'd been outmaneuvered by abominable snowmen settling in his gut like bad clams. Tall shadows ran over the snowpack and down the incline, a massive figure lunging toward a smaller one—Biggie. A gurgled roar, and when the shadows were almost touching one disappeared.

Biggie leaped back down the slope, feet first, arms out before him. He slid into Mina, who careened into Wes, and the three companions skidded down the hill, crashing into the mud and slush in a jumble of arms, legs, and pride. Curses and screams as the trio untangled, the wind laughing and chanting at them.

When he was a boy Chance read that playing video games could improve eye-hand coordination. That was all he had needed. It was a bazooka in the ongoing war with his mom about how much time he was allowed to waste in front of the TV directing a digital hero through mazes and castles, dragons roaring at him. Like balance and coordination, fast decision making was key to success when boarding, and in the time it took his heart to beat twice, he decided what to do.

Chance jumped, turning himself around as he slid down the slope. He patted Colin on the back, smiled at Tina as he zipped past, and landed next to Biggie with a splash of mud and slush.

Tina and Colin landed beside him.

Then everyone was moving, running toward their snow holes as if some type of protection could be found there.

Chance stood staring after his companions, knees aching, blood dripping down his arm into his glove. The fire's embers were fading, cold and time doing their work, and the puddles farther away from the heat were freezing, the stars, moon, and encroaching clouds reflected therein. He didn't know what to do. Or was it that he didn't want to do anything because he no longer cared? Sorrow washed over him as he stared at the line of blood and entrails in the mud and slush. Bomber's corpse had been hauled away into the blackness.

The wind laughed and sang.

"You coming?" Biggie yelled.

Chance said nothing. Where was there to go?

Biggie stomped back through the mud and grabbed Chance's arm. "It's time. Let's go."

Anger rifled through him. Who the hell was this asshole to tell him what to do? He thought of the pill in his jacket pocket, tuned out the cajoling wind and menacing darkness. His grandfather, his parents, Amy, all arguing, stating their cases, telling him what he should do. Chance opened his mouth to scream, his brain preparing to jerk his arm from Biggie's grasp, but the order wasn't issued, and Chance said nothing. His friend . . . *friend* . . . was trying to help him.

Chance nodded.

"Whatever you think you need, you better grab it fast," Biggie said. "We're strapped in and gone in ninety seconds."

His stomach sank again. Ninety seconds wasn't a very long time, or it could be a lifetime. He was happy Biggie was taking control. Chance didn't think he was capable . . . or wanted to be the answer man anymore. He followed Biggie into their snow hole and balled up his mylar blanket and stuffed it in his jacket pocket. He had his boots and gloves on, but when he saw the glint of his replacement goggles, he slipped them on. His backpack and other belongings would have to remain behind. Boarding with the pack on was difficult due to his injury and, truth be told, he didn't need the stuff anymore, so he left it all behind.

Mina, Wes, and Tina waited by the snowboards, which were stuck end up in the side of the slope like decorated tombstones on a snowy hillside.

"I can't ride," Wes said. "I just know how to talk like I do."

"Take one anyway, ja?" Mina said. Chance thought that may have been the first time he'd heard the woman speak. Tear streaks lined her dirty face. Her brother dead and gone, yet she was still thinking about her agent.

Chance grabbed his replacement board, its nose cracked and ragged. He hadn't had an opportunity to fix it—that bitch time again—but he wasn't concerned as he bent and tied his boots tight before stepping into the undersized bindings.

Biggie and the others grabbed boards without a word. There was nothing left to say. There was no more hiding, no more hunkering down and waiting for daylight.

The confusion and turmoil at the dormitory hadn't settled down. White smoke leaked from windows, people screamed and screeched, and beyond it, the tangle of metal and burnt wood that had been the storage warehouse looked on as if relishing its role as the first domino to fall.

"Here," Wes said. "I believe this is yours?"

Chance received his grandfather's knife. He'd forgotten all about it. "Thank you."

"Found it in the mud."

Chance held the closed blade in his gloved palm, fighting back the tear struggling to break free and slide down his face. "You're not going to try and ride?" he said.

Wes looked away, staring at the moon where it settled

on the southwest horizon. Mina stood next to him. She wasn't leaving her agent, brother's death or no, and Chance had to laugh to himself.

"Let's go," Biggie yelled.

Three minutes had passed since Biggie leaped down the snowdrift and started the retreat.

"We'll be right behind you," Wes said.

Biggie inched forward, his board shrieking in the mud as it ran over stones and debris that had been buried beneath the snowpack. The road ran west out of the valley—the easiest route out of Fort Fortune.

Chance hoped the beasts didn't realize that.

When they glided around the glowing remains of the barracks, Chance saw footprints, and the tracks of the snowmobiles and snowcat trailing west, turning south as the road plunged five hundred feet in a quarter mile.

Chance thought of his grandfather, the old Willys he and his partner had used to get to Fort Fortune on their fateful trip. He'd ridden in it once when he was very young. His father had kept it in the garage like an ancient relic, and now that Chance was older, he'd realized that's exactly what the old Jeep had been.

Tops of trees and stones stuck from the snowbank along the road. Chance worked his legs back and forth as he sliced through the coating of loose powder, bumping over chunks of ice kicked up by the snowmobiles and the snowcat. He got low, tucking in his broken wing, and holding the knife out in the fighting stance with his other hand.

Biggie led, Tina in his wake, Colin behind Chance. He looked back and barely saw Wes and Mina as they trudged through the snow, their two silhouettes shrinking into darkness. Chance thought of Trevor, Stefan, Shelly, all the people he knew at Fort Fortune. Suddenly everyone who had been together were now on their own.

Ice shrieked as he cut around a turn, throwing a wave of powder. Funny how that worked. People had no problem being together when sharing a common obsession, yet when it came to life, to the things that really mattered, everyone was on their own. He remembered his mother explaining this to him as he sat next to her on the subway. The train had screeched, and the lights went out as they often did when the train entered the station. The woman next to him had clutched his young arm, bony fingers digging in flesh, and he'd almost screamed, but young boys needed to be tougher than that, so he'd held it in. He hadn't understood why a stranger would touch him like that, like she needed his help. When the lights came back on, she released him, the danger past, everyone on their own again. But in that moment, with darkness working its magic, everyone in that train car was together, everyone in the same boat.

A huge menacing dark shape slipped from behind a stone and blocked Biggie's path.

Chance tried to scream, but instead his dry mouth only croaked.

Biggie jerked his board horizontal in one smooth motion, changing direction, avoiding the creature but putting himself on course to hit an enormous boulder that stuck from the snowbank like a stop sign at an intersection. He leaned forward, pushing his legs back, outward, and up, his board lifting from the snow as it rode the side of the rock, Biggie horizontal to the ground. He straightened, board back in the powder, and launched off a ledge and disappeared down the southern slope, the beast's hairy white head and searching eyes silhouetted against the moon.

Tina had more time to react, and drove her board hard, spraying snow as she rode the side of the snowbank that ran along the road. Her motions were fluid and practiced, and she pulled right, slid around the white hairy outstretched arm that threatened to take her head off, brought her board straight, and continued on.

Colin hooted, his shadow banking hard left, launching

off a low section in the snowbank and careening down the south slope.

The creature stood in the center of the road, wind tearing at its straggly locks, a large boulder to its left, a tall snowbank to its right. It stared through the gloom, the low growl of anticipation rumbling over the snow-packed road.

The monster was twenty feet away.

Snow hissed beneath his board, the wind laughed and celebrated, whistling and howling, spinning snowy specters.

Mom and Dad argued. "We never should have let him ride in the first place, give up on school."

As if they would have been able to stop him.

"It wasn't our call. He's got to make his own choices." His father's occasional voice of reason.

Amy joined in, yelling about how she should be the most important thing in his life, how he needed to grow up, sit at the adult table.

The yammering of his parents and Amy fell away, replaced with his grandfather's steady voice. "To get off this hill you have to turn your addiction inward. Focus and fortitude. Do not look back. Only ahead. Forge your own path." Just words, but good words.

Ten feet.

Chance had no space left, and he hunkered down on his board, pulling it straight and lifting the ragged nose just a hair as he brought up the knife, his injured arm pressed to his side. He breathed, relaxing as he coiled, pushing himself down onto the board, bindings creaking as he built-up force.

The beast roared, its massive hand coming at Chance, flashes of light shone through its fingers, dark three-inch claws glinting in the pale moonlight. The mitt overshot Chance's head, but the beast's forearm connected, knocking Chance to the side as he hopped and turned, bringing the board horizontal, forcing its sharp metal edge into the beast's legs.

It was like hitting a brick wall, and the creature's

muscled arm stopped Chance in midair, his head snapping back, the board lifting from the snow as he was swiped aside like a bug.

Even as Chance fell, cartwheeling through a black and white whirlwind, knowing he only had a few precious seconds left to live, he threw his grandfather's knife, a last desperate effort to best a creature that so far had proven his superior.

Whether it was Chance's grandfather guiding the knife from beyond, luck, or just the odds finally favoring him, the blade pierced the monster's right cheek. It wailed—the sound a cross between a pig squealing and a horse dealing with a veterinarian's arm up its ass—as dark blood leaked down the creature's face.

Chance wasn't around to see the monster fall, because he landed face first on the mountainside, the ragged tip of the board catching on an evergreen branch and splitting the fiberglass covered wood. He plummeted, out of control as he worked his legs, trying in vain to use the broken snowboard as a brake. He careened into a boulder, eyeballs shaking, and a ringing rose in his head until he heard no other sound. Chance tumbled down the slope, injured arm screaming, hot blood making him think of happier times as he was lost in a maelstrom of white, and his eyes saw no more.

27

February 3rd, 2019, Park City, UT—Elevation 7,000 feet

THE ANNOUNCER TAPPED the microphone, his slick blonde hair glistening under the harsh stage lights. "Welcome to the debut of Tragedy on Abominable Peak directed by Tatiana Crow. This film is under consideration in the documentary category here at Sundance." Light clapping. "Without further ado, I'm pleased to ask Director Tatiana Crow to the stage."

The lights in the theater dimmed as Tatiana slipped through the drawn curtains. Her black hair shone, her sleek black dress accented with a large sparkling rose brooch. A hushed silence fell over the crowd as the announcer handed her the microphone and disappeared off the stage.

"Welcome to the debut of Tragedy on Abominable Peak," she said. Riotous cheering answered, and Tatiana heard Biggie's sharp whistle and Tina yelling her name. "I know you've all heard the rumors, seen some of the footage, but today's film is the product of many people's efforts. First, I have to thank Reality Groove Films, for their support of the project from day one, before . . . " She trailed away. "Before the story became something else. Special thanks to my crew, Ju Ju and Maggie. Stand up, people." Ju Ju stood, his orange tie standing out in the dim light, Maggie looking uncomfortable in a form-fit dress. "Without them what you see here today wouldn't have been possible."

The rear door opened, and someone grunted, a faint "sorry" echoing through the theatre.

"We'll start off with the past, bring us current, and show you what we found when we returned to Fort Fortune. Fair warning, it's not easy viewing, though the corpses had been removed by State Police during their initial investigation, everything else—all the memories and horrors—were left behind." Tatiana paused as she dabbed at her eye with her shirtsleeve. "Our run time today is forty-one minutes, but before we get going, let's observe a moment of silence for the twenty-five people that weren't as lucky as me and sadly died at Fort Fortune."

Someone in the crowd sniffled, a cough, air pushed from the HVAC system. Tatiana made her way down a narrow set of steps to her seat in the front row, where Ju Ju, Maggie, Biggie, Tina, and Colin waited.

The stage lights went dark as the curtains drew back, revealing the large white screen. The Reality Groove Films logo appeared over black, creepy violin music dipping and rising as the scene shifted and cycled through cinematic sugar, a series of aerial shots of Abominable Peak. Opening credits laid over long dramatic shots, finishing with a close-up of the peak's cornice, the line Abominable Peak, elevation 16,971 feet on the bottom of the screen.

The music faded as a cross dissolve transition sharpened into Tatiana walking toward Fort Fortune, the snowdrifts along the side of the road like dirty stone. The temperature had been mild for mid-March. She went on about the mining camps history, Lucky Strike Number One and Two. Then, she stopped, staring straight into the camera. "Parts of what happened here are a mystery, and we'll share what the police found, plus what we discover, in an attempt to set the record straight."

Tatiana paused and dropped into a catcher's crouch, the camera following her. She pointed at the ground. "There—" she said, "—is where this was found." She produced a red utility knife and held it out to the camera. "This was Charles 'Chance' Hance's knife, which was passed down to him from his father, who got it from his dad, Jesse Hance." In an attempt to draw sympathy and emotion, she added, "I have not been able to return it to him."

The camera followed her as she talked, all the details about the first ski expedition to Abominable Peak, how Roland and Jesse had driven up this very road, stood in the same spot.

"But as you can see, if Roland or Jesse were here now, they wouldn't recognize the place." The black mounds that had been the barrack and the warehouse stood out in the dirty snow. The cinderblock dormitory was stained black, all its windows broken.

"How did this happen? How did we get here? That's the story I'm here to tell," she said. The camera panned away from her face and zoomed in on a mangled backpack half-buried in snow and mud, ash swirling in the wind.

She went on about the legend of the Metoh, how the Indian Chief Nefitti led his followers into the mountains before winter. How they all died, except the chief, whose heart turned to pure ice.

"It's said he walks the mountaintop searching for prey, a massive hairy thing with glowing red eyes," Tatiana said, staring into the camera. She went on to describe Roland and Jesse's trip as she walked through the desolation that had been Fort Fortune. Her voice continued, but the picture shifted to a large four-toed footprint in the snow, then to a picture of Jesse carving on the mountainside, then to the picture of Roland and Jesse standing on the peak, Roland's arm around his partner.

"But everything wasn't what it seemed, even between the two partners," Tatiana paused for effect. "And this is where things went off the rails."

At this point, the film went through a brief recounting of others who had died on the peak as Tatiana made the case that the Metoh had killed before. “Despite all this, Roland and Jesse were determined to see their goal through,” she narrated.

The scene shifted to Chance, sitting in a snow hole, Tatiana’s voice pushing through the howling wind and shifting snow. “What do you think happened to your grandad up here?”

Chance stared into the camera, eyes tired. He shrugged. “I only know what I’ve been told, I wasn’t even born yet. The section of snowpack where Grandad set up his camera fell away, and he was lost.”

“And you believe that?”

Chance didn’t respond as he stared at something out of the camera’s view.

The scene shifted to a wizened and broken Roland, his liver spot freckled face filling the screen, his blue eyes still bright with life, even at ninety-two. Tatiana narrated over the image,

“And now for the first time, Roland Harvey promises to give a full account of the events that led to Jesse Hance’s death.”

Whispering and murmurs in the crowd. Tatiana looked to her right, and Maggie and Ju Ju’s attention was locked on the screen, but when she looked left, she found Biggie, Colin, and Tina watching her.

Roland spoke, his voice cracking as he stared into the camera as if on trial, his cheeks red with busted blood vessels. “First, I must apologize. The tale you’ll hear now is the true story, and if others have heard me tell it differently, I ask that they forgive me and forget it. Back then, I didn’t understand. I was young, and I didn’t think I’d done anything wrong, but now at the end of my life I realize the truth must be told.”

Silence as Roland’s face filled the screen and a tear slipped down his fat cheek. “For my part, Jesse was always my friend. Even after I won the right to ski Abominable

Peak, he stuck with me. Found a way to support me, though he made it clear that he was jealous of my opportunity. We argued often, but I sit here today because of him. He saved my life."

A cough, air streaming from vents.

"I didn't fall on the lower section of the mountain. That was a lie. I never skied Abominable Peak."

Intakes of breath, calls of what and why, the crowd murmuring like a hive of bees.

"I fell right away. Busted myself up real bad, and Jesse risked his life to save me. He could've left me there, but he didn't. He dug me out and saved me, what happened next . . . " Roland dabbed his sweaty forehead with a handkerchief. "We ended up slipping down the face of the peak, clinging to each other. We saved each other several times . . . but in the end . . . " Roland wiped his eyes. "I had to let him go. If I hadn't, we both would have died. I had no choice, but I thought folks wouldn't understand. That they would think I . . . that I hadn't done everything I could have. I did, but in the end it wasn't enough."

The interviewer asked, "Why did you lie about skiing the peak?"

Roland shrugged. "After everything that had happened, I didn't want it all to be for nothing, but that was just me convincing myself. I wanted the glory. The fame. The money."

A brief pause, Roland's wet eyes blazing into the camera.

"How did you make it down with all your injuries?"

Roland went on about how he used the sled, how lucky he was.

"Do you have anything else to say?"

Roland leaned forward for emphasis, staring straight into the camera. "Chance, if you are out there, I'm sorry."

The screen faded to black.

An image of Abominable Peak emerged from the

blackness as Aerosmith crooned about sweet emotions, Abominable Peak—2018 appearing in black below the image. Stock footage of boarders and skiers riding the peak rolled across the screen, epic jumps, rail rides on trees, and bombs into powder. One of the cuts was of Colin launching off a boulder and grabbing his board.

Tatiana heard him yawp.

A picture of Chance in his riding gear filled the screen, Tatiana's voiceover chilling. "But then things took a turn for the worst, just as it had for Chance's grandfather."

Chance's image materialized on screen. He sat in the same snow hole, talking about how he fell through the snowpack into the crevasse. When he got to the part about seeing the red eyes, he paused, looking down.

"You okay?" The voice was Biggie's.

Chance nodded, and went on, the red eyes, how the creature had attacked, injured his arm, which he held up as evidence. "I thought I was done, but I guess I was luckier than Grandad. My buddy, Jibber, wasn't."

Next was a fast montage of people talking about what they thought when Chance got back and told his tale. Stefan, Trevor, Shelly, the crew . . . everyone talking about how they believed, or didn't, how the mountain can do strange things, make people see stuff that's not there.

Back to Tatiana standing before the Lucky Strike saloon. "When Lima Haplin was taken outside her lodging, I entered the story. Chance agreed to allow me to go up the mountain with him in search of the beast who he believed had killed his friend Jibber and taken Lima. I interviewed him inside our snow hole on that journey."

Pictures of Jibber and Lima appeared with the dates of their births and deaths.

Back to Tatiana as she said, "What you're about to see is very disturbing."

The footage selected was shaky and dark, from the portion of the trek to the snow beast's cave when Tatiana was working the camera. Flashes of light on snow, dark drips of blood, everywhere the camera's light found nothing but white and stone dappled with dark pinpricks.

The footage steadied, and Tatiana narrated as the camera entered the cave through the ice wall, the image bouncing around as she climbed. There were many fast cuts to charge the drama, and because when Tatiana had sat down at the editing bay to go through the three hours of footage, not very much was useable. All the nuances of shadow and light were lost under the klieg light stare of the camera's light, everything washed out and painted in harsh black and white, no depth or contrast.

But she'd captured the finding of Lima and Terry's death, the creature's blood-soaked face filling the screen at one point, the audience shrieking and crying out. Tatiana smiled.

Tatiana strolled along a mountain path, Abominable Peak in the backdrop. "With no doubts left, we fled, but what we found when we returned to Fort Fortune was worse than anything we could have imagined."

A series of cell phone pictures and video clips, supplemented by the video Tatiana had shot upon her return, spilled across the screen. The crowd in the theatre squirmed and squeaked and made all those sounds uncomfortable people make. Again, she smiled. She'd considered long and hard about the commercial viability of her movie—or rather the movie company had—and it had been decided to let this sequence run long. Drive home the horror.

The barrack burned, then the new dormitory, the smoldering ruins of the warehouse in the background. People clogged the snow-packed paths, some rushing, others lost in conversation as if they didn't quite believe what was happening and were on their way to the saloon to play their violins like the trio on the sinking Titanic.

The screen faded to white, and Biggie's face appeared.

"It was nuts," he said. "The creatures were coming at us from all angles. We had no idea how many there were."

Then Stefan, hair disheveled, dark bags beneath his eyes. "We'd heard the rumors, the stories, but I never believed any of it. Bears. That's what I thought." He chuckled a low cackle that sounded a little unhinged.

The interviews continued, spilling out in an endless line, like witnesses being rolled out in court. Trevor explaining his theory that the creatures had targeted the warehouse because they knew that was where the helicopter was kept. Tina, Colin, many others lending their stories.

When they circled back to Biggie, the bearded man was weeping. "When we lost Bomber, it was like . . . like a piece of me had been torn out. I'd seen Jibber's body, and it was horrible. But Bomber . . . that one happened up close and personal."

The scene shifted back to Tatiana as she stood on the spot where Bomber was killed. The snowdrift with their snow holes was melted, garbage and forlorn supplies half-buried in muck. "The state police arrived to find nineteen bodies. Six people are still considered missing, including Chance Hance."

Footage of when the police arrived cycled across the screen like a bad dream; charred bodies, giant bloody patches in the snow all around Fort Fortune, burnt-out buildings, everyone gone.

"I was lucky," Tatiana said, staring into the camera for effect. Behind her, piles of abandoned gear and trash marked the spot where Chance and his crew camped for a short time.

"The mystery of the Metoh, I fear, is one that requires more investigation, but we are left with another question: is Charles 'Chance' Hance alive?"

A picture of Chance spraying snow on a competition run filled the screen.

"He was last seen that night, and is presumed dead,

though his body wasn't found, and rumors and sightings have persisted in the last year. So, we asked those closest to him what they think."

An abrupt cut to Biggie.

"Do you think Chance is alive? Will you see him again?" Tatiana's voiceover asked.

Biggie nodded vigorously and smiled, holding up a postcard. "I know I will."

"What's that?"

"I got this a month after I got home. It's a postcard from Sarasota Springs, FL. It's blank."

Cut to Tina, her smile as bright as a perfect sunrise. She shrugged at the questions. "I got this strange phone call a few months ago, but . . . " She paused, dabbed a tear from her eye. "I hope so."

Colin's face filled the screen. "I got this invitation to go to a fight in Vegas? Really weird. No name on it, no nothing."

"Did you go?"

"Oh, yeah. Great card."

"But Chance wasn't there?"

Colin smirked. "Naw, not that I saw."

Biggie's face filled the screen again, dark bags hanging beneath his bright eyes.

"If he is alive, why hide?"

Biggie laughed long and hard. "Who doesn't want to disappear sometimes?"

Sideways bump-cut to Tina, who said, "Maybe he wanted a fresh start. Leave all his baggage at the station kind of thing."

Colin didn't respond right away. He chuckled and looked down. Finally, he said, "No clue, but I know whatever reason he might have, it's a good one. My boy went through mucho shit. Maybe he doesn't want the world watching his every goddamn move anymore."

The camera's eye faded to black, then bloomed white,

and Tatiana stood before the remains of Fort Fortune, her face solemn. "Soon, the gold mine will be back in business, and some of the wounds will heal, but we may never know what happened here. What we do know is many people lost their lives, and this film is dedicated to them."

Fade to black, rolling white credits.

The audience erupted, clapping, screaming, "Bravo! Bravo!"

Tatiana marinated in adulation as Biggie, Colin, Tina, Maggie, and Ju Ju surrounded her, hugging, kissing, praising, and crying. It was celebration time, but she didn't feel much like celebrating, and she still had one more task to complete.

The lights came up, and she covered her eyes, cameras snapping, people yelling. She slipped from the crowd, escaping behind the stage, where she paused and caught her breath. She reached in her pocket, felt the metal.

A cold breeze met her as she left via the rear entrance, a light snow falling and covering everything in a thin coating of powder. A man wrapped in a head scarf and wearing tinted goggles was pulling a Burton Reaper from a board rack.

"Yo," she cooed.

The man turned, his face reflected in his goggles lenses.

"So, what did you think, Chance?"

Chance glanced around, shrugged, but said nothing.

"Here." She fished out Chance's grandfather's knife and handed it to him.

He turned it over in his gloved hand before slipping it into a jacket pocket. "Thank you," he said. "For everything."

"Don't mention it." She saw him pat his breast pocket, then look at the ground. "I left out the part you told me about the pain pill you carry. Didn't think it had relevance."

Chance chuckled, and it was a welcome sound. "Good thing," he said. "I threw it away." He dropped his board in the snow at his feet, bent, and strapped in.

People streamed from the theatre, hooting, hollering, and laughing.

The wind picked up, blowing snowy clouds from rooftops, a white haze falling over Park City.

"Will I see you again?" she asked, and for the first time, she cared about the answer.

Chance pushed off, gliding through the new-fallen snow down the street. He looked over his shoulder and said, "Time will allow it, or it won't." He saluted and cut hard right, swirling frozen mist wrapping him in its embrace.

Tatiana laughed as Chance rode into the snowy haze, a new trail . . . a new life to blaze.

THE END?

Not if you want to dive into more of Crystal Lake Publishing's Tales from the Darkest Depths!

Check out our amazing website and online store. https://www.crystallakepub.com

We always have great new projects and content on the website to dive into, as well as a newsletter, behind the scenes options, social media platforms, our own dark fiction shared-world series and our very own webstore. If you use the IGotMyCLPBook! coupon code in the store (at the checkout), you'll get a one-time-only 50% discount on your first eBook purchase!

Our webstore even has categories specifically for KU books, non-fiction, anthologies, and of course more novels and novellas.

ABOUT THE AUTHOR

Edward J. McFadden III's recent novels include *Hell Creek, Too Much Grit, The Cryptid Club, Keepers of the Flame, Quick Sands, Sandbagged, Dogs Get Ten Lives, Barracuda Swarm, Dinosaur Red, Drop Off*, and *Jurassic Ark*. His sea thrillers, *The Breach* and *Shadow of the Abyss* were Amazon #1 Best Sellers and the audio version of *The Breach* was a #1 Hot New Release. His other novels include *Throwback, Sea Tremors, Primeval Valley, AWAKE, The Black Death of Babylon*, and *HOAXERS*. He lives on Long Island with his wife Dawn, and their daughter Samantha.

Readers . . .

Thank you for reading *Terror Peak*. We hope you enjoyed this novel.

If you have a moment, please review *Terror Peak* at the store where you bought it.

Help other readers by telling them why you enjoyed this book. No need to write an in-depth discussion. Even a single sentence will be greatly appreciated. Reviews go a long way to helping a book sell, and is great for an author's career. It'll also help us to continue publishing quality books. You can also share a photo of yourself holding this book with the hashtag #IGotMyCLPBook!

Thank you again for taking the time to journey with Crystal Lake Publishing.

Visit our Linktree page for a list of our social media platforms. https://linktr.ee/CrystalLakePublishing

Our Mission Statement:

Since its founding in August 2012, Crystal Lake Publishing has quickly become one of the world's leading publishers of Dark Fiction and Horror books in print, eBook, and audio formats.

While we strive to present only the highest quality fiction and entertainment, we also endeavour to support authors along their writing journey. We offer our time and experience in non-fiction projects, as well as author mentoring and services, at competitive prices.

With several Bram Stoker Award wins and many other wins and nominations (including the HWA's Specialty Press Award), Crystal Lake Publishing puts integrity, honor, and respect at the forefront of our publishing operations.

We strive for each book and outreach program we spearhead to not only entertain and touch or comment on issues that affect our readers, but also to strengthen and support the Dark Fiction field and its authors.

Not only do we find and publish authors we believe are destined for greatness, but we strive to work with men and woman who endeavour to be decent human beings who care more for others than themselves, while still being hard working, driven, and passionate artists and storytellers.

Crystal Lake Publishing is and will always be a beacon of what passion and dedication, combined with overwhelming teamwork and respect, can accomplish. We endeavour to know each and every one of our readers, while building personal relationships with our authors, reviewers, bloggers, podcasters, bookstores, and libraries.

We will be as trustworthy, forthright, and transparent as any business can be, while also keeping most of the headaches away from our authors, since it's our job to solve the problems so they can stay in a creative mind. Which of course also means paying our authors.

We do not just publish books, we present to you worlds within your world, doors within your mind, from talented authors who sacrifice so much for a moment of your time.

There are some amazing small presses out there, and through collaboration and open forums we will continue to support other presses in the goal of helping authors and showing the world what quality small presses are capable of accomplishing. No one wins when a small press goes down, so we will always be there to support hardworking, legitimate presses and their authors. We don't see Crystal Lake as the best press out there, but we will always strive to be the best, strive to be the most interactive and grateful, and even blessed press around. No matter what happens over time, we will also take our mission very seriously while appreciating where we are and enjoying the journey.

What do we offer our authors that they can't do for themselves through self-publishing?

We are big supporters of self-publishing (especially hybrid publishing), if done with care, patience, and planning. However, not every author has the time or inclination to do market research, advertise, and set up book launch strategies. Although a lot of authors are successful in doing it all, strong small presses will always be there for the authors who just want to do what they do best: write.

What we offer is experience, industry knowledge, contacts and trust built up over years. And due to our strong brand and trusting fanbase, every Crystal Lake Publishing book comes with weight of respect. In time our fans begin to trust our judgment and will try a new author purely based on our support of said author.

With each launch we strive to fine-tune our approach, learn from our mistakes, and increase our reach. We continue to assure our authors that we're here for them and that we'll carry the weight of the launch and dealing with third parties while they focus on their strengths—be it writing, interviews, blogs, signings, etc.

We also offer several mentoring packages to authors that include knowledge and skills they can use in both traditional and self-publishing endeavours.

We look forward to launching many new careers.

This is what we believe in. What we stand for. This will be our legacy.

Welcome to Crystal Lake Publishing—
Tales from the Darkest Depths.

www.ingramcontent.com/pod-product-compliance
Lightning Source LLC
Chambersburg PA
CBHW071247190726
48292CB00007B/2445

* 9 7 8 1 9 5 7 1 3 3 0 2 7 *